MURDER
IN PARADISE

JAMES PATTERSON is one of the best-known and biggest-selling writers of all time. His books have sold in excess of 375 million copies worldwide. He is the author of some of the most popular series of the past two decades – the Alex Cross, Women's Murder Club, Detective Michael Bennett and Private novels – and he has written many other number one bestsellers including romance novels and stand-alone thrillers.

James is passionate about encouraging children to read. Inspired by his own son who was a reluctant reader, he also writes a range of books for young readers including the Middle School, I Funny, Treasure Hunters, House of Robots, Confessions and Maximum Ride series. James has donated millions in grants to independent bookshops and he has been the most borrowed author of adult fiction in UK libraries for the past eleven years in a row. He lives in Florida with his wife and son.

MURDER
IN PARADISE

JAMES
PATTERSON

WITH DOUG ALLYN, CONNOR HYDE
AND DUANE SWIERCZYNSKI

arrow books

7 9 10 8

Arrow Books
20 Vauxhall Bridge Road
London SW1V 2SA

Arrow Books is part of the Penguin Random House group of companies
whose addresses can be found at global.penguinrandomhouse.com.

Copyright © James Patterson 2018

James Patterson has asserted his right to be identified
as the author of this Work in accordance with the Copyright,
Designs and Patents Act 1988

This is a work of fiction. All characters and descriptions of events
are the products of the author's imagination and any resemblance to
actual persons is entirely coincidental

The Lawyer Lifeguard first published as ebook
by Cornerstone Digital in 2017
The Shut-In first published in paperback by BookShots in 2017
This edition published by Arrow Books in 2018

www.penguin.co.uk

A CIP catalogue record for this book is available from the British Library.

ISBN 9781787461727

Printed and bound in Great Britain by Clays Ltd, Elcograf S.p.A.

CONTENTS

THE LAWYER LIFEGUARD

JAMES PATTERSON
WITH DOUG ALLYN

CHAPTER 1

IT WAS A clear afternoon on the Lake Huron shore during the last weekend in May, so there weren't many swimmers. Whitecaps slapped against the sand, goosed in by a mild breeze. Gulls keened in the sky overhead.

Down the beach, a kid was throwing a softball for his dog. The big yellow Lab was having a blast, splashing through the shallows, snapping up the ball, and fetching it back to the boy.

Farther out, three teens were waist deep in the breakers, tossing a Frisbee around. A lifeguard in a tower chair was on duty—sort of. He seemed to be more interested in chatting up a gaggle of summer girls in micro-bikinis.

It was a gorgeous afternoon on the darkest day of my life.

And it was going to be my last.

I was sitting on a low sand hill behind my family's beachfront cottage, still dazed, dressed for court in a three-piece Armani pinstripe suit. It was scorched and torn, and spattered with blood.

I had a pistol in my lap.

I wasn't sure whose blood was on me. My fiancée's? Or mine? It didn't matter. The blood was on me.

Hours ago, my fiancée died in a car bombing. I'd managed to escape, yet I knew one thing for certain. Her death was my fault.

And I couldn't live with myself because of it.

Immediately after the accident, I came here. As a boy, the Port Vale shore was my favorite place on the planet. I spent my summers here, swimming, running with my buds, and combing the beach for soda cans to earn ten cents a pop.

In high school, I was a lifeguard. It was a magical job. I got twelve bucks an hour to tone my tan, and scope out the summer girls from my tower chair. At sunset, I enjoyed beers and bonfires on the beach. I was Lord of the Shore in those days.

They were the best times of my life.

And this was the perfect place to finish things up.

I looked down at the pistol again. It was a battered Japanese Nambu automatic my grandfather brought home from Vietnam. "Imagine the stories it could tell," he used to say. Now it would have one more.

Except...

Guns leave a god-awful mess. My first week as an assistant DA, I was called to an Iraq vet's suicide. The poor guy did his best to go out clean. He parked a kitchen chair on a tarp in the middle of his garage, then

4

wrapped himself in a plastic sheet before putting the muzzle of a 12 gauge in his mouth...

But...

He'd overlooked the laws of physics. The blast sprayed the garage ceiling with his blood and brains. The cops, the coroner, the EMTs, and I all had to do our jobs in a steady drip, drip, drip of red goo and gray matter.

I burned my suit afterward.

Here on my hill, the sand would soak up most of the blood, but...a body's an awful thing for a little kid to find.

So.

Forget the gun. The surf would do. I'd walk out in the breakers, slip under and breathe in deep.

Maybe they'd never find me at all.

Laying the pistol aside, I rose on shaky legs, swaying slightly. I couldn't focus. I knew I was forgetting something big. Was it the laws of physics? No. But something just as important. My head was thumping like a bass drum. I couldn't remember...

Drawing a ragged breath, I took a last look down the shore...

And in that moment, I swear I saw Death. Not the guy with the scythe, wearing the cowl. More like a dark distortion, hovering above the waves, in deep water.

Crouched, poised, ready to strike.

Waiting...

But not for me.

CHAPTER 2

THE BOY'S SOFTBALL had splashed down near one of the Frisbee players, who tossed it farther out. Naturally, his Lab chased after it, dog-paddling into deeper water, and into deep trouble.

As she lunged for the ball, a wave broke over her. And with the ball in her jaws, she couldn't close her mouth.

Gagging, in a panic, the Lab thrashed about wildly, attempting to keep her head above water, and then she slipped below the surface.

That's when something in me snapped.

On pure reflex, I went reeling down the beach, barely able to keep steady on my feet. I staggered into the surf after the drowning dog.

The kid was screaming now. The lifeguard looked up, baffled by the racket. He clearly had no freaking idea what was happening.

After splashing through the shallows, I plunged into the surf, swimming desperately toward the spot where the Lab went under. The icy water cleared my foggy mind as I bulled through the waves, fighting the breakers and the drag created from my sodden business suit.

When I popped my head above the water, I'd lost sight of the dog. She'd disappeared completely.

Damn it! If she'd sunk to the bottom, there was a chance I'd never find her—

Suddenly, she exploded to the surface of the water. She was hacking and gagging, but she still had the damned ball clamped in her jaws.

Desperate to reach her before she went down again, I sprinted toward her. But the dog started frantically snapping her head back and forth, trying to spot the shore. She kept paddling farther out and as I raced after her, I felt my strength fading fast. With a last, despairing surge, I lunged for the Lab's collar.

Grabbing it, I yanked her head around, trying to swing her toward the beach, and the ball popped out.

But she was out of her mind with fear and rage. The moment I touched her, she whirled on me, savagely snapping. She bit down on my arm, sending a sharp blaze of pain through my body.

Sweet Jesus, she was going to drown us both! Cursing, I pushed at her with my free hand, trying to break her hold, but she clamped down even harder.

And that's what saved her life.

With her jaws locked on my arm, she couldn't swallow any more water. But I couldn't swim, either.

Rolling over, I managed to support her as I side-stroked back to the shallows with my free arm, hauling her with me until my feet brushed the bottom.

Even then, she wouldn't let go, so I gathered her up. I staggered ashore with the exhausted dog cradled in my arms, her jaws still clamped on me.

Not a soul came to help me. They were all too busy filming the whole episode with their phones.

I dropped to my knees in the sand. The second the Lab's paws touched solid ground, she squirmed free of my arms, and went tearing off to the boy and a woman who were both crying and yelling.

Suddenly the lifeguard was in my face, hauling me to my feet by my lapels.

"Are you out of your freakin' mind?" he shouted. "What the hell were you doing out there?"

"Your damn job!" I roared back. Pushing him off me, I took a wild swing at his jaw that missed the muscle-bound clown by a foot and dropped me to my knees in the sand.

As I struggled to rise, I realized the Lab had ripped my arm open. Christ, blood was everywhere.

I felt my body sinking.

Then the sun winked out...

CHAPTER 3

I WOKE IN a world of white. White ceiling tiles, sterile white walls, white machines beside my bed. One was for oxygen, I think. The others were…complicated. I had no idea what they were for.

My bracelet was silver, though, because my right wrist was handcuffed to the bed frame.

A heavyset woman in blue hospital scrubs was swabbing down my left arm with disinfectant. She was a big woman with legs like tree trunks and no waist at all. A black flat-top buzz cut, kept boot camp short, adorned her head. She had a tattoo on one bicep and an LGBT tattoo on the other. Three more icons decorated her skin, proclaiming: Man, Woman, Equal. It worked for me.

I tried to sit up, but it was a bad mistake. I sagged back into the pillow, stifling a groan.

"Stay still, sport," she said without looking up.

"Mess up my handiwork and I'll bite open your other arm. What happened to you? A big dog tear you up?"

"Yes."

"But that's not all that happened." It wasn't a question.

"No ma'am," I admitted. "Not all."

"In addition to the dog bite, we treated you for a dozen contusions and lesions, plus third-degree burns. I've seen injuries like yours before in Helmand Province, Afghanistan. Car bomb?"

I managed a nod.

"But not in Helmand, right?"

"In Detroit. Where the hell am I?"

"You're in the Port Vale Samaritan ER, sport. I'm Dr. Lucille Crane. My friends call me Lucy, but you'll call me Dr. Crane. You're Brian Lord, aren't you? The lawyer who got blown up with your girlfriend a few days ago? It's been all over the news."

I nodded.

"I thought so. The police are waiting outside, dying to talk to you. You might want to put that conversation on hold."

"Why?"

She leaned in close, making sure I could read her eyes. "Listen up, Mr. Lord. You are in shock. I suspect you have been since the explosion. You may have sustained a concussion as well. But a minute ago, just before you came to? You were talking to somebody named Serena, like she was actually here. Was that your girlfriend?"

"Serena Rossi was my fiancée, Doc. She's dead. It's my fault and that's the simple truth. So bring on the cops. I really don't care."

"It's your funeral," she shrugged.

But she was wrong about that. It wasn't my funeral. It was Serena's.

CHAPTER 4

THREE COPS CAME into the room. The first was a slim red-head in a black Donna Karan jacket and matching skirt. It was stylish, but practical. Her skin was pale as alabaster and if she was wearing makeup, I couldn't see it.

She introduced herself as Lieutenant Beverly Hilliard of Detroit Metro homicide. It made sense, since the car bombing happened in Detroit. Though Port Vale is a beachfront community twenty miles up the Lake Huron shore, Motown detectives work with locals all the time.

Her partner, Stan Buchek, was from the Metro bomb squad. He wore a brush cut, a tweed Sears sport coat, and looked as square and dense as a cement block.

A policewoman trailed them in, but stayed by the door. She was tall and lanky, and a bit older. She was dressed like a nun in a blue shirt and navy skirt. Maybe she worked hospital security. Buchek and Hilliard ignored her.

Buchek started the good cop, bad cop show. He

played the bully, which suited him. Hilliard played the sympathetic sister. I knew the game better than they did. I've run it a million times myself.

Buchek threatened me with arrest that included a million years in prison. I didn't say anything till he began reading me the Miranda warning. Literally. He had it on a card. "You have the right to remain silent—"

Blah, blah.

"Save it," I managed. "I'm an officer of the court. I know my rights, and I'm waiving them. I'll help you any way I can. Got questions? Fire away."

"Waiving?" Buchek echoed, looking to Hilliard. "Can he do that?"

"He just did," Hilliard nodded, edging him aside. "Can you tell us what happened the day of the bombing, Mr. Lord?"

"I'm—shaky on that," I said, trying to focus. "I was carrying a suitcase out to the car…" I could feel my eyes closing.

"Snap out of it, pal!" Buchek said, prodding my shoulder sharply.

"Whoa up, Sarge," the tall policewoman by the door said. "That's enough of that."

"What? Who the hell are you, lady?"

"That's *Chief* lady to you, Sergeant. Chief Jean Paquette, Vale County PD. You two are operating in my jurisdiction, or were, anyway. Now I'm thinking we need a word. Outside. Please."

Buchek glanced at Hilliard in exasperation.

"What the hell is this?"

CHAPTER 5

Buchek, Hilliard, Paquette

IN THE CORRIDOR, the chief turned to face them. She was taller than most men at six foot plus and as slender as a riding crop. She wore her silver hair in a loose mane and had gray eyes. Buchek had to look up to meet those eyes, and then he looked away. Staring into her line of sight was like staring into a laser.

"Look, lady, or Chief or whatever you are," he blustered. "You got a quaint little town here, but this beef is out of your league. It's a murder case, and that mutt in there's a suspect—"

"He looks more like a victim to me," Chief Paquette said. "Either way, you don't lay hands on a fella in a hospital bed."

"I was getting his attention—"

"You got mine, instead. Did you two ride up together?"

"What? No," Buchek said, surprised at the question. "We're from different divisions. We drove separately. Why?"

"Good," the chief said. "I won't have to spare a patrolman to drive you home. You're eighty-sixed, Sergeant. I want you out of my town. Sharing jurisdiction is a privilege, and I'm revoking yours. Go back to Detroit. Lieutenant Hilliard can keep you up to speed on any developments."

Buchek opened his mouth to argue, then bit it off. There was no point. He couldn't muscle her. It would be like scrapping with your grandmother; there was no way to win. He closed his mouth and stalked off to the elevators, shaking his head the whole way.

"What about me?" Hilliard asked.

"You're not axed. But let's clear the air. Detroit averages a killing a day. In Port Vale, we get two or three a year, mostly domestic disputes that get out of hand. My perps are usually waiting for me on their front steps, bawling their eyes out when I roll up. So Buchek had one thing right. A car bomb is definitely over my head. I've never worked one. So catch me up. Where are we on this?"

"Since the Towers and with ISIS, every bombing triggers Federal attention," Hilliard said. "TSA, ATF, the whole alphabet shows up whenever they happen. The teams checked the car, did the forensics, and then went back to Quantico or DC or wherever they came from. This one wasn't a terrorist attack."

"How do they know that?"

"The mope who crafted the bomb is already doing triple life in Jackson Prison, but a few of his builds are still on the market. Strictly local street gang stuff."

"So this is a gang thing?"

"We don't know what it was," Hilliard shrugged. "Brian Lord's fiancée was killed. It looks like he was flattened, roughed up pretty good. He's a defense attorney with a lot of low-rent clients. There's a good chance he pissed one of them off."

"So they might try again? Terrific. That's all we need to kick off tourist season. Fireworks. When a bomb goes off in Motown, it barely makes the papers, but not here. Port Vale's a resort town. Peace and quiet's what we sell. Lord's a local boy. His family is here. Whatever he got himself into in your city, I don't want it showing up on my streets like a stray cat. Are we clear?"

"Crystal," Hilliard nodded.

"Good. Then let's try to get something useful out of him."

"What do you have in mind?"

"Definitely not muscle. I don't mind bouncing a perp off the walls if he's got it coming, but Lord's an Afghan vet *and* an attorney. Tick him off, and all we'll get is his name, rank, and serial number."

"So?" Hilliard asked cautiously.

"Let's try making nice instead," Paquette said sweetly. "We'll feed that boy a whole lotta rope. See if he hangs himself with it."

CHAPTER 6

"**BRIAN?**" **THE OLDER** woman said, pulling a plastic chair up beside my bed. "How are you, son? Do you remember me?"

"I should," I said. "You look fam—you're Chief Paquette's wife, right?"

"I was," she nodded. "Arlo blew out his pump a few years ago chasing down a crack dealer. As head of the 911 division, I was next in line. I believe you were in Afghanistan at the time with my Bobby Ray. Thank you for your service, son."

"You're welcome."

I felt my eyes closing…

"Stay with us, Mr. Lord," Hilliard said. "Can you tell us what happened the day of the bombing?"

What happened? I tried to think. My head was throbbing and—

"Serena was going to the beach," I said quickly, before I faded out. "She wanted to stay at my family's cottage over the weekend."

"Alone?" the chief asked.

"We'd been squabbling, so we thought taking a break might help, but—" I shook my head and pain flashed across my eyes.

"Mr. Lord," Doctor Crane sighed, "you really should wait awhile before you—"

"No," I managed, "I can do this. I need to. Serena had packed enough crap for a European tour and I was late for court. I was griping about her luggage as I hauled her suitcase to the car, and—"

I stopped and stared up at the chief and the lieutenant.

"That's all I've got. Everything's a blur after that."

"That suitcase saved your life," Hilliard said. "It absorbed most of the blast. The explosion shattered every window on the block. You were thrown backward twenty feet, and landed behind a garden wall. It shielded you from the secondary blast."

"Secondary?"

"When the gas tank blew up," she added. "The car was on fire."

"Fire? My god, was Serena—?"

"The coroner's report was inconclusive," Hilliard said quickly. "Her family took her body home to LA. The ceremony is tomorrow. Closed casket. You, um, you are specifically not invited, Mr. Lord."

I didn't say anything to that. There was nothing to say.

"That's enough," the doc said. "This man has multiple contusions, third-degree burns, and may be concussed. He needs rest. Don't you people have hearts?"

Hearts.

"Hearts," I echoed, wonderingly. *That was it!* For a swirling moment I could actually see one. A big red heart, on a card. And then...it vanished like mist.

"What is it, Mr. Lord?" Hilliard asked.

"I had it. Just for a second. Couldn't hold on to it."

"Steady down, son," the chief said. "It'll come back."

"You really should stop this now," the doc said.

"No," I said. "I want to help. I need to."

"Go on, Mr. Lord," Hilliard prompted. "Anything at all."

"Um, after the blast? I woke up in a hospital in Detroit. Henry Ford, I think. It was the middle of the night and nobody was around. A bedside TV was on, and I realized from a newscast that days had passed and Serena"—I swallowed—"had been killed. But it seemed impossible—I mean, she had been leaving for the goddamn beach!"

I broke off, about to lose it completely. Dr. Crane started to interrupt, but the chief waved her off. After a moment, I pulled it together and went on.

"I guess I wasn't thinking straight—"

"Which is symptomatic of a concussion, sir," Dr. Crane said.

"All I could think was, it was all a mistake. That if I could get to my folks' cottage at the beach, Serena would be there..." I trailed off again, realizing how loony that sounded.

"How *did* you get here?" Hilliard asked.

"Uber. Hired a ride."

"With your suit all splattered with blood?"

"It was a Detroit hospital," I said.

That explained the situation. Even the chief smiled.

"Do you have any idea who planted that bomb, Mr. Lord?" Hilliard asked. "An enemy? A disgruntled client, or—" She stopped speaking because I was staring at her.

"A client," I said. "That's it."

"What is it?" Hilliard asked.

"Just before," I said. "The image of a heart came to mind. A valentine. This is about Valentine."

"What kind of a valentine?" the chief asked.

"Not a what," Hilliard said. "Valentine's a who."

CHAPTER 7

"JIMMY VALENTINE IS a loser of a client," I explained. "When I left the prosecutor's office to work for Garner and Mackey, Jimmy was on the list of castoffs that came with the job."

"Garner's offices are on Cadillac Square," Hilliard said, nodding. "Big step up for an ADA."

"I didn't make it on my own. Serena was a paralegal with Garner for years. When we started dating, she got me in. But new hires are bottom of the food chain so I inherited the shit list, the clients nobody else wanted. Jimmy Valentine topped that list."

"Who is he?"

"Nobody. Jimmy's a small-time loan shark out of Warsaw Heights. Got busted in a gambling raid in Dearborn. His case is an open and shut loser. Unfortunately for him, it's also his third fall."

"So he's facing a stiff sentence as a repeat offender," the chief said. "That's his fault, not yours. Why would this Valentine have a beef with you?"

"He doesn't. But he thought I could get him a deal with the DA's office. Offered to swap some evidence against Bruno Corzine."

That got their attention.

Hilliard's eyes widened. "Jesus," she said. "Corzine's an underboss with the Zeman crime family. How is Valentine connected to him?"

I almost said "a murder," but caught myself in time. I shook my head. "Sorry. Valentine's information falls under attorney–client privilege. Corzine's not a client, so I can give you what I know about him, but that's as far as I can go."

"What about your late fiancée?" Chief Paquette asked. "Does she get a vote in this?"

"Serena's death is on me," I conceded, "but I can't compromise Valentine's rights without spitting on everything I believe in."

"Lawyers are bound by legal restrictions," Hilliard said. "We get that, Counselor. So what *can* you tell us?"

"My old boss, Assistant DA Leon Stolz, caught Jimmy's case. I called Leon, offered to trade what Jimmy knew for a plea bargain. He said he'd get back to me. But word must have leaked out. Next day, Corzine and two thugs were waiting by my car. He warned me to blow off Valentine's deal, or I'd be sorry. And he was right. I am sorry I ever heard of Jimmy Valentine."

"Where did this confrontation with Corzine happen?" Hilliard asked.

"My firm's parking garage, off Cadillac Square."

"Were there any witnesses?"

"Only the thugs with Corzine."

"Did they lay hands on you? Rough you up at all?"

"Bruno's goons held him back. Thank God, or he would have torn my arms off. Why are you wasting time with this crap? You want to know who planted that bomb? I'm telling you who planted it."

"No, son," the chief said mildly. "You're telling us about a dust-up between you and a couple thugs in a parking garage. With no witnesses to back your story, and no hard evidence it happened at all."

"Your evidence is being buried in LA tomorrow, lady. She's my deceased fiancée."

"You were an ADA, Brian," Hilliard put in. "How many cases did you prosecute?"

"I'm…not sure. I was second chair to Stolz for…maybe a hundred. I flew solo on forty or fifty more after that."

"Then you know the rules of evidence. If we hauled this Corzine into a courtroom right now, what kind of a case could you make against him?"

I started to argue, then slowly closed my mouth because she was right. I had nothing.

Damn! I wanted to punch the wall or something, but I couldn't. I was still handcuffed to the bed frame.

"Corzine aside," Chief Paquette said. "Could one of your other clients have done this?"

"I—guess that's possible. Haven't thought about it."

"If we could take a quick look through your files…?" Hilliard began.

"Attorney–client privilege, Lieutenant. You know I can't turn them over."

"Can't? Or won't?"

"Even losers have rights," I said. "Sometimes, it's all they've got. Am I under arrest?"

"No," Hilliard said, "not at this time."

"But I'm under suspicion, right?"

The fact that she didn't answer was answer enough.

"If I'm not busted, then could you please uncuff me and leave?" I said, closing my eyes. "I've got a killer headache."

CHAPTER 8

Hilliard, Paquette

OUTSIDE IN THE corridor, the two policewomen faced each other.

"No confession, no big breakthrough," Bev Hilliard said. "But you got a lot more out of him than Buchek would have."

"Not nearly enough, though," the chief said grimly. "The coffee they serve here's terrible, but at least it's hot. Let me buy you a cup."

They rode the elevator down to the cafeteria in silence, both mulling over what Brian Lord had told them. In the bright, noisy cafeteria, they filled paper cups at a tall urn, then took a table in a corner, away from the other diners.

"Have you worked with Buchek long?" Chief Paquette asked, eyeing Hilliard over the rim of her coffee cup.

"Not at all," Hilliard countered. "We're on different units, so I just met him today. Frankly, I didn't like him much."

"Me neither. He's pushy."

"Bet you didn't like when he was razzing on Port Vale."

"No, he was right about it being a small town. We're forty thousand in summer, half that when the snow flies. But we're only twenty-five miles up the road from the most violent city in America."

"You're not from Port Vale, though," Hilliard said. "Not with that accent."

"South Alabama. I met Arlo at a police convention in Mobile. After three dates, I married him and moved up here. But I was Alabama Highway Patrol twelve years before that. I run a small-town force, but I ain't no hobby cop."

"So I'm gathering," Bev nodded.

"So this Corzine Lord talked about," the chief said, "do you know him?"

"Know *of* him," Hilliard said. "He's a thug on the rise in the Zeman crime family."

"The Zemans I've heard of," Paquette said. "Last of the old Purple Gang. They used to run hooch across the lake ice from Canada during Prohibition. Locals say some of those trucks are still at the bottom of the lake with their skeletons sittin' at the wheel."

"I'll bet their hooch is better than this coffee," Hilliard said, and both women laughed, relaxing a little.

"Thing is, these days the mob's mostly into white-collar crime," Hilliard said. "Union skims, credit card fraud, identity theft. Scams that work best when they don't draw attention."

"And bombs draw a whole lot of attention," the chief nodded. "Is this Corzine that stupid, do you think?"

"He has a rep as a dangerous man to cross, but he's no fool. He's never done time."

"Maybe we can fix that," the chief said. "But we'd best get a move on. That boy upstairs? He did two tours overseas. I got two officers who did time in the Sandbox. It ain't like our daddy's wars, where you served your hitch and then came home. Nowadays, they go back tour after tour, in combat almost the whole time. A lot of these heroes come back and have a hard time adjusting, and if Brian believes Corzine did this thing, there's a chance he won't wait long for us to settle up. He might decide to settle it himself, up close and personal. And if he does, his life will be over no matter how it comes out."

"Then we'd better beat him to it, Chief," Hilliard said. "If we're going to work this together, I'll need a desk and a connection to the enforcement nets."

"Come downtown, use my office," the chief said. "We got computers, Wi-Fi, the works. I only play Angry Birds on 'em myself, but my people can hook you up."

"You've never played Angry Birds in your life."

"Never once," Chief Paquette admitted. "But I designed our 911 Emergency System."

"My god," Hilliard said, "all that cornpone's just a front, isn't it?"

"No ma'am, I'm redneck to the bone and proud of

it. But up here, if you sound like you're from Alabama, folks automatically subtract twenty points off your IQ. It used to piss me off somethin' fierce. Now? I find it real useful sometimes."

"You take 'em by surprise," Hilliard said.

"See? You're a smart city girl. Two minutes and you've already got me figured out."

"Not even close," Hilliard smiled. "But we're making a start."

CHAPTER 9

AFTER THE TWO policewomen left, I slept like a dead man. Which was appropriate, because when I woke…

Bruno Corzine was standing beside my bed, glaring down at me.

Gasping, I bolted upright.

"Hey, hey!" a woman's voice said. "Take it easy!"

I slowly released her, blinking as Corzine's shape shifted into that of a tall, slim, African American nurse in hospital scrubs. She was only checking my pulse.

She couldn't have looked less like Bruno Corzine if her hair had been dyed purple.

Still, his image lingered in the room after she left. And I wondered how long it would take for the real Bruno to track me down and finish the job.

I needed to get the hell out of here. The sooner the better.

But nothing's ever simple.

At six in the morning, Dr. Crane popped in to check her handiwork, then had an orderly help me into a wheelchair and roll me off to an elevator to the basement lab.

A cheerful neurosurgeon gave me a thorough examination. I read charts with slanted lines, and followed the path of her fingertip back, forth, up, down, and sideways.

Did I know what year it was? *Yes.*

And the president's name? *Knew that, too.*

How about the day of the week? *A little foggy on that one.*

In the end, even though she said I was the healthiest bombing victim she'd ever treated, she opted for an MRI anyway, just to be on the safe side.

Afterward, I got some good news and bad news. The good news: though I'd suffered a number of physical traumas in the explosion, I was *not* concussed. If the radiologist's report confirmed her diagnosis, they could cut me loose later in the day.

The bad news? When they rolled me back to my room, Marvin Garner, the senior partner at Garner and Mackey of Cadillac Square, was waiting for me, and I could read my future at the company in his plastic, executioner's smile.

CHAPTER 10

"BRIAN, MY BOY," Garner said. "How are they treating you?"

"Fine," I said. "I'll be out of here in a few hours."

"No rush, of course," he said, glancing around uncomfortably. "You'll need time to rest and recover."

"Not in here," I said. "I hate hospitals."

"I suppose not." He flashed me that plastic smile again. I'd only met him one other time, on the day I signed on at Garner and Mackey. After that, I'd seen him around the office occasionally, at a distance. With his shock of silver hair and a three-thousand-dollar suit, I thought he looked vaguely presidential. But today? Up close? He looked sleek and slick, and I was empty and aching, and in no mood for phony sympathy.

"Look, Mr. Garner, let's just get to it. Why are you here?"

"To—settle up," he said evenly, all pretense of amiability gone. "No one blames you for Serena's death, of course—"

"Good to know."

"But," he continued, annoyed at being interrupted, "she was with us for many years. She's been with you a matter of months, and, well, here we are. The inference is obvious."

"Not to me."

"Then you're not as bright as she promised you were, when she conned me into hiring you away from the District Attorney's Office. Clearly that was a mistake. A fatal one for her. Some gangster or mental case you convicted lashed out at you, and Serena paid the price."

"You're half right. But the client wasn't from my past. He was one of the hand-me-downs I got at your firm. Does Valentine ring a bell?"

"Look, today's a holiday, so I'll cut to the chase, Brian. The partners have met and voted. Given the appalling incident and publicity? They've opted to sever our relationship. Nothing personal. It's purely a business decision, I assure you."

He handed me an envelope. I opened it and found a single sheet of legal paper. A Separation Document. I've served them myself.

Effective immediately, Brian Lord is terminated from Garner and Mackey for associations and behavior deemed detrimental to the firm.

"You'll receive a severance package with ninety days' salary. Your medical insurance coverage will continue for the same period. We don't wish to seem vindictive."

"That's good," I said, "because I have one last favor to ask. In the time I've been with the firm, I've had a half dozen clients assigned to me."

"Ten, actually. I checked."

"I'd like to retain them."

"I...don't see any problem with that," Garner shrugged. "They're not cases any of the partners would want anyway. Anything else?"

There wasn't. We said polite good-byes and he left, taking my visions of a brilliant legal career at Cadillac Square with him. We didn't bother to shake hands.

It didn't matter. We both got what we wanted. Garner got rid of a public-relations disaster for the price of a severance package.

But I got something too. Clients. A loser's list, maybe, but I wanted them. After my midnight vision of Corzine, I'd lain awake for hours, mulling it over.

Corzine was the obvious suspect. But I've learned a few things about the obvious answer.

Like never to trust it.

For most of my time as an assistant DA, I'd worked as second chair for Leon Stolz, a guy who never won a popularity contest in his life. In court, he was the one making charges, working for convictions, grilling the perps in the holding tanks. If someone we'd convicted back then had a beef, they'd be mad at Leon, not me.

The cases I'd prosecuted as a solo were strictly minor league stuff. DUIs, deadbeat dads, petty theft.

Other than a few barroom scuffles, I couldn't think of a single case that involved overt violence. So the bomber probably *wasn't* some loser out of my past.

He was more likely to be a current client or someone connected to them. Corzine qualified, but he might not be the only candidate. Someone tried to kill me, and murdered Serena instead.

I damn sure intended to find out who, and would settle up with them.

Legally or otherwise.

CHAPTER 11

DR. CRANE WAS giving me a final exam when Lieutenant Hilliard and Chief Paquette visited.

"For a guy who's been blown up, I've seen worse," Hilliard said.

"Worse is getting buried today, like my fiancée is?" I countered, then sighed. "What can I do for you, Lieutenant?"

"Actually, it's what I can do for you," Hilliard said. "I did some serious digging into the name you gave us. Bruno Corzine?"

"And?"

"Because of who he is, it's not uncommon for a law enforcement agency to have eyes on him. Ever hear of the Riviera Social Club?"

"It's a Detroit mob hangout," I said, nodding.

"At the time of the bombing, a dozen witnesses, including two of ours, can place Bruno Corzine at the Riviera Social Club, playing cards with his cronies. He couldn't have been directly involved."

"The key word being 'directly,'" the chief added. "I've noticed a funny thing about alibis over the years. Innocent people almost never have 'em. They're walking the dog or home watching TV. Can't remember which program because they don't expect to be asked. A thug like Corzine? It'd be more surprising if he *didn't* have a rock-solid alibi."

"I don't care if he was playing pinochle with the pope. It doesn't get him off the hook. I appreciate your efforts, though. Thank you."

"It wasn't an effort, Mr. Lord," Hilliard said. "Corzine is a suspect in an ongoing investigation now. I don't know what you might be thinking, but you need to just let us do our jobs. I know you're angry and scared, but if you go anywhere near him, you'll wind up in traction or a cell. I want your word that you'll leave this alone."

I just looked at them. Both Hilliard and the chief seemed straight to me. It was a rare thing in the criminal justice system. I didn't want to lie to them.

So I didn't.

I didn't say anything at all.

They exchanged a glance, then left me to the tender mercies of Dr. Crane.

On her way out, Chief Paquette paused in the doorway. "You need to be careful now, Brian," she said. "If you get sideways of this thing, I'll truly hate locking you up. But I will do it. You understand?"

"Yes, ma'am," I said.

CHAPTER 12

THAT AFTERNOON, I was pacing the hospital sunroom, when I got my first pleasant surprise in a while.

"I'll be damned," Carly Delaney said from the doorway, "Brian, the Lord of the Shore. Do your friends still call you that?"

"I don't have many friends left these days."

"You've got one, at least," Carly said, sweeping me into her arms in a fierce hug.

"Easy," I groaned, "I'm a tad fragile."

"Sorry," she said, releasing me. "It's been a long time."

And it had been. We both took a step back, looking each other up and down.

"The line you're looking for is 'gee, Carly, you haven't changed a bit,'" she said.

"It wouldn't be true. You've definitely changed a lot, all for the better."

It was true. Her smile lines were a bit deeper, and she still wore her cinnamon hair short enough to comb with her fingertips, but she wasn't my tomboy beach buddy from my days as a lifeguard. Not anymore.

Carly'd grown up, and the difference was striking. As a girl she'd been cute as a bug. As a grown woman, she was drop-dead gorgeous.

But as impish as ever.

"You've changed some," she said frankly, her smile fading a bit. "Skipping past the bandages, you look—"

"Like I've been run through a wood chipper?"

"Sort of," she nodded, "but the big difference is your eyes. You seem wiped, my friend."

"I've had better weeks."

"I've been following your adventures online. I'm sorry about—hell, Brian. Everything."

"Thanks. How are you doing?"

"A lot better than I could be, thanks to you."

"To me? How so?"

"That yellow Labrador you rescued? She belonged to my nephew, Tim, my sister Rhonda's boy. Do you remember her?"

"I remember a cute little butterball we called Help Me Rhonda. She can't be old enough to date yet, let alone have a kid?"

"She has two, a boy and a girl. And she's twenty-six."

"Jesus, we're dinosaurs."

"Speak for yourself, I'm in my prime. I'm Vale County Parks Director now, and on behalf of parks management and staff, I'd like to thank you for your amazing rescue last week. Jerry Koval, the lifeguard on duty, had promised me he'd keep a close eye on Timmy and his dog, but he's easily distracted. Beach girls, I imagine."

"He's a lousy lifeguard, Carly."

"He's an ex-lifeguard now," she sighed. "I had to fire him. Normally, I hate that part of my job, but the dunce tried to lie to me about what happened when the video is all over the web. So, he's a terrible lifeguard *and* a liar. They don't make them like they used to. And unfortunately, I have to get back to the office to find a replacement. I definitely owe you a 'thank you' lunch, though. It'll give us a chance to catch up."

"I'd love that but...look, if you're serious about owing me? What are my chances of getting my old job back?"

"You mean as a lifeguard? But aren't you a lawyer now?"

"What I am is in between jobs, Carly. And to tell you the truth, hauling that dog out of the surf was the first *worthwhile* thing I've done since I got out of the army. I really need to feel useful again and you need a replacement lifeguard. So? Win-win, right?"

"Win-lose, you mean," she snorted. "Look, I'll concede that because your video went viral, you're probably the most famous lifeguard on the planet, but...No offense, Brian, you said it yourself. You look like you've been through a wood chipper."

"I've got a few dings, but they're mostly cosmetic. I'm in better shape than I look."

"You'd have to be. For openers, you'd have to be recertified and it's been years since you tested. Do you remember what the qualification tests are like?"

"More or less."

"They haven't gotten any easier."

"I need to work, Carly. I'll retest, get recertified, whatever you say."

"Jesus, you're serious, aren't you?"

"Serious as a heart attack. I need this, Carly. And you said you owe me."

"Not this way, I don't."

"At least let me try. You owe me that much."

"Fine, I'll give you a shot. Be at the park at dawn tomorrow. And don't be late."

"At dawn? Is this something like a duel?"

"No. It's *exactly* like a duel," she said.

CHAPTER 13

A FEW MINUTES after Carly left, I was paged down to the front desk. My uncle Josh and my older brother, Tall Paul, were there waiting for me. And they were clearly worried about me.

We embraced fiercely, a miniature Lord family reunion. Uncle Josh is sixty, a construction boss. His brush cut is steel-gray and he's a bit grizzled, but he's lean as an axe handle and just as hard. He doesn't smile a lot. Today, he wasn't smiling at all.

Tall Paul is two years my senior and is six foot seven inches to my six foot flat. He's my big brother in every way. We were hometown basketball heroes for the Port Vale Vikes, which is appropriate since Tall Paul, with his blond beard, actually looks like a Viking and played like one, too. He took no prisoners. We were State Class B champions my sophomore year.

Those were the glory days. After school, I followed Paul into the army. There was no glory there. Paul lost a leg below the knee in Iraq. He still looks like a Viking raider, but these days he runs a shoreline bar and grill called the Beachfront Bistro.

I was a lot luckier. I took two tours in Afghanistan with the military police and made it through without a scratch.

I guess my injuries occurred during life as a civilian.

Outside, Uncle Josh's '70 Chevy step-side pickup was parked in a tow-away zone. We piled in, and I took the middle seat, as usual. Josh was at the wheel with Paul riding shotgun. Neither of them said a word to me until we were rolling through traffic.

"I found that on top of the dune behind the cottage," Paul said as he fished the old Nambu semi-automatic out of his jacket and dropped it in my lap. "Was that where you left it?"

I nodded. "I was having a really bad day. I was still pretty rocky from the car bomb."

"Must have been," Paul agreed. "You've always been wild, Brian, but not that kind of wild. Were you seriously considering—"

"I *thought* about it, Paul. But that's all I did."

"Any man who ain't *considered* eatin' a weapon at least once has led a pretty quiet life," Uncle Josh said dryly. "Are you past all that now? Or do we have to keep an eye on you?"

"I'm okay now, Unc. Not a hundred percent, maybe, but better than I was. I blamed myself for what happened to Serena. We were fighting that day. That's why she was in the car and I wasn't. That's on me, and always will be."

"Any idea who might have done it?" Paul asked.

"A Motown hood named Corzine is top of my list. He threatened me just before it happened. But he has a pretty fair alibi. The police were watching him at the time."

"So he didn't do it himself," Uncle Josh said.

"Or he didn't do it at all," Paul added. "Who else?"

"The detectives think one of my clients might have done it, and it's possible they're right. They want to check through my files, but I can't allow that."

"Why not?" Paul asked. "I mean, what if one of them's guilty?"

"And what if he's not? If the law's looking for a bomber, but finds something else, it's not like they'll just forget it. My clients trust me to protect their rights and their privacy. I can't just hand them over. But…?"

They both glanced at me.

"Nothing's stopping *me* from looking through my own case files. With a little help from my discreet family and friends."

"And if one of your clients looks good for it?" Paul asked.

"Then we turn them over to the law."

"And if that doesn't work out?" Uncle Josh asked. His tone was neutral, but he's not the subtle type.

"Then I guess we'll try something else."

CHAPTER 14

THE LORD FAMILY cottage is a two-story relic on Vale Beach, a few hundred yards up the shore from the park. My great grandfather built it by hand out of rough planks and natural stone.

And that's why the new cardboard boxes stacked on the porch steps looked totally out of place.

"Wait here," Paul said, "I know a bit about bombs." Climbing out, he edged warily up to the boxes. The box on top was open. Paul leaned over and peered in.

"What is it?" Uncle Josh demanded.

"Office stuff," Paul said. "Brian's, I'm guessing."

He was right. The top box held my law license and various papers from my office. Fountain pens, legal pads, and my Rolodex. The others were filled with my client files.

There wasn't even a note, but the message was clear enough. *"Good riddance, from your former employers, Garner and Mackey, Cadillac Square."* That note sealed my fate. It had finally sunk in that I was actually fired.

But at least I was home again. We carried the boxes into the cottage. It was a comfy old barn of a place, with a country kitchen and great room downstairs, and bedrooms above. Every room has a grand view of the big lake.

Home sweet home. My favorite safe haven.

Upstairs, I changed into jeans and a faded Mötley Crüe T-shirt while Paul busied himself in the kitchen, making sandwiches. Uncle Josh made calls to his construction crews.

Then we gathered at the kitchen table with the stack of files in the center.

"How do we do this?" Uncle Josh asked.

"We divide them up, read through them one at a time," I said, dealing out the files as if they were an oversized poker hand.

"I'm a chef, not a lawyer," Paul said, shoving a steaming tuna melt into my mouth. It was utterly delicious, especially after a few days of hospital chow. "What should I be looking for?"

"A bomb," I said flatly. "Any connection to explosives. Military experience, mining, blasting. Or anybody who seems batshit crazy enough to use one. I'm sure we'll know it when we see it."

"I'm not sure I'll know mad bombers when I see them," Paul said.

"Think back to Iraq," Uncle Josh said. "You knew a few then."

We settled into the job at hand, scarfing lunch while we winnowed my client list of losers down to a manageable number.

My personal favorite was still Jimmy Valentine. Because he threatened to rat out Corzine, he made the gangster or one of his goons prime candidates. No lawyer, no deal. I set him aside, saving him for last.

Paul's first two were easy to pass over. A vagrant hoping to sue a hit-and-run driver and a lush suing Walmart to get his greeter's job back. Neither case involved violence, or any reason to lash out at me. Most of the cases were similar, bottom of the barrel beefs. Nuisance lawsuits, plain and simple. In twenty minutes of sorting, we culled my client list down to a final three.

Paul came across a file for "Crazy Jack" Bruske, a young outlaw biker who was facing prison time for marijuana possession. His crew, the Iron Disciples, are mad dogs on motorcycles, and notoriously violent, so they might have access to some dangerous material, and have the ability to construct a bomb. And though Jack's crime seemed pretty low-level to me, and though I couldn't think of a rational reason they'd want to blow me up, I couldn't stop focusing on the biker's name. A rational guy nicknamed "Crazy"? It's a contradiction in terms.

Uncle Josh came up with Sherry Molinere, a young woman trying to divorce her domineering husband, Dex, who happens to be a corporal in the state police. Dex had been gaming the system to stalk her. He'd filed a blizzard of bogus charges on her, so I fired back with a restraining order and complaints to his department. He had plenty of cause to want me gone. As a tenure cop, Dex may not know about the munitions himself, but he would have sources who would.

Two new names. I read their case files again, thoroughly.

"Well?" Uncle Josh asked.

"It could be any of them—including Corzine," I said. "Drugs, money, and jealousy are all in play here. But killing me? It seems a little over the top."

"Let's say it's not about you personally," Josh said. "What if it's strictly business? What would taking you out of the picture accomplish?"

"Other than making the world a better place," Paul joked.

I thought about that one. "Corporal Molinere is trying to control his wife. He's already bullied a public defender into dropping her case. Without me, she's alone and he wins. The others? At most, it could delay their cases, kick them back to square one."

"Would that help any of them?"

"It might. Evidence can be time sensitive. Memories fade, witnesses move on. It might be some small detail, and not all the evidence is in these files."

"Then where's the rest of it?" Paul asked.

"In the prosecutor's office. My clients tell me their side of the story, and then the DA hears the rest from witnesses and the police. They're supposed to share evidence, but things get held back. Accidentally or on purpose."

"Like hole cards," Josh nodded. "How do we get a look at 'em?"

"I can set up a meeting with my old boss to work out plea deals. He'll try to trump my offer by dumping any dirt he's been holding back. Maybe something will link up."

"It better," Josh said. "Because the guy who missed might try again. Does anybody know you're here?"

"No."

"Good," Paul said. "I'll sleep downstairs on the couch tonight."

"You don't have to do that."

"Yeah," he said. "I definitely do."

CHAPTER 15

THE NEXT MORNING, I arrived at the park at first light, while the sun was breaking over the horizon and the surf was driven onshore by the wind.

Carly Delaney was waiting for me at the tower chair, looking fine, fit, and deadly serious.

"You're on time," she said, checking off the first box on her waterproof clipboard. "That's a good start. And before you even ask? I'm going to do you a big favor—"

"I don't want any special treatment—"

"Great! Because that's my big favor," she finished brightly. "I'm gonna bust your ass, my friend. Not because I want you to fail. But as a pal? It's better if you wash out here than have some citizen drown on your watch."

"Got it," I nodded grimly. "Do your worst."

She peeled off her baggy T-shirt and stepped out of her surfing shorts to reveal a taut, toned frame in a skintight swimsuit.

Slipping the clipboard over her shoulder on a carry

strap, Carly sprinted off through the shallows into the surf, then plunged in, swimming hard for the third raft, permanently moored seventy yards offshore, in water fifteen to twenty feet deep.

Watching her slide through the water like a shark gave me serious pause. Ten years had sped by since my last lifeguard certification test, and getting back in the swim wasn't *anything* like riding a bicycle.

The test is an ordeal designed to thin the herd. Let the games begin.

The first test is toughest of all. I had to tread water in place for half an hour with both thumbs in the air. Carly made it even tougher by needling me and joking around. It's not easy to laugh and swim at the same time, but I managed. Barely.

Next I swam four quarter-mile stints in the surf at top speed, doing breaststroke, sidestroke, backstroke, and front crawl. Then I swam them again, towing Carly on a plastic rescue board as she pretended to be my victim. Said victim was razzing me the whole time.

At eighteen, the test had been a challenge. At twenty-eight, it was taking every ounce of concentration I had just to keep from drowning. Carly knew it, too. But instead of lightening up, she did her best to make every segment as grueling as possible. She fell off the rescue board at mistimed moments, and struggled desperately as I tried to keep her afloat.

"Had enough?" she panted, halfway through.

"Hell, no," I said, gasping for breath. "Is that all you've got?"

"It's your funeral."

"People keep telling me that. Bring it!"

And she did. She worked me through every possible contingency, until finally we reached the last line on her clipboard. She crossed it out even though we hadn't done a thing.

"What was that?" I gasped, only a few breaths away from sinking like a rock. "No special treatment, remember?"

"That box is for attitude, my friend, and you've got plenty of that. C'mon, take my hand."

Reaching out, she hauled me up onto the raft, then swiveled around so I could rest my shoulders against hers, back to back. I was freezing, and Carly's skin radiated warmth like a space heater.

I was so exhausted I could scarcely breathe, but at the same time, I felt elated. The damned test had taken every scrap of energy I had, but somehow, I'd survived.

I was reminded of a simpler life, before the army and law school, when we used to have *fun* on the beach. We sat for a time, resting, both lost in our own thoughts.

"Can I ask you something?" Carly said.

"Sure, shoot."

"It's dumb, but it's always bothered me. Back in the day? You know how we were great friends, partied together, and ran in the same crew?"

"Yeah."

"You never hit on me. Why was that? Was something wrong with me?"

I was tempted to wisecrack, but her tone told me it wasn't the day for it.

"The truth? You were my best friend, Carly. In some ways, you were like a sister."

"Wow, that's the kiss of death."

"Besides, every time I got my courage up to make a move on you, you were with somebody else. We had great times, but terrible timing. You married Denny Delaney; I wound up in Afghanistan."

"Two fails," she agreed. "But even after you came home, you didn't say a word to me. The next thing I hear, you were engaged, working in Detroit."

"I came out of the army like a rocket, in a big hurry to make up for lost time. I picked up my bachelor's in the service, then doubled up my law school classes and finished in twenty months. Directly from there, I was hired into the prosecutor's office as an ADA. Another big mistake, by the way."

"How so?"

"I'd rather help people out when they're in trouble than lock 'em up. Anyway, then I met Serena…And maybe we were both in too big a hurry. She came on strong and got me a great job at her firm. And now I'm in this god-awful mess."

"I'm sorry, I didn't mean to—"

"It's okay, I'm still sorting it all out myself. The truth is, we weren't getting along, and if we'd been honest with each other, and admitted it wasn't working, she might still be alive."

"You don't know that."

"No, I don't," I admitted. "Any other annoying questions?"

"Nope, because our timing definitely hasn't improved," she sighed. "After today, I'm going to be your boss. And the department has got strict rules about bosses and subordinates fraternizing."

It took a moment for what she said to sink in. "Wait, you're saying I passed? Everything? I'm hired?"

"If you still want the job."

"Hell, yes, I want it!"

"Then it's yours," she said, standing up, slipping the clipboard strap over her shoulder. "C'mon, I'll race you in." She shot off the raft in a perfect swan dive, swimming hard for the shore, using every wave as an accelerator.

I watched her go, making no attempt to chase her. I was so low on gas, I'd probably drown. Instead I slid into the water, using the last dregs of my stamina to manage a slow sidestroke to shore.

Still, I felt good. The best I'd felt in…hell, a very long time. It had been a tough test. I'd been lucky to live through it.

I just hoped I'd be as lucky to survive the next test.

The meeting with my old boss, Assistant District Attorney Leon Stolz.

CHAPTER 16

WHILE I WAS driving into Detroit in my uncle's truck, I kept getting flashes of Bruno Corzine. I saw him raging at me in the parking garage, held back by his men. Then, looming over my hospital bed.

Except he was never really in my room, of course. Hell, according to Hilliard, he was never anywhere but the Riviera Club, playing cards in front of witnesses. He'd given himself a bulletproof alibi. It didn't make him innocent, but smart.

Really smart...

Hilliard said he was seen at the club the day of the bombing.

Seen by whom? By cops. The Riviera was a well-known mob hangout. So notorious, that feds or Detroit's Organized Crime Division probably had it under surveillance 24/7.

Corzine would have known that. He probably counted on the staked-out cops to confirm his foolproof alibi. If he knew the place was staked out, he'd expect any phone calls made from the club to be monitored. So he wouldn't have given any orders by phone, not even a burner. Because anyone could be listening in.

He would have to send his messages some other way. Something foolproof like a gofer. Because what could be safer and simpler than a messenger?

I straightened in the seat, my hands tightening on the wheel. With all the surveillance tech out there, he'd *have* to pass his orders along the old-fashioned way. And *that* was his weak spot.

He wouldn't have been able to use serious hoods as delivery boys, so he probably used some half-baked wannabe. Maybe the same one every time. If I could figure out which punk Corzine was using to carry his messages, I could charge him as an accessory to murder and get him to flip on his boss.

But first I'd have to find him…

And I couldn't do it myself. I'd already had a run-in with Corzine—he knew me by sight.

That made it harder, but not impossible.

I knew I had to meet with the ADA, but the appointment was going to have to wait a few more moments. I took out my cell phone, and tapped one of my favorites. Grady Baker, *the invisible man*.

CHAPTER 17

GRADY WAS AN investigator who worked for Garner and Mackey by digging up dirt on witnesses, perps, and victims. He said he'd be at a Starbucks near his apartment so I went there to meet him. The place was busy, so I carried my cup to a window seat to wait.

Grady walked past me twice before I realized who he was. Carrying my java, I fell in step with him on the sidewalk.

"Showoff," I said.

"You're lucky I'm not a hit man," Grady said. "You were a sitting duck in that window." Grady is a nondescript guy, like anyone on the street. There's nothing about him that's memorable. Most of us work hard at being noticed, but Grady's perfected the opposite skill.

I explained my problem. He snorted.

"Stake out a mob guy in a mob joint? Why not shoot me in the head now and save Corzine the trouble of cutting my throat?"

"Are you saying it can't be done?"

"Nope. But it'll be a lot trickier than tailing a suburban dad with a hankering for hookers. It'll cost Garner and Mackey double my usual rates, and lately—"

"Bill me personally. I don't work there anymore."

"Seriously? Good for you."

I glanced at him. He wasn't kidding. "Why? What's up?"

Grady pursed his lips, choosing his words carefully. "Garner and Mackey were solid clients for years. Until their checks started bouncing."

"I thought Garner was loaded."

"He was. But he also likes gambling. A lot. To recoup, he's been taking on clients he wouldn't have touched in the old days. Suddenly, the firm's flush again. The situation makes me uneasy. Investigators walk a fine line between the law and the bad guys. I can't risk being on the wrong side of it."

"What do you think's going on?"

"Don't know and don't want to. You know how lawyers have rules? Well, gumshoes have a few of our own, too, like not talking out of school. I'm on the Corzine thing, Brian. I'll call you when I've got something. Until I do? You might want to stay away from window seats."

CHAPTER 18

THE WAYNE COUNTY prosecutor has offices on the top floor of the Frank Murphy Hall of Justice in downtown Detroit. The place boasts of stained glass windows, walnut wainscoting, and ten-thousand-dollar desks.

Or so I've been told.

I've never actually been to the top floor. ADAs like Leon Stolz cut their plea deals in basement cubicles, where every whisper goes on record and corrections officers are only a shout away.

My old boss was waiting for me. Chunky, surly, and sour, Leon Stolz always needs a shave, and you can guess his lunch by checking his necktie. He treats his staff like serfs, and after I quit to join Garner and Mackey, he branded me a traitor who left public service to cross to the dark side, a defense practice. Winning my first few cases only threw salt in the wound.

I expected to have trouble with him. He didn't disappoint.

"Mr. Brian Lord," he nodded, sliding into a metal chair, facing me across a battered table that looked like war surplus. "Which of your miscreant clients are we throwing under the bus of justice today?"

"Let's start with Jimmy Valentine. He's offering to trade information about a mobster for—"

"Valentine's off the table," he said flatly. "No deal. Who's next?"

"Whoa, hold on, Leon—"

"That's *Mr.* Stolz to you."

"Fine. Jimmy has incriminating evidence on a mob capo, and all he's asking in exchange is a pass on a petty gambling beef. It's a freaking *gift,* Le—Mr. Stolz."

"But it's one I can't take. While I'd love to hear you pule and whine about it, I'll cut to the chase. Word from the top floor is, no deals for anyone in Zeman's crew, *especially* Corzine."

"Since when?"

"Since he became the prime suspect in a certain… explosives case. There's talk on the street that Corzine was responsible for that bomb, Brian. The DA can't look weak on this. My orders are explicit. No deals, no wiggle room."

I leaned back in my chair, eyeing him. "Is something in the wind with that crew? Federal task force? OCB?"

"If I knew, you'd be the last person I'd tell. You're a Garner and Mackey hack now. You represent the enemy. You're lucky I'm sharing this at all."

"I'm not with Garner anymore, actually. I'm on my own."

"They canned your ass? What a surprise. Same message still applies. No plea deals for anyone in that crew. I hope you didn't come down here with just one lonely loser. Who's next on your laptop?"

I didn't answer for a moment and eyed him instead. "Can I ask you one question, totally off the record? Just two guys in a room, who used to work together?"

"You can try."

"Turn off the video recorders."

He thought about that one, then flipped the switch below the desk. "Okay, we're private. What is it?"

"You've seen my client list, and ADAs always know more about suspects than the defense does. They hear comments by arresting officers, off-the-cuff remarks, facts not entered into evidence..."

He nodded, waiting.

"You know details about the bombing—"

"It's not my case, Brian—"

"But you've *heard* things!"

"Dammit, Brian, you know I can't—"

"I'm asking you like this, as two guys in a room. Is anyone *else* on my client list connected to that case? Am I in danger, Leon? Is my *family* at risk?"

He started to protest, then bit it off. Looked away instead, thinking.

"Those are two separate questions," he said, facing me again. "First, about connections to the bombing? The honest answer is, no, not to my knowledge."

"But you've gotten orders about Corzine—"

"And I've told you what I know, Brian. My orders are

to keep a safe distance from that crew, which is probably good advice. The second question, are you at risk?" He shook his head. "You've got some *very* problematic clients. One or two are…almost *certainly* dangerous."

"What does that mean?"

"Exactly what I said, and it's all I can say without breaking protocol. I'm turning the cameras and recorders back on. Now can we get back to the business at hand?"

And we did.

I ran down my list. Leon bargained hard, but since trials cost money the city doesn't have, he couldn't pass up a chance to cut his caseload.

We struck deals on the Walmart greeter who'd shown up to work inebriated, and a woman who'd mistakenly backed into a homeless man, and in her panic, fled the scene. But Leon wouldn't offer a deal for Crazy Jack the biker.

"Next," he said, sliding a file out of his briefcase. "Sherry Molinere—"

"She isn't on my list—"

"This isn't *your* list, it's mine. My office has received an allegation of an improper relationship between you and this client. I see you're handling the case pro bono. A generous gesture for a guy who isn't with a firm."

"Check your records. The public defender's office kicked her case because of a *previous* allegation of improper conduct filed by her husband. He's a state trooper, Leon. He's gaming the system. He knows which buttons to push—"

"So your response is—?"

"Sherry Molinere is a client. That's the beginning and end of our relationship. And," I added, leaning forward, locking onto his eyes, "I'd think twice before you parrot any of her husband's bullshit to my face. I've had a bad week, Leon. I'm not in the mood."

"Are you threatening me?"

"Why not? Dex Molinere is using you to threaten me. You're his bitch, Leon, and you don't even know it."

"Accusations of misconduct still have to be forwarded to the bar—"

"Unless you deem them frivolous," I said, "which they damn well are."

He didn't say anything for moment, reading my mood, choosing his words.

"I never liked you much, Brian. You're cocky, and you wanted too much too soon. Quitting the DA for Garner and Mackey? That was a betrayal."

I didn't say anything to that. He was probably right.

"But now? You really need to watch your step. You're dancing barefoot in a roomful of broken glass."

CHAPTER 19

Garner

WHEN THE MAN found the email, it was like discovering his own obituary.

He'd been lounging by the Olympic-sized pool of his Port Vale mansion in a silk robe, but he sat bolt upright when he saw a sender that no longer existed.

It was from a dead woman. A ghost.

He opened it, but there was no message. Only a blank page with an attachment. Swallowing hard, he downloaded the document.

And instantly recognized it.

It was a page copied from a ledger listing fund transfers from the Virgin Islands to the Nacional Banco de Panama. Every single one was from his personal accounts.

Taken by itself, the page wasn't incriminating. But the message was clear, because it came from the middle of the ledger. Whoever sent it had the whole file.

The extortion was beginning all over again, but with a major difference.

A new player must have taken over the game, because the last blackmailer was dead.

After a moment's musing, the man realized who it must be. And exactly how to deal with him.

Still a bit shaken, he glanced around. His estate looked as posh as it had for the past century, a flat roofed tri-level, à la Frank Lloyd Wright.

His new mistress was swimming laps in the pool, nude as a Titian Venus. She was ten years younger than his last mistress, and beautiful, but not exceptionally bright. It was for the best. Sharing your life and secrets with a clever woman can be tiring—and sometimes dangerous.

In the driveway, his hired help was washing the Morgan Plus 8, a classically styled roadster, complete with a leather strap over the hood. The man admired the car, but rarely drove it. Driving was for his inferiors.

And so was the task at hand.

He called for his hired help. The gaunt man perked up and sauntered over.

"Sir?" he asked, smirking a little as he spoke. Both men knew his true role at the estate. He was a gift from a Serbian arms dealer. He drove the man around, protected him, and dealt with the messier aspects of his business. Including blackmail and murder.

The man outlined the problem to the assassin, speaking slowly and distinctly, to be sure the Serbian man understood. A new player had the stolen file. It was probably on a thumb drive by now. The assassin was to find the drive, find the player, and eliminate both of them.

"How will I know this man?" asked the assassin.

"That part's easy. He's famous."

The man swiveled the notebook to show the assassin the screen. A video was playing of a man in a three-piece suit, soaking wet, and staggering out of the surf with a dog in his arms.

CHAPTER 20

NO SHIRT, NO SHOES, NO PROBLEM.

The sign over the door of the Beachfront Bistro says it all. It dates from the lumber baron days, built of pine logs that were probably dropped on the spot. The bar offers beers and burgers, and has a jukebox that thumps out pop tunes from the Summer of Love.

Locals love the joint. It's a second home for everyone in the area code.

Tall Paul bought the place with his separation money from the army. He practically lives there. But at least it makes him easy to find.

Paul and my uncle Josh were at a table just outside the office, both suitably dressed for fine beachfront dining. They were barefoot, wearing shorts and Hawaiian shirts. Paul nodded at the barmaid as I walked in, and a cold Budweiser, cheeseburger, and fries arrived as I sat down.

"How did it go?" Uncle Josh asked.

"Bad news, and no news," I said around a mouthful of juicy burger. I explained about the DA's new hands-off policy toward Corzine's crew, and told them about his warning.

"I managed to cut deals for a few clients, but Stolz wouldn't budge on the others. Or give up any info that isn't in the files."

"This warning? Do you think it was about the biker?" Paul asked. "He's not much more than a kid, but he's got the likeliest connections for a bombing. Outlaw crews play rough."

"If Jack's ticked off at me, he's about to be more so," I said, chasing a mouthful of fries with a swig of Bud. "No deal for him, either. Leon wants to look tough for the cameras, and Crazy Jack's a perfect photo op. His cell's already booked."

"But it might get un-booked if his lawyer had an unfortunate accident, right?" Uncle Josh said. "What would happen then?"

"He…would get a continuance to seek new counsel," I conceded. "Then another delay while he brought him or her up to speed. Meanwhile, charges could lapse, his underage girlfriend keeps getting older, maybe changes her mind about testifying…The whole thing could go away."

"Sounds like a plan to me," Josh said, then stopped. "What is it?"

I'd held up my hand like a traffic cop. *Stop.* They both turned to see what I was staring at.

A blond woman, slim as a whisper in a summer shift

and flip-flops, was standing in the club doorway, scanning the crowd...for me.

"Sherry?" I called, standing up and waving. "I'm over here!"

"God," she said, hurrying to our table and clinging to me.

"You're shaking," I said, easing her into a chair. "What's wrong?"

"Dex found me again," she managed. Paul passed her his drink, and she guzzled it down without caring what it was.

"Slow down," I said, sitting down beside her. "What happened? Where did he find you?"

"At the Glazers, that job you got me in Royal Oak. As a freaking nanny, for chrissake! I have a degree in software engineering."

"Easy now, easy," I said. "Remember? Engineers have to submit job histories, background checks. He could've tracked you—"

"He tracked me anyway!" she wailed. "He came to the house this morning in his freaking *uniform!* As a state trooper, he told the Glazers that I was mentally unstable, and a danger to myself and others. Then he showed them my old mug shot..."

She broke down, sobbing like a child. I touched her shoulder, and didn't know what else to do.

But Uncle Josh did.

"Easy now, miss," he rumbled in his deep bass voice, the way he's been soothing Paul and me all our lives. "He found you, but now you've found us, and you're home free. You're safe. Everything's gonna be fine. You just take another long slug of whatever this was." He tapped Paul's empty glass, motioning to the barmaid, who quickly brought over a refill. Sherry chugged that one at a gulp, too, wincing as she did it.

"Christ, what is this crap?"

"Single malt Glenfiddich," Paul sighed, "twelve years old."

"Scotch? I hate Scotch."

"Could've fooled me," Paul said, eyeing her empty glass. "Would you like something else?"

"Not here," Uncle Josh said, rising. "If her ex-husband found her once, he might be following along. I will be leaving with this lady."

"Where are you going?" I asked. Sherry didn't even bother. She was already collecting her purse. Uncle Josh is like that. People in need of help are drawn to him, like metal to a magnet.

"If I told you, and someone asks where she is, you'd have to lie, Brian. And you're a lousy liar, which is shocking for a lawyer. You should practice more. If you need me, you've got my cell number."

He took Sherry's arm and ushered her out. And she didn't even look back.

CHAPTER 21

"WHERE WILL HE take her?" I asked Paul.

"Unc's got a half dozen rehab and remodel projects going, mostly for summer people. She'll be safe at one of those, and untraceable for a while, at least. What are you going to do?"

"Haven't a clue," I said honestly. "Her husband's got her on the run. Every time she lights somewhere, he shows up. I don't know how he does it."

"He's a state cop, right?" Paul said. "Molinere? So it ain't supernatural. He's probably got contacts we can't even dream about. But he'd better hope they don't work this time."

"How do you mean?"

"Uncle Josh is a sweetheart and I love him. But if that cop shows up and tries to bully that girl? He'd better have his major medical paid up, because bad things are gonna happen."

"They already have," I said. "Molinere's filed a complaint with the Wayne County DA, trying to get me removed as her attorney. He knows the system, and he's playing it."

"So what do we do?"

"Nothing, yet. He filed the complaint with my old boss. Leon may be a jerk, but he's good at his job. He promised to take a closer look at the guy, and I think he will."

"If he's so good at his job, why is your pal Corzine still walking around?"

"Because his flunkies handle the rough stuff while he plays cards in a public place, surrounded by witnesses." I went on to explain my hunch about the messengers, and that I'd set Grady on the trail.

"How good is this Grady?" Paul asked.

"If you ever meet him, you won't remember him five seconds later," I said. "That's how good he is."

We sat quietly for half an hour, sipping our drinks and catching up. Then I excused myself, and walked up the beach to the cottage. It had been a rough day, and tomorrow would probably be even tougher.

I desperately needed to rest.

So naturally, sleep didn't come when I laid in my bed.

I kept thinking about Grady, who was working the Riviera Club alone. Corzine was no fool. He was a rising star in the mob world and a dangerous man.

Had I pushed Grady too close to the problem? Being invisible to cheating husbands or embezzlers is one thing, but would it be so easy around a thug like Corzine?

Damn it.

Grady was the ultimate pro, though. He was practically a legend in the business. I had to trust his talents.

But as soon as I put Grady aside, thoughts of Serena took his place. She'd seemed so…overwhelmingly perfect at first. Smart, pretty, dressed like a runway model. She had a great job with Garner and Mackey at Cadillac Square. After the army, law school, and my crappy job as an ADA, having a woman like her seemed almost too good to be true…

And of course, it was. Our lightning engagement was her idea, and in hindsight, I realized our whole relationship was basically her idea. One that began to sour the day I gave her the ring.

She'd traded it in for a larger stone. She'd paid the difference, and said that she just wanted to impress her girlfriends at work. As though it was all for show.

But it wasn't. Not to me. Before long, we were squabbling almost nonstop. But what if we'd faced up to it, admitted we'd made a mistake, and broken things off?

Maybe she wouldn't have been in the car that day. And that was on me.

It was almost dawn when I finally dropped off. The alarm woke me fifteen minutes later.

I sprung out of bed because I had a big day in store. I was starting a job I hadn't held since high school.

CHAPTER 22

THE MORNING SUN was barely breaking across the bay when I got to the beach. It cut a shimmering silvery path across the gentle surf.

I checked the bonfire pits first, collecting the empties, picking up broken glass, and kicking sand over the charred pits.

For the most part, the shore was in good shape. Beach folks generally police up after themselves, but there are always a few who party late.

I found a young couple under a beach blanket, sound asleep in each other's arms and without a stitch of clothing on their bodies. I told them the beach wasn't open yet, and that they might want to find their clothes before the kids started showing up. When I left them, they were still holding each other, watching the sun rise out over the surf.

My day brightened when I saw Carly coming down the beach, dressed for work. She was barefoot, and in shorts and a Hawaiian shirt. It was the uniform of the day.

"You made it," she said, brightly. "I thought you might change your mind."

"Why would you think that?"

"Because you've been through a heck of a lot, Brian," she said, falling into step beside me. "Hell, you've been blown up. I'm just saying, if you do change your mind—"

"Wow. If this is your 'go get 'em, tiger' pep talk, it needs work."

"Okay, okay," she said, raising her hands in mock surrender. "You're where you need to be. At least for now. If you need me, I'll be in my office. I'll be back at noon to rotate you out for lunch. Otherwise, you're on your own, pal. Good luck."

I watched her walk away, a dynamo of a woman in a coltish frame. She was really something. But once again, our timing was totally askew. I wondered if we'd always be out of sync—a day early, or ten years too late.

I didn't worry about it for long, though, because the first invaders were already hitting the beach. A steady stream of cars rolled into the parking lot, and screaming kids spilled out, while their moms followed behind in floppy hats and shades toting lawn chairs and blankets and sunblock. There were tots with pails and shovels, and tweens and teens with cell phones and ear buds who were scarcely aware of the water.

I climbed the short ladder up to my tower chair and settled in. I took my first long look up and down the shore. Kids were daring each other to test the waters.

And then I felt myself relaxing, *really* relaxing. I felt

the knots that have been wound around my heart since Afghanistan loosen their hold a little. I was fully alert, mindful of every single soul on that shore, but at the same time, I was basking in the beauty of the day. The surf, the wheeling gulls, the laughter of children.

It got better. Women started arriving, but instead of sunning themselves or trolling for men, they were gathering around my chair, chatting me up, taking selfies with me in the background.

I knew that it was only because I was temporarily famous. I was the guy who saved the dog in the video, but still, I was enjoying my fifteen minutes of stardom...

Until I saw the first kid make a fatal mistake.

I was up, out of my chair, sprinting into the surf before I finished my conversation with a beach bunny. Something was wrong. Something serious.

A minute before, a little kid had been paddling around the first raft. It was moored thirty yards offshore in shallow water, only a few feet deep. He was having a great time, plunging into the breakers like a seal.

But he hadn't surfaced. He'd been down too damn long. And then suddenly, he shot out of the water, hacking and gagging, half-drowned. With one arm, I grabbed him before the next breaker could roll him under. I held him clear of the water, letting him breathe and encouraging him to cough the water out of his windpipe. He was good to go in less than a minute, which is exactly how long it would have taken him to drown. He could have been gone just that quickly.

I asked him where his mom was, and he pointed her out. She was on her feet, rushing toward us. I waved that he was okay, then gave her a split-finger "eyes on" signal, and she nodded. I took a deep breath. The boy was my first save.

I went back to my chair.

The sun was still high, the lakeshore was still beautiful, but I'd just been reminded how quickly things can go wrong at the beach.

Or anywhere.

CHAPTER 23

CARLY CAME BY at noon, and I took my lunch break at the Bistro. I had an omelet and coffee, because I didn't want to have anything heavy while I was on duty. I carried my plate out to the patio deck and took a table by the railing. It offered a view of the beach, and a better view of Carly, who was down the shore in the tower. Beautiful on both counts.

Paul popped out of the kitchen. "Hey, lifeguard. Uncle Josh called in at ten. Your friend had a quiet night, and all's well. No sign of her husband. How's your first day on the job going?"

"The best I've felt in a long time," I said around a mouthful. "Almost as good as I do now. You're a great cook."

"I am, brother, which is why I have to get back. No rest for the wick—aw, crap. Here we go."

I swiveled in my seat to follow his stare. Two police cars had pulled into the Bistro lot. One was from the Port Vale PD, and the second was unmarked. Chief

Paquette and Lieutenant Bev Hilliard got out separately, but marched in together, heading straight for me. Paul vanished into the kitchen, not an easy thing to do when you're six seven, wearing a toque.

"Mr. Lord," the chief nodded, pulling up a chair, "do you mind?"

"Not at all. I'd recommend—"

"This isn't social," Hilliard said, taking the seat beside the chief. "As you've probably guessed, you're still very much a person of interest in the car bombing."

"I'd be surprised if I wasn't. The husband, the wife, the partner, are always prime suspects. But then again, since I was almost blown to hell myself...? Anyway, why all the muscle, Lieutenant? What is it you want?"

"I'm hoping to get a straight answer out of you for once. Your client, Jimmy Valentine? When did you speak with him last?"

"Not...for a few days. Why?"

"Is that unusual?"

"Jimmy doesn't punch a time clock. Why are you asking about him?"

"He was under surveillance by the Organized Crime Unit until last night when he...dropped out of sight."

"They lost him? Where?"

"An after-hours poker game on Dequinder. They couldn't exactly follow him into a closed room. The other players said he left to use the bathroom, and then he never came back."

"Did he ditch them on purpose? Or was he abducted?"

Hilliard shrugged.

"Why were they tailing him?"

"Since he's trying to buy himself a deal by dealing dirt on Corzine, the boss's people are looking for him."

"And you were watching *Jimmy*? Instead of Corzine?"

"We were watching both of them. Corzine's the easy one, because he hangs around his club. But Valentine—"

"Is in the wind. Can you blame him? You have to find him before Corzine's crew does."

"Then help us."

"I can't. I have no idea where Jimmy is, and no way to contact him. If he calls, I can tell him you're looking for him. Whether he chooses to contact you is up to him."

"That's not good enough."

"It has to be. Anything he says to me, including his whereabouts, falls under attorney–client privilege."

"You're being obstructive."

"I'm protecting my client, which I'm damned well required to do, by law and oath. I'll help if I can, Lieutenant, but not by selling Jimmy out."

"Is he still a client? You're working as a lifeguard, for god's sake. Are you even a practicing attorney anymore?"

"I'm a lawyer because I passed the state bar, Lieutenant. Not because I had an office on Cadillac Square. I work for my clients, until they choose to take me off their cases."

"I doubt many judges will take you seriously if you show up in cut-offs and flip-flops."

"I take courtrooms seriously, Lieutenant. Besides, if I screw up a case, it can be appealed. On the beach, if some kid makes a little mistake, and I miss it? There's no mistrial, no appeal. There's only a funeral. So I take both of my jobs seriously. And if your guys had paid closer attention to theirs, maybe they wouldn't have lost Jimmy."

CHAPTER 24

HILLIARD ROSE, GLOWERING down at me, then wheeled and stalked out. I expected Chief Paquette to follow, but she just shook her head. "You don't have enough enemies? Trying to add one more?"

"Are you gonna bust my chops, too, Chief?"

"Not about Valentine," she said, pushing a police file and a mug shot of a haggard, red-eyed woman over to me. "Do you know who this is?"

"Sure. Her name's Sherry Molinere, and she's a client who was recently busted for possession. That mug shot is six years out of date."

"And that's all she is to you? A client?"

"Here we go," I sighed.

"Meaning what?"

"Meaning, you've received allegations of mental instability and illegal drug use. You've heard claims that she's a danger to herself and others. Off the record? Maybe there have been a few suggestions of improper advances by her attorney, me, toward this client. All filed by her husband, Dexter Molinere, a ten-year corporal in the state police."

"So far, you're batting a thousand."

"Let's see what your average is. Does anything strike you odd about all this?"

"Sure. The mug shot. Your client was what? Twenty when it was taken, and strung-out at the time. I doubt she looks much like this anymore."

"She was a college kid who got messed up on meth and oxy, and got busted for possession. While she was in Midland Rehab, the arresting officer, Corporal Molinere, visited regularly and brought her flowers. He seemed to be the only one who cared about her—a white knight. They were married three weeks after her release."

"But...?" the chief prompted.

"Sherry thought he was a bit stiff at first, but it was a welcome relief after the life she'd been in. Then his white hat fell off. Dexter Molinere's a control freak. He dictated every aspect of their lives, clothes, meals, friends. She was practically a hostage. And when she finally filed for divorce?" I gestured toward the mug shot.

"She suddenly gets busted for possession again."

"For drugs that were planted by her husband."

"Can you prove that?"

"Of course not. He knows the system, Chief. He's part of it. The Staties gave Sherry a toxic screening when she was arrested, but then it disappeared."

"A buddy protecting a fellow officer's wife?"

"It wasn't ditched to *protect* her. I think she tested clean, which would prove the charges are bogus. Look, I can understand you feeling sympathetic toward the officer's situation—"

"Sympathetic?" she echoed, raising her eyebrows.

"A cop with wife trouble? Do tell. Divorce rates in law enforcement rank right up there with rock stars. You're a career cop, who's the widow of a cop—"

"With a son on the force, and a nephew who's applied to the academy," she finished. "Which means I know cops a hell of a lot better than you ever will, sonny. My Arlo had a theory about cops. Wanna hear it?"

"Go ahead."

"Some join the force because it's a family business, the way citizens become butchers or coal miners. Others think it's a good job—do your twenty-five, then collect your pension. Some want to serve and protect, and if they weren't cops, they'd be firemen or EMTs. But an unhappy few, like Corporal Molinere? They're bullies. They like pushing people around and the badge gives 'em a license to do it."

"You sound like you know him."

"Only the type. This mug shot tells me a lot more about him than it does her." She tapped the photo with a fingertip. "No man who really loved a woman would *ever* want people to see his wife like this. Still, I've got an official BOLO request from the state police. I have to honor it."

"Are you going to arrest her?"

"Oddly enough, the request is only procedural," she said, leaning back in her chair. "We're here to locate and inform. Is Molinere physically abusive?"

"Not to my knowledge. Sherry's afraid of being brought home. He doesn't want to hurt her. He wants to own her."

The chief mulled that a moment, then shook her head. "He may not be a danger to her, but that doesn't mean you're bulletproof."

"Meaning...?"

"Most officers serve their whole careers without drawing a weapon. Corporal Molinere's been involved in two shootings in the past three years. Both perps were armed. One was threatening to massacre his family with a machete, and the other had already fired on officers, probably hoping for suicide by cop. There's no question both shoots were justified, but...?" She leaned forward, lowering her voice.

I leaned in, too.

"The thing is, Counselor? Molinere was on the force eight years before his first shooting. Only nine months before the second. He knows how easy it is to pull a trigger now. Maybe he's developing a taste for it. If you get crossways of him, you'd best keep that in mind."

"I'll remember," I said.

"You'd damned well better," she said.

CHAPTER 25

THAT NIGHT, I snapped awake in the dark. My eyes were wide open as I sat motionless in bed, listening. Then I heard it again. A muffled thump and voices that were coming from downstairs.

Molinere?

If so, he wasn't alone.

Slipping out of bed, I padded silently to the closet, and picked up the Louisville Slugger I'd bought with beach bottle money when I was ten. It's still perfectly balanced and swings like it's part of my arm.

I carefully tiptoed down the stairs, keeping close to the wall to avoid squeaks. Not that I needed to. I could see two figures blundering about the kitchen in the dark. They clearly didn't care if I heard them.

I switched on the light, startling the crap out of both of them. It was a bad idea, because one second later, both men had guns aimed at my head.

They were wearing jeans, boots, and black leather vests over their sleeveless T-shirts. Both were decked in Iron Disciples colors. Bikers.

Crazy Jack Bruske's blond mane fell to his shoulders and tangled in his scruffy beard.

The second man looked like Attila the Hun's cousin. He might as well have been a berserker who'd stepped out of a ninth-century time warp. He had wild hair and a beard that would impress ZZ Top.

"Hey, Brian," Jack said, sliding his weapon back into a concealed-carry shoulder holster. "What's the bat for? Gonna pop up a few flies?"

I'd forgotten I had the Slugger in my hand. The Hun hadn't. His gun was still aimed at my head. I put the bat down.

"What the hell are you doing here, Jack? It's two in the morning."

"We need to talk," he said. "Had to wait for your watchdogs to nod off."

"What watchdogs?"

"Two guys in a blacked-out van, off the road, maybe a hundred yards from the house," the Hun said. "They got you staked out. We stashed our bikes beyond them, and walked in. Are they cops?"

"I don't know. Maybe. Somebody tried to kill me a week ago. I could be on somebody's watch list."

"I don't think so," Jack said doubtfully. "I've seen that van before. They've been on you for a while, brother. And I ain't so sure they're law."

"License plate's muddied up so you can't make it out," the second biker added. "They're pros, whoever they are."

"This here's Cujo," Jack said. "He's with the Iron Disciples, too. An enforcer."

The Hun nodded. Neither of us offered to shake hands.

"You got beers?" Jack asked.

"In the fridge," I said. They helped themselves. We sat at the kitchen table, warily facing each other.

"What's so important it couldn't wait till morning, Jack?"

"You were gonna talk to that ADA about my case? Schulz?"

"Stolz," I said. "Look—"

"No deals," Cujo growled.

"What?"

"You heard me. Jack can't take no deal."

"Stolz didn't offer one."

"Whoa, wait a minute. Isn't there anything you can do?"

"Stolz wants to put you away on the six o' clock news, Jack, and wants to slap the cuffs on you himself. So unless you've got something to trade…?"

"I said no deals," Cujo said.

"You're not my client, pal, and you won't be the one doing the time."

"How much time?" Jack asked.

"At most, it'll be a year."

"Okay, look, I can do the year, Brian. Hell, it'll probably give me some street cred in the group. Besides, I'd only be, what? Twenty-three when I get out?" He shook his mane slowly as he accepted his fate.

"It's tough, kid," Cujo said. "But if you trade in anything on the crew, you'll get shanked before you hit your bunk. And I'll get clipped for being your running buddy."

"You're saying your own crew will kill you?" I asked.

"It's the life we're in, man," Jack shrugged. "You're my lawyer. What's your hotshot legal advice?"

"Do the time. It's only a year, and if you're on your best behavior while you're in there, you stand a good chance to get out early."

Jack nodded again. "Thanks, Brian. I'll go with your advice then."

"I'd appreciate it," I said, as I walked them out. "Jack? You said something earlier about seeing my watchdog van before. Did you mean before the bombing?"

"Yeah. I stopped by your office last week, but I seen the truck on the street and kept goin'. Thought they might be cops, looking to pick me up, but now? They're definitely on you, Brian. Watch yourself."

CHAPTER 26

AT FIRST LIGHT, I was up and at 'em. I didn't have breakfast because there wasn't any time for it. Instead, I stalked out to the garage at the rear of the property and uncovered the battered Jeep CJ-7 we keep there as a beach buggy. I fired up the old L6 engine as though it had been run yesterday, instead of sometime last summer.

I came roaring out of the garage, racing down the back trail to the rear of the property where Jack and Cujo had said the black van had been parked the night before. I was hoping to take them by surprise.

But there was no one in sight.

Somebody *had* been there, though. I saw tire tracks that led off the road into an area concealed by brush, one that offered a clear view of the cottage. There were oil spots on the ground. A vehicle had definitely been parked there.

The bikers were right. Somebody was watching the

cottage. The black van they'd mentioned sounded ominous, because it indicated that more than one person was doing it. Maybe it was a crew—a band of cops, protecting me? Or maybe it was a posse looking to finish the job the bomber botched?

As I roared out the long dirt road to the highway, a blue sedan pulled out of a brushy area, spraying gravel. It quickly gained speed, tailgating me. Once the lights went on, I knew exactly who it was.

I pulled off on the shoulder and he did the same. He was driving a navy-blue sedan, unmarked, but equipped with a full bank of flashing LEDs in the grille. The cop stepped out in full uniform, including his equipment belt. A Glock automatic, flashlight, and a nightstick, which he drew as he walked up to the Jeep. He paused to casually smash the taillight, then sheathed the stick.

"That's the official reason why you've been stopped," Dex Molinere said, not bothering to conceal a smirk. "Broken taillight. Don't feel too bad. The video-cam on my cruiser's broken too."

Up close, Molinere was smaller than I'd expected, barely above the five eight department minimum, and a hundred and fifty pounds. But the gun and nightstick gave him all the weight he needed.

"Do you know who I am?" he demanded.

"Corporal Molinere," I sighed. "The famous tail-light breaker."

"I can break a lot more than that—"

"Actually, you can't," I said.

"Why? You think being a lawyer gives you some kind of immunity?"

"The law's got nothing to do with it. Over the past week, every scratch and dent on my body has been X-rayed, photographed, and catalogued. If I have one more bruise after this conversation? You'll be swapping that uniform for a jailhouse jump suit."

He looked away a moment, considering that. He was weak jawed and watery eyed, and seemed to be the type that probably got pushed around every damn day back in grade school. And that probably made him what he was now.

Armed and dangerous.

"You're assuming you'll be around to tell 'em we talked," he said, resting his palm on his gun butt. I didn't bother to answer.

"I'll make it simple, pal. Just tell me where my wife is—"

"I don't know where she is."

"Then you won't mind if I take a quick look through your place, just to be sure—"

"That's not gonna happen."

"How do you sleep at night? You're breaking up a marriage—"

"She practically spits when she says your name, Dex. All she wants is to get away. It's called a divorce. They happen about half the time nowadays. Deal with it. Let her go."

"She's bangin' you already, isn't she?"

"That's not true, and you know it."

"What I know is, somebody tried to kill you and missed, which is lucky for you. But even luckier for me."

"How do you figure?"

"Because it makes you fair game now, Counselor. I could pop you right here, right now. The local yokel cops will assume it's connected to the last time. My name wouldn't even come up."

"Sure it would. The Port Vale police have already questioned me about you, Dex. Framing Sherry with a bogus possession bust was a mistake. It'll blow back on you eventually. You're going to lose everything. Your job, maybe your freedom. Unless you let her go."

"Jesus, you don't get it," he said, shaking his head. "Whoever tried to take you out probably ain't done trying. My Sherry, your family, everybody around you is in danger because you're still breathing. I won't let you put my wife in danger. I'll put you in the goddamn ground first. You understand me?"

I understood that Molinere was only one wrong word away from losing control and putting a bullet in my skull. So I didn't say a word. I looked away, avoiding his eyes. I wasn't proud of it, but it beat the alternative.

And maybe it worked.

"Think it over," he said, stuffing a business card in my breast pocket, "and if you decide you want to hand her over, call me."

It took every ounce of my self-control to keep from punching him in the face.

"And better make it real soon," he said. "The next time I see you? I'll break a helluva lot more than a tail-light."

Jerking out his nightstick, he smashed the Jeep's other taillight before he stalked back to his cruiser.

CHAPTER 27

PORT VALE PD headquarters is housed in a Greek Revival temple in the heart of the Olde Towne district, surrounded by retro shops and offices that date back to the nineteenth century. It's quaint, cute, and touristy.

None of that mattered as I stormed up the stone steps three at a time, blew through the heavy oak doors, and ran straight into trouble. Lieutenant Bev Hilliard was making a call at a desk a few steps from the greeting counter. She slammed down her phone as soon as she saw me.

"Mr. Lord? I need a word. Now."

When a cop uses that tone in the middle of a police station, every head turns. The sergeant at the counter rested his hand on his weapon, but Hilliard waved him off, motioning me to her desk.

"Has Valentine contacted you?" she asked.

"Not yet. If you want to know where Jimmy is, ask Bruno Corzine. I've got troubles of my own. Where's the chief?"

"She's in a meeting upstairs and should be down in a minute. Can I show you something?"

"Sure."

"It's a video. It'll only take a minute. In here, please."

I followed her into a glassed-in office with Chief Paquette's name on the door. There were file cabinets in the corner, a wall full of framed awards and photographs, and a Spartan metal desk with a laptop on top of it. She switched on the laptop, then swiveled the screen toward me.

It took me a moment to grasp what she was showing me. It was a dining room in a crowded restaurant, a bar in the background lined with blue-collar types. Bruno Corzine was at a table in the far corner, playing cards with three other goons.

"The Riviera Club," I said. "You've got it wired."

"Note the time line in the corner of the screen."

"What about it?"

"This video spans nearly seven hours, yesterday, with Corzine in view the whole time. And Valentine went missing during the first two hours."

"So? Corzine gets a pass because he's drinking with his buddies on camera at the time? Bin Laden was in Pakistan when the Towers came down. He still got it done."

"And if Corzine was involved with Valentine's disappearance, or with what happened to your fiancée, we'll get him for it. You can see that we're on him."

It was true, they were. But that wasn't all I saw. At the far end of the bar, a nondescript little guy in a baseball cap was nursing a beer, watching the Tigers on TV.

Grady Baker. Mr. Invisible was on the job, too. And Hilliard clearly didn't know who he was. Score one for our team.

"Okay, you're on it," I conceded. "What do you want from me?"

"Work with us, Brian. Tell Valentine to turn himself in. We can protect him."

"I already told you. If he contacts me, I can tell him what you're suggesting. That's the best I can do."

"Damn it, that's—"

"Hey!" Chief Paquette said, poking her head in. "If you two want a license to fight, the county clerk is on the third floor. What's the problem here?" She stepped inside, closing the door behind her.

"No problem," Hilliard said as she glared at me.

"I definitely have a problem," I said, "but not with the lieutenant. I just got pulled over by a psycho state trooper." I quickly recounted my run-in with Dex Molinere.

"Did any witnesses see what happened?" the chief asked.

"The cottage sits on forty wooded acres, so no, no witnesses."

"You're an attorney, so you know the procedure, Mr. Lord. File a complaint, and I'll find the corporal and have a talk with him. But unless he's dumb enough to admit to it..."

"It's his word against mine," I sighed.

"Not quite. He was here yesterday. Paid me a courtesy call, in fact, in full uniform."

"What did he want?"

"You know what he wanted. To locate his wife. He wasn't wearing a sidearm."

"What?"

"He left his weapon in his car to impress the hick town police chief with how harmless he was. Popping in unarmed."

"Were you impressed?"

"Sonny, we're only a few miles up the shore from a town they call Murder City. Firearms aren't optional in my department, and I know that Staties are required to carry, even off duty. Molinere ignored his own unit's regulations in order to blow smoke at me, which had the same effect on me as seeing that six-year-old mug shot. This guy's a wrong cop, which makes him dangerous."

"What are you going to do?"

"Follow up on your complaint. I'll pick him up, have a serious talk with him, and hopefully, send him packing. In the meantime, tell your uncle Josh to move his lady friend again. The neighbors have noticed."

"You know about that?"

"I'm the chief of police. In this town, I know almost everything. Except for one important piece of information."

"And what's that?"

"Molinere," she said simply. "Any idea where he is now?"

CHAPTER 28

Dex

CROUCHED IN A cluster of cedars across from the Lord cottage, Corporal Dexter Molinere wiped the sweat from his eyes. He'd swapped his uniform for his National Guard jungle camouflage, which made him nearly invisible in the piney woods behind the Lord cottage, but the outfit was made of rip-proof canvas that didn't breathe, and he was already sweating, despite the early hour.

He'd been in place for an hour, watching for any sign of life within. A shadow, a blind quivering—any sign from Sherry that gave her away.

She was in there. He damn well *knew* it. And she was alone, now that he'd chased her hotshot boyfriend away. The thought of the two of them together, Sherry opening her robe in front of him, baring her breasts—

His jaw locked. At the same time, he couldn't help savoring the image. He wondered how it would *feel* to watch Sherry put out for someone else.

Maybe they could try that to loosen things up a little.

Sherry was always complaining he was too uptight, too controlling. He'd show her how loose he could get and bring a little excitement to the sack.

But first, he had to find her and get her home. Away from the bastard who'd—

He shook off the anger that threatened to take him over. First things first. *Find Sherry. Force her to come back.*

Moving out of the pines, he trotted up the driveway to the house. Casing the cottage was easy, because most blinds were up and the curtains were open to the morning sun.

Slinking around the building warily, he peered through every window, keeping low and using his police training to remain unobserved.

He made a full circle of the house without seeing Sherry or any other sign of life. There were no indications anyone was using the place but the lifeguard.

There was one coffee cup on the kitchen table, not two. No blankets or pillows on the sofa, but they'd probably be sleeping together anyway, up in Lord's bedroom.

The second-floor blinds were drawn and there was no easy access to the room. He couldn't see anything he could climb—no trellis or ladder or trees close enough to the building to give him a quick look.

He'd have to break in.

Damn. Dex didn't like the idea. It was risky, especially since he'd already leaned hard on Lord. The chump could be coming back any sec with the local yokel law, and no explanation would cover his ass if they caught him inside the house. Still...

He *had* to know if Sherry was in there. And there was only one way to find out.

He circled the house to the front porch that faced the beach. With luck, he'd hear a vehicle approaching in time to get away without being spotted. The beach was all but deserted, with a lone person strolling along the water in the distance. But the person was too far down the shore for Dex to see.

Moving quickly, he trotted up the steps to the front door, took a packet of lock picks out of his breast pocket, and went to work on the deadbolt. Christ, the damn thing had to be a hundred years old. The tumblers were rusty and hard to turn, and some interior springs were likely broken.

Twice he thought he had it, but the door wouldn't budge. Not a hair. Sweat was dripping on the backs of his hands as he worked. He decided to give it one last try. If he couldn't pop it, he'd circle around and have a go at the kitchen door.

Taking a deep breath to steady himself, he glanced quickly down the beach—Goddamn! A person was headed straight for the house, barely a hundred yards off now. Was he coming here or just strolling this way? Dex couldn't be sure, but he couldn't get caught on this porch.

Keeping to the shadows, he edged around the corner of the house, crossed the drive to the pines, and then crouched down in the shadows.

He waited to see which way the beach stroller went.

And hoped to hell it was Sherry.

CHAPTER 29

SOMEONE WAS IN *the house.*

I knew it the moment I stepped in the kitchen door. I've been coming home to the cottage my whole life. I know every groan and grumble, and the way it *feels* when it's empty.

But it wasn't. Someone was here. I snatched up my Louisville Slugger and circled the ground floor. I slid through the kitchen, the dining area, and the living room, hoping I'd find Molinere lurking...

A floorboard creaked and I froze and listened carefully. No. It wasn't a floorboard.

It was the front porch swing, creaking in the breeze. Only there was no breeze.

I yanked open the door, expecting to find the trooper—

"Hey," Carly Delaney said.

"Hey, yourself. What are you doing here?"

"I've been thinking. After your test? When we talked, on the raft? What you said about...old times?"

"What about it?"

"It's been bugging me. I haven't been able to get it out of my mind. Come sit by me. Please." She patted the seat tentatively, as though she expected me to say no.

I sat down beside her, and the swing fell into an automatic rhythm that put us in sync. That was the way it had always been with us, back when we were too young to know how rare and fine a thing that really was.

Neither of us spoke for a bit. She was lost in thought. I was curious but unwilling to push things. That was something else I remembered from those old days. Pushing Carly was not a good idea.

"So here's the thing," she said abruptly, turning to me. "What you said about our timing being off, back in the day?"

I nodded.

"You were right, it was. Looking back now, it's almost comical to think about those stupid teenybopper relationships that all seemed so terribly important at the time, that turned out to be...well, to not matter much."

"You married one of yours," I pointed out.

"Not for long," she sighed. "I swear I knew it was a huge mistake right when my dad walked me down the aisle. But the church was full, our friends and families were there. So...? We said till death us do part and split up within the year. Dennis is in real estate now, in Houston, with a new pre-fab family, two of hers, one of theirs. He sends me Christmas cards."

"Staying in touch? Or rubbing it in?"

"A little of both, I imagine." She laughed with more regret than humor. But then she cocked her head. "Marrying Dennis was a mistake," she continued, "but it wasn't the biggest one I made. You know, back in the day, I almost asked you not to go."

"What are you talking about?"

"Before you enlisted? I knew you were leaving, and I was—afraid for you, of course, but more than that? I was afraid we'd miss our chance. And we did."

"Carly…"

"Look, I know we were just kids. If I'd told you how I felt, it probably wouldn't have changed a thing. But if you'd asked me to wait for you, I would have. I wouldn't have made the mistake of marrying Dennis."

She waited a beat, letting her words sink in. Then she sighed. "Maybe our timing's all wrong again now, and it's too late. Maybe we had our moment and missed it. But this time, I'm not letting us miss out on something because I didn't tell you how I feel."

I didn't say anything because there was nothing to say. I'd known Carly all my life, but suddenly, I wasn't sure I knew her at all.

She was right, our timing was terrible. Again. But deep down?

I didn't care.

She'd bared her heart to me. It was an incredibly brave thing to do. And right now, I was in no position to say anything in response. I think she got that.

"Look at the time," she said, glancing at her watch

and rising from the swing. "Your shift starts in twenty. Can I walk you down?"

"That...would be great," I said, standing up. "I'll just lock up."

We walked down the shore to the park together, barefoot in the sand. Somewhere along the way, we were holding hands. It felt so natural, I'm not certain she even noticed.

But I did.

CHAPTER 30

Dex

AS HE LURKED in the shadows, Molinere watched Brian stroll off toward the park with that woman. For a manic second, he'd thought she was Sherry, but a quick glimpse confirmed that he'd been wrong.

He'd drawn his weapon on reflex, but then slid it under his belt at the small of his back. The last thing he wanted was to explain a sidearm to some yokel cop, but it was a chance he'd have to take.

As Dex watched Brian walk away, he realized he had a window of opportunity. He had enough time to get into the house for a quick, thorough search. He'd take Sherry at gunpoint if necessary and get the hell out of Vale County.

After slipping out of the trees, he trotted across the drive to the kitchen door. That lock was new, well-oiled, and he was inside in under a minute.

He closed the door quietly behind him, drew his weapon, and made a quick search of the first floor, clearing each room in turn.

Nothing. No sign of Sherry.

With his weapon leading the way, Dex tiptoed silently up the stairs, pausing at the second floor landing to listen. For a moment he thought he heard a sound from outside. The crunch of gravel? A car rolling up?

He edged to a window that offered a view of the driveway and couldn't see a car, or anything out of place.

He picked up his pace, searching each of the upstairs rooms. Still nothing. Only one room even appeared to be in use. He looked at the graduation pictures of the lawyer with his mom and dad, and another with the lawyer and a taller man in basketball uniforms. This had to be Brian Lord's room.

Dex took special pains to look for any sign that Sherry had been there. He checked the bathroom for her perfume or shampoo, looked under the bed for her suitcase, and peeked into the closets.

But again, there was nothing. Not the slightest hint of her. As his frustration mounted, he grew less and less careful with his search, yanking out dresser drawers, dumping them on the bed, and pawing through them for any trace of his wife.

Shit! Dex lost it, hurling a nightstand across the room to smash the mirror on a closet door.

In a rage now, he dropped to his knees, groping between the mattress and a box spring. He upended the bed, dumping it on its side.

He *knew* she'd been here. He wanted to scream. He wanted to smash every piece of furniture in the place—but he froze.

Damn. There it was again. The same noise he'd heard before. Maybe it wasn't outside the house, though. Was it inside?

He'd searched downstairs so he knew those rooms were empty...

Regardless, it was time to get the hell out. He couldn't risk being caught here.

But as he started down the stairs, he heard the damn noise once more, and realized why he couldn't place it before. It was coming from *inside* the house, and it was muffled. Someone was shifting around in the closet at the foot of the stairs.

Had he checked it? He should have, but he'd been in such a big hurry to get upstairs...he must have walked right past it. And he could only think of one person who'd be scared and dumb enough to hide in a closet.

Taking the final steps two at a time, he jerked open the closet door.

"Surprise!"

But it wasn't Sherry.

A skinny guy in a black suit with dark hair and widow's peak emerged from the closet. He was holding an automatic, aimed straight at Dex's head. The gun was big, about 10 mil or a .45.

But it didn't matter. There was no time for finesse. Molinere had trained for this a million times...

Police procedure 101: Take control.

"Lower your weapon!" Dex roared, dropping to a combat crouch with his hand poised above his gun belt. "Get on your knees! Now!"

But that was when he realized his hand wasn't poised over a sidearm. He wasn't wearing a gun belt. Or a uniform. He was in camo, and his automatic was concealed in the small of his back.

The guy in the closet didn't even blink. "Or what?" he asked mildly. "You'll bleed on me when I blow your head off?"

"I'm a police officer," Dex managed. "I'm going to show you my identification."

"You move your hands and I'll show you what your brain looks like," the man said. "I heard you searching around up there. Did you find the file?"

Dex blinked, trying to craft an answer. Then realized it was already too late.

The man cocked his weapon. Dex wasn't sure which was worse, staring into the gun muzzle, or the eyes of the man who held it. They were both lifeless.

"You don't have any idea what I'm talking about, do you?" he said.

"I—no. I don't know about any file," Dex said, swallowing. "I'm looking for my wife."

"Under the bed?" the man snorted. "Did you find her?"

"No."

"That sounds like a predicament—for both of us. What am I supposed to do with you?"

CHAPTER 31

THE SKY WAS DARK, gloomy, and overcast on my second day as a lifeguard. But it wasn't necessarily a bad thing.

With a chill breeze coming off the lake, the sun had barely peeked out before it disappeared behind a wall of dark clouds. A few moms showed up with their kids in tow, gamely unfolding their lawn chairs, and handing out pails and shovels. They were hoping the clouds would burn off.

They didn't.

By midafternoon, some teens got a volleyball game going. A few people gathered to watch, but not a soul dipped a toe in the water.

The empty day gave me plenty of time to stare out over the surf. I thought about Jimmy Valentine going missing and Corporal Molinere showing up.

But mostly, I thought about Carly, and the way she'd laid her heart on the line.

In a way, it was like the bomb had sent my life pinwheeling back through time, and crash-landed me on this beach.

But somehow, it didn't *feel* like a step back. Being on the beach felt like the most natural thing in the world to me. It felt like I was fated to be here, almost. As though I were getting a do-over, a second chance to live my life. This time, I could do things better and get them right...

Suddenly, my cell phone rang. It was Grady Baker.

"Hey Grady, what's up?"

"A lot. I've been working the Riviera Club, watching our friend. I was able to snap a picture of his gofer, but I've got no idea who he is, and Corzine may have spotted me. I think I'm burned, man."

"Jesus! Are you okay?"

"No. I'm in my car, headed for my apartment to pack a bag. I'm bailing out, Brian. If you want the picture, pick it up quick. Once I'm gone, I'm staying off the grid. There's an Irish pub on the corner near my place called Riley's. I'll wait as long as I can, but you need to get here yesterday, man. I got a bad feeling about this."

"On my way," I said, standing up. I checked the beach automatically, remembering that I was still on the job.

I dialed Carly immediately. "Hey, I've got trouble. Can you find a sub for me? And loan me your car?"

She didn't hesitate a second. "I've got a kid here looking for more hours. I'll bring him with me. You can use my car, but I'm coming with it."

I didn't argue.

But I should have.

CHAPTER 32

CARLY DROVE, ROCKETING down I-94 in her tiny Mini Cooper convertible. As we raced along, I told her who Grady was, what he'd been doing, and the danger he might be in.

It was a danger she might be in as well. Above all, I told her that I needed her to stay clear of this. No arguments.

She promised to drop me at the pub, then circle the block. If I came out alone, she'd pick me up. If I was in trouble or waved her off, she'd bail out, and call 911. It wasn't a brilliant plan, but in the army, troops bet their lives every day on these KISS tactics: Keep It Simple, Stupid.

In the city, we drove slowly, past Riley's Pub. I could see Grady sitting alone at a corner table, a beer in front of him. The restaurant was empty otherwise, despite it being lunch hour, which was odd.

"Okay," I said, "drop me at the corner and remember…?"

"KISS," Carly said. And we did. It was natural and wonderful and much too quick. In the next second, I was gone, and so was she.

I pushed into the pub, and headed for Grady's table. He looked on edge, and had a right to be. As I sat, he avoided my eyes.

And in that instant, I *knew*.

The question was, why had he sold me out? I didn't have to wait long to find out.

Damn. Bruno Corzine came out of the kitchen. He was pulling Carly with him.

Double damn.

I rose to my feet. "Are you okay?"

"She's fine, Counselor," Bruno said as the trio took a booth across the room. "And she'll stay fine, if you play it smart. Sit your ass down."

I sat. I didn't have a choice. There were four of them, and they were all armed. I wasn't. And I couldn't think of a single move that wouldn't get us all killed.

Not that it mattered.

Because we were probably dead anyway.

CHAPTER 33

I TURNED TO Bruno Corzine. Up close, he looked even rougher than I remembered. He had a brutal face and a trunk wide as a Mack truck. He was wearing a black silk running suit, though I doubted he was a jogger. Chances were, he was dressed for a funeral. Our funeral. And there wasn't a thing I could do about it.

"I'll do whatever you say, but the lady's got no part in this. She just gave me a lift."

"She's safe, Counselor, as long as you behave. I only want to talk."

"Then talk. What do you want?"

"To get you off my back," he said bluntly. "You're going to get us both killed."

"What are you talking about—?"

"My name isn't Corzine," he said, cutting me off. "It's Benedetto. Detective Anthony Charles Benedetto from the Chicago Organized Crime Unit."

I just stared. "You're a narc? Funny, because the last

time we talked, you threatened to tear my arms off. And then my car blew up a few weeks later."

"I had nothing to do with that."

"Right. Because you're undercover. Am I supposed to just take your word for it?"

The pub doors pushed open and we both swiveled in our seats.

Lieutenant Bev Hilliard walked in wearing her black Donna Karan jacket and slacks.

What the hell?

"If you won't take my word," Bruno said, turning to face me again, "maybe you'll take hers."

CHAPTER 34

"HEY, LIEUTENANT," CORZINE said, as Hilliard pulled up a chair facing me. "Would you please tell this man who I am?"

"He's Detective Tony Benedetto, on temporary duty out of Chicago," Hilliard said. "And that information stays in this room. Life or death."

I glanced from him to her and back again. She was dead serious. And that's when I realized Tony Benedetto was telling the truth. Corzine was a made-up identity.

"I've been infiltrating the Zeman crime family for months," Benedetto said. "You know who they are?"

"I was an ADA, of course I know who they are."

"Benedetto's risen higher in the crew than any undercover ever has before," Hilliard offered.

"And it's mostly thanks to you, Counselor," Benedetto said.

"To me?"

"Terrible as it was, that car bombing *made* my reputation," Benedetto said. "Zeman's crew are mad dogs. I tangle with you, then somebody blows you to hell? They all think *I* did it. It put me in with that bunch instantly."

"Glad we could help out," I said bitterly. "Remind me to mention it to Serena."

"I'm not trying to make light of what happened," Benedetto said. "I am sorry for your loss."

I brushed him off and said, "Okay, so you're a narc. Why are we here? What do you want from us?"

"We need you and that investigator to back off before this gets out of control," Hilliard said. "You blamed Corzine for Serena Rossi's death. Clearly, he wasn't involved, seeing as Corzine doesn't really exist."

"Because if the Riviera crew knew a PI was tailing me inside the club?" Benedetto said. "Somebody could've ended up dead."

"Maybe somebody already has," I said. "Any chance one of your new running buddies tried to do you a solid by lighting me up?"

"I know for a fact none of the Zeman crew was involved," Benedetto said flatly. "My unit's got more lines on all of them, and besides, it wouldn't make sense for them to stick out their necks like that."

"Why not?"

"Jimmy Valentine is the one making trouble, not you. If the Zemans were going to cap somebody, it'd be Jimmy. And they will, if we don't fix this. That's why I'm here. We need your help with him."

"*My* help?" I echoed.

"My guys have Jimmy stashed in a safe house in Dearborn. I can't tell him who I really am, because I don't trust him."

"I doubt he trusts you, either. He saw you beat a man to death."

Benedetto scoffed. "He dreamt up that cock and bull story to get himself a plea deal."

"Tony's under surveillance twenty-four-seven for his own safety," Hilliard added. "So we can confirm that it never happened."

"He's still my client. If you want him to drop his story, what does he get in return?"

"Are you serious?" Benedetto demanded. "He's lying."

"You want something, so does he," I said. "That's why it's called a plea *bargain*."

"How about this?" Hilliard cut in. "Valentine stands mute at his hearing, and we withdraw the gambling charges on a technicality. He walks with no time and no fine. Will that satisfy you?"

I mulled that a moment, but it was only for show. I didn't have any wiggle room.

"Deal," I nodded. Nobody offered to shake hands.

Benedetto rose, glowering down at me.

"What?" I asked.

"I'm gonna remember this," he said. "If I ever get jammed up and need a lawyer? I'll give you a call."

"Sorry about the cloak and dagger," Hilliard said, rising. "It was necessary. We had to hold your friend hostage because we thought you might destroy the operation otherwise. No offense, but you've been known to act rash. Just look at your past actions. You've been sticking your nose where it doesn't belong."

I didn't bother to answer. She followed Benedetto out, leaving me with Grady Baker.

Carly had a terrified look on her face, but was taking deep breaths, trying to figure out what was going on.

"I didn't know they were cops, Brian," he said, holding up his hands in mock surrender. "They grabbed me, told me to call you and get you here. I was just trying to stay alive for five more minutes."

"I get it, Grady. No problem."

"Maybe I can make it up to you," he said. "But I'll let you see to your girlfriend first. She looks pretty pissed. I'll be waiting outside."

CHAPTER 35

AFTER CARLY AND I talked, we went outside, where Grady was waiting for me. Carly was clearly upset, and was now sitting in her car, fuming.

"Thanks for showing up tonight," Grady said. "That could have gone badly if you hadn't."

"I shouldn't have gotten you involved."

"You didn't. You offered me a job, and I took it. I knew the Riviera Club was risky. I liked the challenge of being invisible in a roomful of goombahs."

"Except the law was there, too," I said. "I should have guessed."

"You're a lawyer, not a cop. After all you've been through? You may not be thinking all that straight."

"About what?"

"The bombing."

"Five minutes ago, I would have sworn Corzine set it up. Now?" I shrugged.

"Yeah," he agreed. "Corzine's new identity changes everything. For me, too."

"How so?"

"Because you're a client who just saved my ass, and who *might* be in the crosshairs of a *former* client. One we both worked for."

"Marvin Garner? What are you trying *not* to tell me?"

"Just this. A few years ago, before you joined the firm? It was nearly bankrupt. Garner's wife left him, then his mistress…"

I couldn't focus on what he was saying. Hilliard had crossed the street to Carly's car, and the two of them were having a *very* heated discussion. Carly got so fired up, in fact, that she revved her Mini Cooper and roared off, leaving Hilliard staring blankly after her.

Terrific.

"…his *longtime* mistress," Grady added pointedly.

I turned back to him and suddenly realized what he was trying to tell me.

"Serena?" I asked. "Are you saying Serena was Garner's mistress?"

"During his divorce, Garner hired me to dig up dirt on his wife. But watching her meant watching him, too, so…Yes, I found out that Garner and Serena Rossi had a longtime thing. I think Serena expected to become the new Mrs. Garner once the divorce was final. Instead, Garner found a new girl."

"Monique Kelso," I said. "I heard gossip around the office about her, but never about Serena."

Grady nodded. "Monique was tight with the boss,

and knew where the bodies were buried, as they say. Now I'm wondering if it's actually true."

"What do you mean?"

"After the divorce, Garner's business flatlined. Then he landed a new client, a Serb arms dealer named Luka Draculic. Overnight, his financial troubles vanished."

"How?"

"I don't know, but it had to involve a lot more than legal representation. As part of the deal, one of Draculic's men became Garner's driver and bodyguard."

This Draculic guy sounded like trouble.

"I ran a background check on him. In Eastern Europe, the guy's the poster boy for organized crime. He has a record with Interpol that's as long as your arm."

"What's he doing here?"

"Whatever Garner says and that's why I quit taking jobs from the firm, not that there were many anyway. Luka handles Marvin's security problems these days."

"By problems, do you mean the bombing?" I asked.

Grady nodded.

"But I've only met Garner twice. Why would he come after me?"

"You're asking me to guess, and I only deal in facts. I've told you every damn thing I know to be a fact. The rest, you'll have to figure out on your own. Look, after getting jammed up between the law and the mob, I'm catching the first bus headed anywhere. Good luck, Brian. You're gonna need it."

We shook hands and that was it. Grady vanished around a corner, the invisible man again.

Across the street, Hilliard was leaning against an unmarked gray sedan with her arms folded. Waiting.

"Need a lift?" she asked.

Damned right I did.

CHAPTER 36

NEITHER OF US spoke for the first few miles of the drive. Hilliard was deep in thought and I was steaming.

"You knew about Benedetto all along," I said.

"I warned you to stay away from him. I did everything I could."

"You could have tried telling me the truth."

"That wasn't an option, and you know it. I had to do everything I could to protect the identity of the undercover cop. I only told you because I no longer had a choice."

When I didn't answer, she added, "We took a big gamble here too, you know. We exposed you to an undercover cop in a very dangerous, unstable crime op. Do you know how risky that was? But we wanted to give you full transparency to the situation so you'd believe us. I'd expect you to appreciate that."

She was right, but that didn't make it any easier to swallow.

"What did you say to Carly?"

"I told her to keep her mouth shut about this, on pain of death or incarceration. Sorry about that. Is she your girlfriend?"

"Yeah. Or at least she is for now."

"She's pretty mad at both of us," Hilliard said. "But mostly you."

"She has a right to be."

"What did Grady tell you?"

"Good-bye. He's blowing town to get clear of this case."

"There is no case, Brian. Since Corzine isn't a real gangster, you're at square one. Exactly where I've been all along. Now that I've shared some very dangerous information with you..."

"Only to protect your undercover."

"Even so, we've trusted you with the truth. Maybe it's time you trusted us."

I chewed on that, but not for long. I hadn't been successful on my own.

"Grady says that before she met me, Serena Rossi was Marvin Garner's longtime mistress."

She glanced at me. "That probably wasn't fun to hear."

"It wasn't all that earthshaking, either. Serena was a few years older than I am, and we didn't meet in a nunnery."

"Where did you meet?"

"At Garner and Mackey. I was an ADA and she was a paralegal, and we worked some cases together. We hit it off. Maybe a bit too quickly."

"Because she was on the rebound?"

"Possibly. Things happened awfully fast, and in hindsight, Serena pushed every decision we made. But I don't see what that has to do with the car bomb."

"Maybe Garner was jealous."

"Of what? He already had a new, younger girlfriend. Besides, he was the opposite of vindictive. He didn't fire Serena, he promoted her, and hired her new boyfriend. I started working there, didn't I?"

Hilliard nods. "He sounds like a prince. I've got an ex-husband. Our breakup was civil, but I can't see him hiring my significant other. I guess he's not as nice as your ex-boss."

"I'm not that nice, either," I conceded. Then I blinked, realizing what I'd just said.

Hilliard caught my expression. "What?"

"The thing is, Garner's kind of a jerk. After the bombing, he made a special trip to the hospital to fire me. Serena's dead, I'm wounded, and Marvin personally handed me a pink slip."

"Did he say why?"

"He implied that I was to blame for her death by saying that one of my riffraff clients probably tried to take me out. He said that if Serena hadn't been involved with me, she'd still be breathing."

"Any chance he was right?"

"I thought so at the time, because I was sure Corzine was behind it. But I've sorted through my other cases, and other than Sherry Molinere's stalker husband, I can't come up with a single client who'd want to punch me out, let alone blow me up. It could be someone else after all. I'm just lucky they missed."

Hilliard fell silent, mulling something over.

"What if…?" She broke off, frowning, then glanced at me sharply. "What if they didn't miss?"

"What do you mean?"

"Look, most of your clients, no offense, really are—"

"Low rent? I'm aware. Some of my cases are even pro bono."

"But a bombing isn't a low-rent enterprise. The device that erased your car had to have been expensive."

I swung my head to the side, glaring at her. She hadn't told me that.

"The thing is," she went on quickly, before I could gripe, "people get murdered in Detroit literally every day. It's one of the most violent cities in the country. But bombs don't go off every day. Most victims are shot, stabbed, or bludgeoned. If you want to kill somebody in Motown, you walk up to 'em on the street, cap 'em, and keep right on going. Detroiters don't call 911, they call Uber. They get in and out, as fast as they can."

"What's your point?"

"A bomb doesn't just kill someone. It erases them. And also erases any…evidence they might be holding. Evidence that might make you hire an old lover's new boyfriend, for instance."

I swiveled in my seat, staring at her.

"You're saying *Serena* was actually the target?"

"I'm not saying anything. I'm thinking out loud. We

checked her background, as part of the investigation. She did well for herself as a paralegal, but she lived well above her means. Expensive apartment, new car. At the time, I didn't think it was relevant, but now—"

She broke off when her cell phone rang. She glanced at the screen, then pressed it to her ear. "Chief Paquette? What can I do for you? Yes. Brian's with me now."

She switched her phone to Speaker.

"One of my guys drove past your cottage an hour ago," the chief said. "He spotted Corporal Molinere's car hidden in the brush behind the house."

"That's right near the spot where he pulled me over," I said. "He's probably staking out my place, looking for his wife, but she isn't there."

"There's no sign of him, either, and my guy can track a mayfly across concrete. Any idea where the corporal might be?"

"Did you check the house?"

"It's locked with no sign of forced entry," Paquette said. "I'm having the car towed to the station. I'll have a word with the corporal when he collects it."

"*If* he collects it. If he figured out where my uncle's got Sherry stashed, he may have changed cars to grab her. A client told me a black van's been tailing me. Maybe Molinere isn't working alone."

I turned to Hilliard, placing my hand on her arm. "We have to turn around. Right now."

CHAPTER 37

WE RACED INTO Port Vale with the lights and sirens blaring. I phoned my uncle Josh on the way. He said that Sherry was fine and that no strangers had been around. He was going to keep an eye out for the corporal, and he knew to dial 911 in an emergency.

But I doubted he'd bother.

Hilliard wanted to take me to Port Vale PD headquarters, but since she could brief the chief as well as I could, I had her drop me at the Vale Parks Department offices. I had a personal fire to put out.

Carly's car was there, but she wasn't. A cheery secretary told me she was at the beach, filling in for…well, me. I thanked her, and marched across the dunes to the park.

It was almost deserted. The overcast was still hanging on, and only a few diehards remained. There was a nanny with three rug rats, and an older woman in a lawn chair reading a Kindle. No swimmers at all.

Carly was in the tower chair, looking out over the water.

"Hey," I called.

"What is it?" she said, without turning.

"You're really mad, huh?"

"You think?" she sighed. "Actually, I'm not. I was mad, now I'm just..." She shrugged.

"Can we talk?"

"I'm on duty."

"I'd be glad to take over. That is, if I still have a job?"

"I'm not *that* mad. On a scale of one to ten, I'm at level four. *Seriously* annoyed. That's down from level seven, where I was after the pub. Ballistic."

"I'll take my chances," I said, climbing up the ladder to sit beside her. "Look, I'm really—"

"Save it," she said. "I know it wasn't your fault."

"What wasn't?"

"Any of—that stuff in the city. I can't actually talk about it or I'll die in prison... That's what that lady cop said, anyway. I was the one who insisted on coming along and you were too desperate to talk me out of it. It's okay, I get that."

"Carly—"

"No! We're both lifeguards. We know how dangerous situations work. You warned me up front, so I knew what I was getting into. I'm not hurt, I'm just..."

"Scared?"

"In way over my head," she admitted, taking a deep breath. "Are you in trouble with the police, Brian?"

I mulled on that a moment. "Not exactly. It's more like... I've been causing some problems for them."

"Really?" she sighed. "I'm shocked. Shocked!"

We both burst out laughing. And then laughed even harder. Not at her lame joke, but in relief. Because whatever the beef was between us, it was going to blow over. After the day we'd had, it felt awfully good to be laughing at anything at all.

We'd both sworn to keep silent about Corzine, but Carly deserved to know the truth about everything else. So I told her all I knew. She offered sympathy in the right places, but also asked pointed questions about the investigation.

I'd forgotten this side of her. Carly was supportive and kind, and very bright. In fact, she was sharp enough to conceal her steel-trap intelligence behind a smile. She hadn't become the Parks Department supervisor by accident.

She listened to my explanation as we sat shoulder to shoulder in the tower chair while the light faded into the mist over the lake. As the purple shadows came on, we rose and took a long last look over our kingdom before climbing down from our throne.

It was truly ours alone now. There wasn't another soul in sight.

Without warning, Carly turned and kissed me hard on the mouth, holding me so fiercely I thought we might fall out of the tower. Then she took a step back, staring up into my eyes. Waiting.

"That was…" I said.

"Important," she said. "Remember it. With the way things are, it might never happen again. So remember it."

"I will."

And I would, because in that moment, I realized that Carly was the woman of my dreams. It was like we were two souls cut from the same cloth and finally stitched together after all these years. I knew I'd do everything I could to make her want to stay in my life this time around.

Carly kissed me again and I felt something rustle in my shirt. I checked my breast pocket, and found the business card Dex Molinere had jammed in there that morning. "Call me," he'd said.

The chief wanted to know where he was. Maybe I could find out.

I dialed the number, and let it ring.

CHAPTER 38

Ruiz

IN THE PARKING lot behind the Port Vale Police Department, Patrolman Gene Ruiz was walking out to his ride when he heard a phone ringing nearby. He followed the sound to the unmarked State Police cruiser that had just been towed in. Had someone dropped a phone? Kneeling, he scanned the ground, and then peered under the car.

Nothing. But the ringing continued. And he realized it was coming from inside the vehicle.

From the trunk.

CHAPTER 39

Paquette, Hilliard, Ruiz

"FETCH A PRY bar, Gene, pop this sucker open," the chief said, scowling. "Something feels wrong."

"I can call the Staties and have them send over a master key," Hilliard suggested. "It'd be easier on the car."

"That boy could be bleeding out in there. Get the goddamn pry bar, Ruiz, and if I hear one damn wise-crack about woman's intuition, you'll be picking up your teeth with your broken arm."

"Yes, ma'am." Ruiz trotted off. Every officer in her department loved the chief like family, she was every-one's favorite Southern gran. But no one ever wanted to cross her.

Paquette and Hilliard stepped aside as Ruiz crammed the bar in the seam just above the license plate and popped the trunk open.

Ruiz took an involuntary step back.

But the chief didn't. She leaned in over the corpse of Dexter Molinere, chewing the corner of her lip, frowning. She pressed a finger against his carotid, though there was clearly no need. His body was already cooling. Cupping his cheek with her palm, she swiveled his head, examining the bloody third eye neatly centered between his original pair.

She whistled softly to herself. "Heavy caliber," she said. "I'd make it a 10 millimeter, or a .45. Definitely overkill. See the smudge around the wound? That's a powder burn. The muzzle was less than an inch away when he fired. At that range, he could've used a brick." She backed out, straightening her lanky frame, and kept frowning down at the body.

"This was an execution," Hilliard said. "The bullet went through, but I don't see any spatter or ricochet marks on the vehicle. He wasn't shot in the trunk."

"I'd guess Molinere was standing near the trunk when he was capped," the chief agreed. "The shooter walked him to the car, turned him around, and *pop!*" She smacked her lips. "Pushed him inside as he fell, barely mussing the dust on the bumper. That tells me he's done this kind of work before. Damn, I hate to leave his body in the dark but..." She carefully closed the trunk.

"Call the State Police, Gene, tell 'em we got one of theirs. They'll want their own CSI team to handle the car, but the crime scene's ours. I want a team back out at the Lord place to scout the ground for blood and find that bullet. We have a dead officer and no one sleeps until we figure out who did this! Now go!"

Ruiz took off at a dead run.

The chief realized Hilliard was staring at her. "Something wrong, Lieutenant?"

"No, ma'am," Bev said shaking her head in wonder. "Not a thing."

A prowl car rolled up, its strobes blazing, Ruiz at the wheel.

"If you're waiting on me, you're already late," the chief said with a feral grin as she slid into the shotgun seat. "God, I love this job. Hit it, Gene." Her car roared out of the lot.

Hilliard scrambled into her own car, racing after the chief, burning rubber all the way.

CHAPTER 40

THE CHIEF WAS already rapping hard on the kitchen door when I came charging up from the beach.

"What happened?" I asked. "What's wrong?"

"A lot," she said, looking me up and down. "But not the thing that worried me the most, since you're still breathing. Are you okay?"

"I'm fine. Why are you here?"

"We found Corporal Molinere's car stashed in a turnout a hundred yards up your road. I had it towed in."

"You think he's here?" I asked, nodding at the cottage.

"Nope. I know exactly where he is. In a body bag on a bus headed to Wayne County Morgue. Somebody capped him, stashed the body in his own trunk."

"Jesus," I said, wincing. "You don't think I—"

"Oh, hell, no. I pretty much have a handle on where you've been all day. I was just concerned you might have run into the same trouble he did. I tried your cell on the way out here. Have you been inside?"

"No, I just came up from the beach."

"Then we'd best take a look. Lieutenant Hilliard's scouting the ground where we found the car. That's most likely where Molinere caught it, but we don't know that for a fact yet. Step aside, please."

She drew her sidearm, a Glock automatic, and tried the knob. It turned, and the door opened.

"Do you normally keep this locked?"

"Usually, but it is Port Vale. So not always."

"Nobody does," she sighed. "They trust their amazing local police force."

She pushed the door open, then paused, listening intently. "Wait out here, please." She eased inside with her weapon at the ready.

Wait out here, my ass. This was my home. I followed her in, and the moment I did, I knew *everything* was wrong.

I glanced around, taking stock, and realized a dozen things were off. Drawers weren't *quite* closed. Closet doors were ajar. Sofa cushions were misaligned, as though they'd been pulled out and then shoved back.

Someone had searched the place thoroughly.

Molinere?

Possibly. But the rogue cop had been looking for his wife. He might have scrounged around for her things, her clothes, maybe a suitcase, but he wouldn't be rummaging under the sofa cushions for her.

Could it be somebody else? Maybe it was the same somebody who stuffed Molinere's corpse in his own trunk...

Chief Paquette was edging silently down the stairs. I hadn't even heard her go up.

"I told you to wait outside."

"Sorry."

"Not as sorry as you're about to be. The bedroom at the top of the stairs has been totally trashed. That one yours?"

I nodded. "That had to be Molinere. He was probably looking for his wife."

"Was she here?"

"Never. This place is in the phone book, for Pete's sake."

"Where is she now?"

I hesitated.

"Mr. Lord, right about now, the county coroner is tweezing shell fragments out of her husband's brain. I need to talk to her."

"My uncle moved her again. She doesn't trust the police, Chief. Every time she's asked for help—"

"Some jerk-off patrolman would call her old man, he'd explain it away as a little tiff with the junkie wife? I get that and I sympathize, Counselor, but this is a murder case now, not a domestic dispute. Your client's delicate sensibilities are way down the list of crap I'm worried about. We don't know who capped her husband or why. She could be next. So blowing me off isn't an option. Clear?"

"Crystal," I nodded.

"Where is she?"

"With my uncle, stashed in one of the homes he's remodeling. I don't know which one."

"I think I do. Don't worry, we'll find him. I'm going to leave a man with you. You're not safe here alone."

I was alone. The realization hit me square in the gut. Carly hadn't followed me in from the beach. And she should have been here by now.

I didn't know what was wrong, but knew something was. And I'd put Carly right in the middle of it.

"I'll be fine," I lied. "I just need to clean the place up. And I'd like to be there when you talk to Sherry."

"She'll be at the station," the chief said, and she headed out without looking back.

I waited until I heard her car rumble off. Then I took a deep breath and stepped out onto the porch.

"Carly?"

There was a cluster of cedars twenty yards from the house. Carly stepped from behind them, into the open.

She wasn't alone. A man in a dark suit was standing slightly behind her.

Luka. Garner's bodyguard. It had to be.

I swallowed hard, because I knew how dangerous he was. He had to have been the one who shot Dex Molinere, and stuffed the man into his own trunk.

"What do you want?" I asked.

"I want things to go smoothly," Luka said. "No trouble. We talk to Mr. Garner, you give him what you stole, we all part as friends." He gave me a faint smile. It wasn't reassuring.

He was holding a gun at his side, instead of pointing it at Carly, or me. But I knew his reflexes were so fast that it wasn't necessary.

"The way you parted as friends with Molinere?"

"Ah. That's why the police were here? They found the body of the man who broke into your house?"

"The police are still here," I said. "They're just up the road, where you left his body."

"I don't know anything about that," Luka shrugged, the smile totally gone. "You break into people's houses, bad things happen."

He gestured with the gun. "I'm parked down the shore on the access road. I think it's time we head to my car."

CHAPTER 41

LUKA FORCED ME behind the wheel of Garner's Lincoln while he and Carly rode in back. I tried to adjust the mirror to see her face, but he shook his head.

"Keep your eyes on the road," he grunted. "If we get stopped, your friend goes first."

I followed Luka's directions to Marvin Garner's lakeshore estate. It was a magnificent, century-old stacked-stone masterpiece. I would have been impressed, but as we rolled past the sculptured hedges that lined the long driveway, all I could think about was Carly, squeezed in the corner of the backseat with the gunman.

I've never felt so totally helpless. I wanted to tear his goddamn arms off.

He caught me watching him in the corner of the rearview mirror, and just smiled. He knew exactly what I was thinking and it didn't worry him a bit. And that worried me a lot.

"Stop here."

We left the car in the driveway, and circled the house on foot. Luka stayed behind me, well out of reach, keeping Carly close to his side. We found Marvin Garner relaxing by his Olympic pool in a red silk robe.

He straightened in his chair as we approached, but it wasn't out of courtesy. Beneath his cool, stony exterior, I could see he was enraged.

"Mr. Lord," he said, laying his tablet aside on a cabana table by his phone. "You're proving to be a huge goddamn problem."

"And having me kidnapped—?"

"You haven't been kidnapped. You've disappeared. You and your girlfriend have taken off for parts unknown. And given your recent troubles, who can blame you?"

"You can't—"

"Shut your mouth! I only want one thing from you. The files Serena took. I know you have them. So where are they?"

"Files?" I echoed, genuinely confused.

But Garner has been a trial lawyer for thirty years. He'd been reading juries before I was born. He knew the truth when he saw it. And he knew I didn't know what he was talking about.

"You don't know what files I mean, do you?" he said, darkly.

"No," I said quickly, "but I can help you find them. We both want the same thing, Marvin. We want to get on the right side of whatever's gone wrong. Walk away in one piece." I glanced involuntarily at Luka as I said it, and he followed my line of vision.

In that instant, I knew there wasn't a prayer they'd let us go. We were all in too deep. But as long as I was talking, Carly was breathing. "Tell me what you need," I said evenly. "Let me help."

He considered that a moment, but seemed to come to the same conclusion I had. Nothing he said to me would matter. It would all end here, one way or the other.

"Serena was my mistress for a time," he shrugged, as if he had nothing to lose. "When my wife left me, Serena assumed she'd take her place, but the last thing I wanted was a new wife. Serena didn't take rejection well. After we ended things, she made copies of proprietary files, then tried to sell them back to me."

"Files involving Luka's boss?" I asked.

"Files that were vital to the firm."

"She was blackmailing you?"

"Serena wasn't shy about getting whatever she wanted," Garner shrugged. "I can see now that you aren't, either."

"Meaning what?"

"Meaning, cut the crap. This isn't a negotiation, Brian. I need those files."

"I get that," I said, "and I get how serious you are, because your goon over there killed a state trooper today."

When Garner didn't even flinch, my last glimmer

of hope vanished. Carly and I had no chance. He wouldn't save us because his head was on the chopping block, too. He would do anything to get the files to save himself.

"Maybe his friend here can tell us," Luka added, seizing Carly's upper arm. "Maybe he'll tell us, if I ask her hard enough."

"*No!*" I blurted. I cursed myself internally, realizing I'd showed them how much Carly meant to me. "Look, I'll get you the damn files," I said. "But first, let her go."

"You don't have the files," Luka said. Then he thrust Carly toward me. I grabbed her to keep her from falling.

"What are you doing?" Garner demanded, getting to his feet. "Don't be an idiot, Luka, you can't do anything at the house. I can't have the police—"

And that's when Carly pushed Garner, sending him into the gunman. During that split second when Garner was in the line of fire, I charged.

Barreling into both of them, I swept them backward, plunging all three of us into the pool.

Both men cursed as they fell. That curse was the last thing Luka ever said. He was struggling to bring his gun around when I drove a fist into his diaphragm. The stiff punch forced the last burst of air from his body.

He gasped, filling his lungs with water. I grabbed his collar, holding his head down in the pool. He struggled for a moment, firing his gun—once, twice—but only in sheer reflex as his life thrashed away.

Finally, he took a final gasp.

I pushed him away from me. His body drifted slowly down to the bottom of the pool, still clutching the gun in his fist. I swam down to get it and kicked back up to the surface of the water.

At the far end of the pool, Carly was keeping Garner at bay with a skim net, smashing his fingers whenever he tried to climb out. I hauled him out, hacking and choking. Then I drew back my fist—

"Don't do it," Carly said.

"Why the hell not?"

"You can't beat him, Brian. It'll complicate things with the police."

She was right. But I really hated that she was.

When the police arrived, Garner was too shaken to lie coherently to Hilliard and the chief, especially with the gunman floating a few feet away in his pool.

They worked together well as the chief asked fresh questions before Garner could invent a workable lie for the one Hilliard had previously asked. Once two of the chief's officers hauled Luka's corpse out of the water, Garner broke down completely, babbling a confession.

Carly and I were at the cabana bar, waiting for our turn to be grilled, when a cell phone rang. I picked it up, assuming it would be one of Garner's accomplices.

But it wasn't.

"Marvin?" a woman asked.

The bottom of my world dropped out. Because I know the voice as well as I know my own.

"Serena?"

She didn't answer, but she didn't have to. The line went so silent, I could hear her breathing.

"Serena? Is that you?"

CHAPTER 42

I SPENT THE next hour in a basement cell at Port Vale PD, stonewalling everyone. They asked questions about Luka, but I had nothing to say.

First, a US marshal named Caldwell tried to bully information out of me, then Hilliard and the chief tried sweet reason to make me talk. I told them I was perfectly willing to explain exactly what happened and my part in it. The whole thing.

But first? There was someone I wanted to talk to. Face-to-face.

They'd get my full cooperation only after I talked to my late fiancée, Serena Rossi.

Finally, they caved. Caldwell led me upstairs to the chief's glassed-in office, but he made me wear handcuffs.

"Sit at the desk, and keep your hands in plain sight at all times," he cautioned. "No sudden movements."

A few minutes later, he ushered Serena in. He held her chair as she sat down, facing me.

No handcuffs for her, I noticed. Caldwell took up a post by the door. He folded his arms and set his face in a permanent scowl.

I'd expected Serena to look train-wreck terrible— as bad as I'd felt in the first days after the bombing. I thought she'd be teary-eyed and sorrowful over the mess she'd made of our lives.

But she looked terrific, albeit strikingly different. Her long dark hair was cropped short and frosted blond. She'd always dressed well, but somehow she managed to look more "uptown" than before. In her short skirt, ecru designer jacket, and stiletto heels, she looked impeccable and even prettier than I remembered.

And yet, far, far less attractive.

I'd loved her once, or thought I had. Now she looked like…a casual acquaintance. She seemed like someone I'd known for a time, and not very well. It wasn't far from the truth.

I was still dressed for the beach, in shorts and a Hawaiian shirt. My whole outfit was sodden from Garner's pool. I'd tried to hold on to my anger long enough to act outraged with her, but I couldn't even manage that.

"You are one great-looking corpse," I joked. "Are you okay?"

"Better than expected," she said. "How much have they told you?"

"Not a thing. What happened?"

"The day that bomb went off, when I was waiting

in the car for you, Marshal Caldwell came charging in to haul me out. He said my life was in danger, and it turned out he wasn't kidding."

"Wait, they knew about the bomb? In advance?"

"We found out a few minutes beforehand," Caldwell interrupted. "I managed to get Miss Rossi to safety, and I was coming back for you when...well. It blew. There was nothing left of the car and no witnesses. You were unconscious. We figured our best chance to keep her alive was to let everyone think she was dead."

"Including me?"

He shrugged, which was answer enough.

"And now?" I asked.

"I cut a deal with the federal prosecutors and the marshals," Serena said. "I'll testify against Marvin and the Serbian crime circle. In return I get witness protection. A new identity, and a new life."

"On your own?"

"Be real, Brian. I hooked up with you because I wanted to make Marvin jealous, and you were the perfect guy for it. Handsome, hungry, and hot. Especially at first. But it wasn't working out for us. We wouldn't have lasted another week, let alone happily ever after."

I couldn't argue the point. She was right.

"And the black van?" I asked Caldwell. "Was that your team? Keeping tabs on me?"

"We were concerned Miss Rossi might try to contact you," Caldwell said. "Witnesses often try to stay in touch with their old lives."

My mind was racing. Serena *had* stayed in touch, but not with me. She must have been the one who blackmailed Garner. And since he thought she was dead, he assumed I'd been doing it.

Serena was the person who'd put me—and Carly—in danger this whole time.

I looked across the table at her, knowing that this conversation could go two ways. I could out her right there, and she could do some hard time in jail.

Or I could keep quiet, and let her go in peace.

She seemed to notice my hesitancy, because a look of horrified shock crossed her face. Her eyes pleaded with me. They asked me not to blame her.

And I truly didn't.

Because she's not the only one who's starting a new life.

CHAPTER 43

THE NEXT DAY, I was back on the beach at first light, raking sand over the bonfire embers, picking up the empties, and watching the sun rise out of the breakers.

I was in my tower chair by nine, the Lord of the Shore again. I was watching, waiting for little kids to make little mistakes so I could save them.

At noon, Carly came by to rotate me out for lunch. She was barefoot and wearing a mauve swimsuit. I didn't want lunch, so I stayed on instead, sharing my throne with her. Both of us gazed out over the lake in silence. After everything that had happened, we were a bit uneasy with each other now.

We'd been kids together and good friends once. And now we were a lot more than that.

We'd shared the most earth-shattering kiss up in the lifeguard tower, on my favorite beach in the world.

But being with me had nearly gotten her killed.

And she'd seen me drown a man at the bottom of the pool.

Yet, here she was. Sitting beside me. In a silence that was killing me.

"So...um...I'm guessing you're still really angry with me, right?" I asked. "Level twenty-something?"

"That depends."

"On?"

"On where your resurrected lady love spent the night."

"Seriously?" I asked. "That's what you're mad about?"

"There's a long list of things I'm not happy about. But at the moment, that's the one that tops my list. So?"

"I wouldn't touch her with a ten-foot pole."

"Really," she said, giving me a look.

"Serena left with the marshals last night, Carly. She's agreed to testify against Garner and the Serbs in exchange for witness protection."

"So she's gone?"

"She's out of my life. Again. And all the way out this time. For good."

She turned to stare at me. "And is it good? Having her out of your life, I mean?"

"Carly, she lied to me, and she nearly got us both killed. I don't wish her harm, but believe me, whatever we had going is definitely over."

"I see," she nodded slowly, turning away. "And what about you? What will you do now?"

I couldn't help smiling at that.

"I'm already doing it. I'm here, with you, watching the breakers roll in. I went to war, and I've been hustling my butt off since I came back, trying to make up for lost time. I thought I was doing okay, but now…?" I broke off, uncertain of how to say what needed to be said.

"But now what?" she prompted. She wasn't looking at me. Instead, she stared straight out across the lake.

"I truly want to start my life over, Carly. Not from the beginning. Just from right…here."

"Lifeguarding is a summer job, Brian."

"I know it's not a career, and I do have options. My ex-boss from the prosecutor's office, Leon Stolz, called last night. He offered me my old job back."

"So you're leaving—"

"Never. I told him I'd think about it, but I was just being polite. I love the law and I'll keep helping clients, but I don't need a cubicle at Murphy Hall to do it. And I definitely don't need an office on Cadillac Square. The view's a lot better here."

"Are you kidding?"

"I'm dead serious. Why should I go to work wearing a three-piece suit when I can be on the beach? Soaking up rays, watching the surf roll in?"

We stared out at the water, and I felt perfectly at peace.

Then I leaned back, looked at her, and said, "Look, I know it won't last forever, but right now? I'm *exactly* where I need to be. A lifeguard lawyer. I don't want my old job back and I don't want a new one. I've already got the sweetest job on the planet. Right here. If that works for you."

She didn't say anything for a bit. She turned away from me, lost in thought. A seagull wheeled over us, keening. It was the loneliest sound in the world.

"What about me?" she asked at last. "What about us? Do I have a place in this brave new world of yours?"

"You're the most important part of it. The only part that matters. Maybe I blew our chance back in the day, but it wasn't our only shot. Serena's starting over, maybe we can, too. Maybe we can get it right…"

But she didn't seem to be listening. She was staring out over the water. Counting off the seconds under her breath.

"Too long," she said abruptly, bolting out of the chair, scrambling down the ladder. "Three kids dove off the second raft. Only two came up. Can't see the other one." And then she was off, sprinting into the surf.

Shit!

Impeccable timing, again.

I was only half a step behind her, racing through the breakers toward the raft. Two kids were on it now, pounding their feet and frantically yelling for their friend.

When the waves hit us chest high, we both dove into them. We swam hard through the surf, taking long breaths to prep ourselves to dive down deep to find the lost boy and save him.

Together.

THE DOCTOR'S PLOT

JAMES PATTERSON
WITH CONNOR HYDE

PROLOGUE

THERE WERE NO clouds that day, but there was a hot air balloon, its red and yellow checkerboard design offset by the blue sky. The sun had risen an hour before, and its low angle cast the balloon's shadow miles away, rippling across the Napa vineyards.

The dawn was cool, and most of the ten people in the basket wore fleece and headbands. The wicker creaked beneath their weight, but the pilot assured them they were safe. They snapped photos, pointing down at the mansions tucked into the forested hills and at the tidy rows of vines that ran up against the tasting rooms and production facilities of the wineries.

They laughed when a hawk drifted by curiously. It flapped its wings, scared away when the propane burner blasted its flame and sent the balloon higher.

Hundreds of feet below, mist ghosted through the vineyards of Whitehall, Rutherford Grove, Provenance. There wasn't much traffic at this early hour, but two vans paced the balloon, chasing down highways and zigzagging along roads, always in sight. The wind determined their course.

After they landed, they would be shuttled off to a champagne breakfast. Several of them were honeymooners, and everyone else introduced themselves as a tourist—except for one man, Paul Bures.

Paul was sixty-five, but a long way from retiring as the medical examiner of Napa County. Silver hair ringed his head. He wore jeans and a windbreaker. His glasses couldn't hide the fatigue in his eyes, dark with exhaustion from the long hours he'd logged the day before. His knuckles were cracked, dried out from the powdered latex gloves he wore at work and from the many times he washed his hands every day.

He carried a long-lensed camera and seemed keenly interested in snapping photos of some of the vineyards. He politely said, "Excuse me," when moving from one side of the basket to the other, but otherwise he barely acknowledged the other passengers.

There was plenty of room in the basket, and at one point nearly everyone was gathered on one side to take in the sunrise. Except for Paul, who took photo after photo of something below. Nobody heard his last words: "Hidden in plain sight."

Nobody saw something buzz past his ear, like a wasp. He flicked a hand to wave it away. But the bullet—fired from below—had already struck its target.

There was a *tink* when it pierced the metal belly of the propane tank. This gave way to a wild exhalation, a hushing roar, as the spark of its entry gave way to a detonation that people reported hearing from as far as thirty miles away.

No one had time to yell "Oh my God!" or "Help!" The basket shattered with the blast. Pieces of wicker rained down, along with the bodies, several of them aflame. Falling like comets.

The balloon was shredded, but it rose suddenly, unburdened of its weight and propelled upward by the blast of heat. The flames were the same color as the red and orange fabric that it ate up—until it was gone, replaced by black smoke that smeared the sky.

Paul Bures silently cut through the air. Flailing his arms as though he might learn to fly. Finally crashing through a tangle of chardonnay grapes and impacting the ground with a damp thud.

The camera lay beside him, the lens shattered, while his blood seeped into the tan soil, feeding the vines' roots.

CHAPTER 1

ABI BRENNER RAN a knife across the seam of the box and split it open. Inside she found a pile of old textbooks on anatomy and biochemistry. "This isn't it either," she said with a sigh.

She was surrounded by so many boxes that the air smelled like cardboard. They cluttered the floor and the counter of the kitchen where she now stood. The moving truck had arrived that morning, and everything was everywhere.

The couch in the living room was a messy jumble of lamps and blankets and photo albums. The bed frame was assembled but the mattress was still in the garage. They had unpacked the board games and the winter jackets, of all things, but nothing they actually needed.

This was their first house—a three-bedroom ranch just outside of Napa—but right now it felt more claustrophobic even than the one-bedroom apartment they'd lived in during med school.

"Jeremy?" she said.

From some far corner of the house his voice shouted back, "Yeah? Just a sec." She heard his footsteps thumping and then he appeared at the end of the hallway. He was a tall man, who slumped his shoulders when he walked as if he was afraid of bumping his head on something. He twirled a screwdriver in his hand. "What's up? You okay?"

That's how he always greeted her these days—"You okay?"—his eyes immediately dropping to her belly. She wasn't pregnant, but they were trying. And failing. And trying again.

She woke up that morning nauseous, but she threw up in the shower so that Jeremy wouldn't hear. She didn't want to get his hopes up. He already worried so much, always fussing over her, spoiling her, rubbing her shoulders and bringing her tea or lemonade and telling her not to work so hard, to take it easy.

But that wasn't in her nature. Work defined her. Maybe it had something to do with having grown up on a dairy farm in Wisconsin, but she couldn't remain idle. Hell, to her, was a cruise ship.

That work ethic—that constant drive to accomplish something—was one of the reasons she applied for the medical examiner position here in Napa. There were only a few hundred such jobs in the country, all of them severely overburdened. Sometimes bodies remained in the freezer for over a year before being processed. She would never have less than a seventy-hour workweek. She knew this when she'd applied for the emergency hire, and it weirdly appealed to her.

When Jeremy entered the kitchen, she lifted her hands and let them fall. "I thought I better get the kitchen set up, but I can't find anything. We were stupid not to label the boxes." She hated the way her voice cracked with emotion. She recognized that she was running on a few hours of sleep. She knew her blood sugar was low from not having eaten any lunch. She felt almost certain she was pregnant, which meant her body was under a hormonal attack. But still. There was nothing worse than feeling weak and jittery, as she did now.

Jeremy set down the screwdriver and pulled her into a hug. He said, "No way are we cooking. We're going out. To celebrate."

"We haven't accomplished anything. Look at this place. What do we have to celebrate?"

He laughed in her ear, and then stepped back to study her at arm's length. "How about that we now live in Napa Valley? That our life is somebody else's vacation? Isn't that too-good-to-be-true enough for you, or do we have to win the lottery too?"

She snorted. It was as close to a laugh as she felt capable right now. "All right," she said. "You haven't officially cheered me up, but you're getting there."

"I'd say we have plenty of reasons to raise a glass. Hop in the shower. Get ready. Let's go."

"It's only three in the afternoon."

"But our stomachs are still on central time."

"Fine. Great," she said, and gestured at the maze of boxes. "But first we have to figure out where we packed our clothes…"

CHAPTER 2

THEY'D FALLEN IN love with California on their honeymoon ten years ago. They couldn't afford the two-week trip—that took them from San Francisco to Monterey to Yosemite to Napa—but their parents had thrown in a thousand dollars. They'd put the rest on the credit card and saved money by alternating nights in hotels and campsites.

They were used to the long, gray-skied winters of the Midwest, and the golden sunshine felt impossibly good on their upturned, smiling faces. They loved the salt spray of the ocean and the way the foothills humped up into mountains and the cross-section of humanity you could encounter walking a single block of Haight-Ashbury.

During the day, they would eat muffins and bananas and cheese sticks and nuts, so that they felt financially and physically justified when feasting every night. The Mustards Grill in Napa was their favorite of any place they'd visited. And that's where they went now.

The restaurant was white sided and blue trimmed with a long bank of windows facing the parking lot. It was a landmark known for its long waits, but it was early enough that they were seated immediately.

Abi wasn't sure she'd ever get used to the fussiness of California cuisine. Even ordering water was a chore. The bearded, tattooed waiter first offered them flat or sparkling water, and when she said, "Flat," he said. "Very good. I'll bring you a bottle of flat water."

"No, no, no," she said. "Flat as in tap."

He raised his eyebrows as though asking her to reconsider. "I see. Tap it is."

Jeremy asked if the restaurant carried any sparkling apple juice. "You know, something that feels like wine. Something celebratory. For her."

The waiter nodded to Abi. "Are congratulations in order?"

"No," she said, and touched her belly instinctively. "But we're trying."

"I see."

She insisted that Jeremy order a glass of cabernet.

"It doesn't feel fair," he said.

"It's fine. We've got the rest of our lives to share a bottle. We'll probably end up sick to death of wine, living here."

The waiter brought them their drinks, then told them the specials and took their order. Pork chops. They had been dreaming about those Mongolian pork chops—served with house-made mustard and sweet-and-sour red cabbage—for over ten years.

"Ten years?" the waiter said. "Well, welcome back."

It was hard to believe they *were* back. She hadn't thought she'd stood a chance of landing the job. She had high marks in med school and strong recommendations from her colleagues in Wisconsin, but she was a young thirty-seven and relatively inexperienced as a forensic pathologist, working for the medical school at UW–Milwaukee. She had no local connections. So few medical examiners were women, and to make matters worse, she had accidentally let slip that she and Jeremy were trying to start a family. She knew that sort of thing wasn't supposed to matter, but it did.

The interview lasted two days and they offered her the position on the way to the airport—and to sweeten the deal, they helped arrange a part-time post at the free clinic for Jeremy.

Abi was too excited to negotiate, to ask if she could have a day or two to think about it. "Yes!" she'd yelled. "Of course I'll take it!"

And now she and Jeremy raised their glasses and chimed them together in a toast. "Feeling better?" he said.

"Much."

Abi had grown up in a superstitious family. Knocking on wood. Tossing spilled salt over her left shoulder. Avoiding black cats. It was bad luck not to drink after making a toast—but when a scream rang out, she dropped her glass.

It shattered on the floor, but no one even looked her way. Everyone in the restaurant was looking at the woman who had slumped forward at her table.

She wore a yellow sundress. Her hair was once the same color, but it was now threaded white. Her body was stiff but shuddering, as though in a seizure, and she leaned sideways and dragged the tablecloth and everything on it with her to the floor.

Across the floor, a bottle of wine rolled in a wide arc, *glug-glug-glugging* a red puddle.

Several people stood from their chairs, but only Abi hurried forward to kneel beside the woman. Her eyes were rolled back, white and edged by red capillaries. She was making a panting noise, her airways clear, so she wasn't choking.

Jeremy joined her now. "What can I do?" She told him to clear away the nearby furniture and call 911.

"Shouldn't you put something in her mouth?" the waiter said. No, that was an old myth. They would wait the seizure out and make sure she didn't hurt herself.

The woman's legs kicked and her body convulsed as if she were being electrocuted.

At her table sat a heavyset man in a golf shirt and khakis. He remained in his chair, his hands still gripping his silverware, his mouth a wide O of surprise.

"Is she epileptic?" Abi said. "Sir! Sir, I need your help."

That woke him up from his daze. He pushed back from the table and hesitantly said, "Mary? Mary, what's wrong?"

"Is this your wife? Mary? Is she epileptic?"

"Yes," he said, and then shook his head. "I mean

no. No, she's not epileptic. Not diabetic. She's nothing. She's perfectly healthy."

As if to argue his point, the woman stopped breathing and her body went stiff, humming like a diving board.

Jeremy was talking to the 911 operator, telling them to hurry.

But it didn't matter. No ambulance could have gotten there quickly enough. A minute later, the woman's body went limp. A minute after that, her pulse stilled.

CHAPTER 3

ABI DIDN'T LIKE to be told what to do. She was very aware of this and thought of it as a weakness as much as a strength. She and Jeremy rarely cooked as a couple—or gardened, or even so much as painted a room together—because they both had strong opinions.

They joked about it often, calling each other *boss* and *chief*. If Jeremy thought the onions needed to be minced instead of chopped, he would have to suggest so indirectly. "Hey, boss. I saw this cool move on the Food Network the other day," he might say. "Can I show you?"

She loved him all the more for this. Because it showed that he understood her and respected her.

Unlike this man. Dean Poole, a deputy with the Napa Valley Sheriff's Department. From the moment he walked into the Mustards Grill, he treated her like she was a suspect, not a colleague. "*You're* the new examiner?" he said upon introduction. He spoke in demands: "What are you doing here of all places?" then

"Tell me what happened," and "Well what did you do?" until finally, "Uh-huh, how about you go stand over there while I secure this scene?"

He was in his midthirties but had a soft, boyish face. Abi thought this must be why he grew out his mustache. It was meant to give him more authority, but it was too thin to do much more than dirty his upper lip.

Abi said, "Why don't you let me help?"

"That won't be necessary."

"But…," she said.

"But what?"

"But I'm the medical examiner."

Dean said, "You haven't even gotten into your office yet. And Millennium should be here any minute."

So she and Jeremy stood in one corner—and the waitstaff and manager in the other, talking in quiet voices, everyone eager to give their statements and go home. Every now and then someone glanced at the body on the floor.

Mary. That was her name. Her mouth and her eyes open. Her arms and legs splayed in an X and her clothes sodden with the red wine that had puddled on the floor.

The EMTs had already done what they could. Nothing. They packed up their kits now and spoke briefly to Dean before heading outside.

Nearby the husband of the dead woman cried softly in a booth, his hands over his face.

Dean pulled on latex gloves and crouched beside the body. He snapped photos. He made notes on a tiny pad. But he was interrupted by a horn blasting outside.

He peered out the window and said, "Excuse me," then pushed out the front door and jogged across the parking lot.

CHAPTER 4

THE ROAD WAS busy with cars and all of them slowed down to gape. But a Cadillac had tried to pull in and continued to blast its horn. Another young deputy blocked his way, saying, "I'm sorry, sir, but the restaurant's closed."

The driver rolled down his window. "What the hell is this? We've got reservations."

"Not anymore you don't," Dean said.

The driver shook his head as if this were Dean's fault. "What are we supposed to do now?"

"I don't care. Go to Burger King." He gestured them out of the way. "Medical examiner's coming through," he said, and made a windmill motion with his arm. "Get moving, get moving."

The Cadillac grumbled off, but not before letting off another loud blast of its horn.

And then a white van pulled into the parking lot. It had black lettering printed across the side that read Millennium Processing.

Abi and Jeremy stood on the porch of the Mustards Grill and watched as a tall, sandy-haired man stepped out of the van. He had a nose too small for his face and wore a white windbreaker that carried the same logo as his vehicle. He and Dean shook hands and clapped each other on the back, both of them smiling.

"Should I be pissed right now?" Abi said. "Because I'm kind of feeling like I just got shrugged off by the good ol' boys club."

"Well, you *could* get pissed," Jeremy said, and hooked an arm around her shoulder to give her a squeeze. "Or you could hunt around for an excuse not to be. Your official start date isn't until tomorrow, right? Maybe you're not legally able to process the body?"

"Yeah," she said. "Maybe."

The deputy gestured toward them then—and the tall man's smile faltered when he studied Abi with a blank expression.

Abi knew Millennium. With about two and a half million people dying every year in the United States— seven thousand a day—and so few medical examiners, corporate groups had popped up to fill in the gaps.

These private coroners were necessary, but they worked for profit, and many considered them messy and unreliable.

The tall man walked toward them now, extended a hand to Abi, and said, "Peter Rustad."

When they shook, she squeezed hard enough to make one of his knuckles pop. "Oh, wow. What a grip." He gave a small giggle.

She pulled her hand away and tucked it in her pocket.

He had a dreamy way of talking and his eyes never really focused on her. "Bad luck, huh?" Peter said. "Dean here tells me you just got into town and somebody already croaked on you. Sorry to ruin your night."

She said, "I'm happy to—"

But Peter made a cutting motion with his hand, as if to slice her words from the air. "Oh, I won't hear of it. Consider this my gift to you. Happy to take over. But you know what I love already? That you're a team player. You head on home. Unpack those boxes. Get settled. You'll have more than enough trouble to deal with tomorrow when you have to clean up the mess your predecessor left behind."

"What do you mean by that?"

Rustad's eyes blinked at shutter speed. "I just mean that he died over a month ago, and that leaves you with quite the backlog." He nodded and continued on toward the restaurant. As he yanked open the door, he yelled over his shoulder, "Now if you'll excuse me, I better get to her while she's still fresh!"

CHAPTER 5

ERIC STELLING PREFERRED the dark. His pale skin burned easily, and the sun made his vision wobble and a headache fork between his eyebrows. That's why his office was underground. Along with all of the wine at Shellsong Estates. The storage and aging took place entirely in the fifty-thousand-square-foot cave system, tunneled into a foothill of the Vaca Mountains. The lighting here was dim and recessed, and the temperature a stable fifty-two degrees.

Occasionally he opened the winery to guests for a special release or a Christmas party or fund-raiser, but it was otherwise closed off from anyone except his employees. He preferred the privacy and the control of his environment.

The tunnels were carved as a series of interconnected parabolas that opened up into chambers. The farther you traveled from the entrance, the wider the tunnels and the larger the chambers grew, the last the size of three basketball courts. The winemakers were centrally located in a lab, and this way they were never more than a few hundred feet from their aging galleries.

He'd gotten the idea for the winery's architecture from an unlikely inspiration: snails. His mother had been a marine biologist who specialized in mollusks. When he was a child, she often gifted him with shells that decorated his bookshelves and windowsills. Some conical, but most a spiraled coil. Spiny, smooth, white, pink, purple, gray. She loved the way they filtered minerals from the water and wove them into a beautiful fortress.

He had been a small boy—often sick, regularly bullied—and when he would pick up the shells to study, he would imagine himself sliding inside them to hide and armor himself.

In a way those daydreams had come true. The winery had become his burrowed fortress, his exquisite shell, and he felt naked and vulnerable whenever he left it. That was why their logo was a shell. And that was why he kept seawater aquariums throughout the subterranean estate, in the floors and walls and even ceilings of the tunnels, all of them knobbed and spined with whelks and limpets and cones.

Eric was sitting at his desk now, holding an empty shell that still smelled like the sea, worrying it with his fingers as though trying to memorize its shape. It kept him occupied while he waited. He stared at the phone. He knew it would soon ring, and when it finally did, he cleared his throat and lifted the receiver to his ear and said, "Yes."

"It's done."

A smile flickered across his face and died. Then he hung up the phone and closed his hand around the shell, making a fist.

CHAPTER 6

IT WAS A strange job, being a doctor for people who were already dead.

Families and police departments requested autopsies because they wanted to be sure. That happened more often than you would think. Yes, there were the homicides, but the list of bodies in the freezer included a woman who died in a car crash, a man who seemingly had a heart attack in a hot tub and whose boiled body was not found until a day later, and a girl who wouldn't wake up when her parents flipped on the lights and told her it was time for school.

Maybe Abi could get through seven or ten autopsies a day. Maybe. A body could take anywhere from forty minutes to two hours to process. She currently had a backlog of one hundred twelve bodies. And could expect more to arrive every day.

With that impossible math in mind, Abi still felt angry about the way she had been treated by the deputy and coroner, but also…weirdly grateful. They dismissed her and treated her like an outsider, yes, but they were right: she didn't have time for another body.

The previous medical examiner—Paul Bures—had left her with a mess that she was going to spend the better part of a year cleaning up.

The pathology lab looked like a cross between a cafeteria kitchen and an operating theater. Stainless steel tables and cabinets edged the room, interrupted by a fridge, a dishwasher, and a deep sink. Surgical gowns and masks and face shields hung from hooks. Here was a scale and a colander for washing organs. Here were rows of saws and shears and mallets and hooks and knives.

At one end of the lab was a big steel door that led to the freezer. And at the other end was a door that led to Paul Bures's office.

Which was now Abi's office, though it hardly felt like it. A windowless room with walls painted the same butter color as every medical clinic and elementary school in the country. There were filing cabinets with open drawers and extra folders stacked on top in perilously leaning piles.

She thought there was a desk buried somewhere beneath all the coffee cups and manila folders and envelopes and loose paperwork, but she couldn't be sure.

Bures must have been a messy person, the working equivalent of someone who didn't make the bed and left his dirty underwear on the floor. But that didn't seem to align with the meticulously clean laboratory.

She didn't know where to begin and for the first few

hours of her day moved between sorting spilled piles of paper and greeting people who popped into the office to introduce themselves. "Good luck," most of them said, looking around at the mess with widened eyes.

Framed photos hung from the walls; Bures was apparently a hobby photographer. There were shots of waves crashing and birds flying and sunsets flaring. She pulled them down from their hooks and set them in a pile to return to his wife.

When she removed a framed photo of a vine-tangled winery, something fell from behind the picture and slapped the floor. A manila envelope. Across which someone had written—in blocky letters—BLACK WINE.

But before she could finger it open, a knock sounded at the open door of her office, and she turned to see a silver-haired, deeply tanned man in a gingham shirt. "Sorry to startle you," he said.

This was Matthew O'Neel, the CEO of the hospital. He smiled and held out a hand to shake. "I see that you're buried, but I wanted to drop by and say welcome."

"Thanks. I'm just…digging my way out." She gestured at the office, the almost archeological layers of paperwork she had to burrow through. She tossed the manila envelope onto a pile that collapsed in a flutter.

"Yes, well," Matthew said, taking in the mess, "I'm sure you'll have this place in order soon enough. That's why we hired you. Because we knew you were up for a challenge."

"Have you met Pete Rustad? Good guy. Knows the

ropes. He'll be your copilot through this transition."
Matthew encouraged her to take full advantage of Millennium. That's why they existed, to help with the impossible workload.

"I'm not looking for help," she said. "I can manage."

"Right," he said. He *tap-tap-tapped* his finger against the doorframe while studying her. She noticed then the ring he wore around his middle finger. A black band.

CHAPTER 7

JEREMY COULD CRUNCH numbers like a calculator, ink his way speedily through crossword puzzles, hear a song once and later play it from memory. But he couldn't remember names. Not for the life of him.

The head nurse—the one with the crooked nose and the smile that took over her whole face—who was she again? Tiffany? Amber? Sharon?

Every time he met someone, he tried to repeat their name aloud, but more often than not, before they finished shaking hands, he had forgotten. It made him look like an uncaring fool.

He was tapping his knuckles against the counter at the nurses' station. "I'm sorry—I've just met so many people so quickly." He screwed his face up in a cringe. "Your name again?"

"Stacie."

"Stacie! So sorry. Stacie Parsons. I'm terrible. Forgive me."

She rolled her chair over to him. "Don't worry about it. What's up?"

"Can you help me out with this kid?"

He felt like an idiot. Because he had forgotten her name. Because he was only a few hours into his first day and already asking for help. And because his career had already plateaued. For eighty dollars an hour, he was working three days a week at the Stelling Free Clinic—offering up TB screening, gyno exams, immunizations, diabetes management, anything, everything. They catered to the poor and undocumented.

He had always liked the idea of volunteering at a free clinic but not working there. This was as good as it was going to get for him. Abi had angled for a spousal hire and the hospital had said no thanks, but how about this?

He was proud of Abi. Of course he was. For landing the medical examiner position. For anchoring their professional life in Napa Valley of all places. Even for making piles more money than him.

His grades were never great as a premed. His MCAT scores weren't stellar. His reviews—as a resident—were kind but never generous. Everyone seemed to think he was a good guy. But only an adequate doctor. He had never been ambitious. He didn't want to perform cutting-edge brain surgery or rise up the ladder to chief executive or present a keynote address at a national conference. He was content with the day-in, day-out routine of listening to someone breathe through a stethoscope, of advising patients on their prescriptions, of jotting down numbers on charts. Helping.

Now Stacie followed him down the hall. The walls were patterned with grape vine borders, but he felt a long way from the luxury of Napa Valley. The clinic smelled like stale urine and iodine. Water stains darkened the ceiling tiles. The doors were splintered. Earlier that morning, the light switch in the bathroom had zapped him when he reached to shut it off.

The door to the exam room was open, and through the crack they could hear the boy whimpering and the mother trying to hush him.

"He's small, but he's strong," he said.

Jeremy had taken Spanish in high school and college, but he couldn't speak or listen as well as he could read and write. The six-year-old boy, Jorge, wouldn't respond to any of his questions, and Jeremy's conversation with the mother had been halting and confused as he tried to explain the immunizations required by the school district. But when he pulled out the syringe, Jorge understood what was happening, leapt out of his mother's arms, and ran for the door.

Jeremy tried to corral him as gently as he could, but the boy balled up his fists and hit him in the chest, bugged his eyes, and screamed until his lungs emptied of air. His mother tried to hold the boy down, but he thrashed in her arms. She was heavily pregnant and the strain of holding her son seemed to pain her. When she said, *"Lo siento,"* Jeremy wasn't sure if she was speaking to him or the boy.

Normally doctors didn't have to deal with this sort of thing, but at the Stelling Free Clinic—Stacie told him—it was all hands on deck. If their volunteers were short, or the other nurses were out sick, he might even find himself answering the phone and manning the front desk.

He had brought Stacie along now to help hold Jorge still. As soon as they entered the room, the boy started screaming again. Tears rivered down his cheeks. He wore camouflage Crocs and one of them went flying off as he kicked his legs and reared back against his mother's grip.

Stacie picked up his chart. "What's he need?"

The syringes were lined up on the countertop next to the sink. "Polio, DTaP, MMR, hep, chicken pox, the works."

She crouched down beside Jorge and softened her voice and in Spanish asked if he liked kittens. This silenced him. *Gatitos?* He nodded uncertainly. *"Sí."*

She pulled out her smartphone and punched at an app that called up a video of kittens playing in a living room. "Hold this." She handed the phone to Jeremy and he positioned the screen for the boy to see.

Jorge wiped away his tears with the back of his hand and his mouth trembled with a smile.

Stacie slid open a drawer and pulled out a bag of M&M's. She explained to Jorge that these were magic M&M's; they worked better than Band-Aids in making pain go away. She would give them to him if he was good. Did he understand?

The boy barely glanced at her, his eyes focused on the kittens tumbling over each other and pawing at each other's tails, but he nodded and only winced a little when she pricked him with the syringe and depressed the plunger. The kittens in the video made more noise than he did, mewling in the background.

"Kittens, huh?" Jeremy said.

Stacie patted him on the shoulder. "Pro tip. Works every time."

She then focused her attention on the mother and her very pregnant belly.

Her name was Sonora. She wore a sleeveless sweatshirt with YOSEMITE printed in faded lettering across the breast. She put her hands on her stomach, as if she could hide it, and said she was five months pregnant, maybe six. No, she hadn't had a gyno exam, and no, she wasn't in their system, and no, she wasn't sure she wanted to be.

Jeremy couldn't keep track of the entire conversation, but the gist of it seemed to be Stacie saying, "We don't care if you're undocumented or not. We just want you to stay healthy."

Stacie asked if Jeremy could watch the boy for a second, while she and Sonora left the room. Jorge continued to watch the screen while absently fingering through the bag of M&M's, popping the candy in his mouth until his teeth were brown with chocolate.

Twenty minutes (and several cat videos) later, when the mother returned and called for the boy, she was rolling her sleeve over a fresh Band-Aid on her shoulder.

Jorge wouldn't look up until Jeremy paused the video and said, "Better get going, bud."

The boy took another handful of M&M's, slid off his seat, and raced past his mother and into the hallway, as if worried that if he lingered one more second, he would be asked to get his toes removed.

"Welcome to the free clinic," Stacie said. "Hey, small request. Can you make sure I get face time with all first-time female patients?"

"Of course." Jeremy handed her back her phone, and when he did, her fingers lingered for a beat on his.

"What did you give her, by the way?" he asked.

Stacie said, "Oh, just what she needed."

CHAPTER 8

THE QUEEN OF the Valley Medical Center was located at the eastern edge of town, where the concrete and asphalt began to give way to vineyards. The parking lot gave off the heat of the day when Abi walked to her car, a Subaru with 140,000 miles on it. She carried her purse in the crook of her elbow. Her hands were busy with the shifting pile of Paul Bures's framed photos, along with some homework, including an orientation packet and the manila envelope that read BLACK WINE.

She could have worked until late into the night, but Matthew insisted she take off early—"They're not in any rush," he'd said, motioning to the freezer—and attend a happy hour gathering hosted by his wife. "We want you to feel welcome here. Taken care of." She couldn't let the job own and ruin her life. That's what had happened to her predecessor.

She had agreed to the happy hour invitation. But first she had something else she wanted to do.

The hospital was under construction—a wing being

added, a new home for the ICU—and a crane was presently hoisting a sign into place. The name of the donor, STELLING, ran across it. The sun winked off the golden letters when she drove off the lot. She called up Google Maps and plugged in the address for the former medical examiner's home.

It was located off Big Ranch Road, in a development called Del Sur. Abi didn't know if Paul's wife still lived there, but like everything else in this small city, it was only a ten-minute drive. She wanted to return the photographs and pay her respects. And maybe ask if Mrs. Bures had any helpful insight into a job that seemed to have overwhelmed her husband.

The development had been built in the eighties and was comprised of half-acre and one-acre lots featuring three- and four-bedroom homes of a similar design, mostly stucco with Spanish tile roofs. Most of the yards were decorated with rocks and thorny bushes and native grasses, but a few had lawns. The grass was a shade of green that would require meticulous fertilizing and watering in this dry climate.

Paul Bures had kept one of those perfectly manicured lawns. She guessed he was the gardener, and not his wife, because the grass had gone to seed and browned to a crisp. The tidy edging and heavy mulch and arrangement of shade plants seemed at odds with the messy office he kept.

The house appeared dark and several newspapers lay on the front porch. Abi rang the doorbell and it sounded a lonely two-toned chime. Thirty seconds passed and she tried knocking. Just when she was about to leave, she heard footsteps inside.

The woman who came to the door could have been sixty or eighty. She had sleep-matted hair, with gray roots grown out into a skunk stripe down the middle of her head. Her eyes were puffed and purpled with exhaustion and her cheek still carried the red lines of her pillow. She wore a T-shirt and no bra with stained lavender pajama pants.

"Mrs. Bures?"

"Who are you?" Her breath smelled like a miserable cocktail of sour milk and whiskey.

"You're the wife of Paul Bures?" Abi asked.

"I was. My name is Neysa."

"I'm sorry to just show up like this. But…" She held out the photos as a way of explanation.

Neysa reached for reading glasses that weren't on top of her head, then leaned forward and squinted. "What's that? Are you trying to sell me something?"

"I'm the new medical examiner. Abi Brenner. I was cleaning out your husband's office and I thought you might like to have some of his things."

Neysa took a step toward her and stumbled on the welcome mat, knocking it askew.

"His photos," she said in a quiet voice, and then her eyes focused severely on Abi. "So you're their patsy?"

"I'm sorry?"

"They bring in a young pretty stupid face. Someone who will do as she's told and not interfere with their nasty business." Her voice grew steadily louder until she was nearly shrieking. She was clearly drunk, the edges of her words slurred.

Abi took a few steps back and set the photos on the porch between them. "I'll just leave them here. I'm sorry to have bothered you."

"Those photos are what got us into trouble in the first place. Paul's meddling." She kicked at the framed photos and they toppled over with a clatter, revealing the manila envelope marked BLACK WINE.

Neysa said, "If you know what you've gotten yourself into, then damn you. And if you don't know what you've gotten yourself into, then you're damned anyway."

A pea gravel path led from the porch to the driveway and Abi began to follow it now, walking backward as if afraid the old woman would chase her down. "I don't know what you're talking about."

"They're killing people!" Neysa said, and retreated into her house once more until she was nearly invisible, just a pale wraith in the wedge of darkness. "That's what I'm talking about."

CHAPTER 9

ABI DIDN'T WANT to go before, and she certainly didn't want to now, but she felt obligated to attend the happy hour gathering hosted by her boss's wife. "She'd love for you to come," Matthew had said. "No pressure, of course. You're obviously overwhelmed, but maybe this is just the dose of medicine you need?"

Abi met them at Fumé Bistro, on an outdoor patio busy with flowering pots and a veranda tangled with wisteria. Ruth was honey blond and yoga-toned, taller and younger than her husband by a decade or more. She wore jewelry that caught the light and flashed when she moved. She kissed Abi on either cheek when she greeted her. "Let me introduce you to everyone. You're one of us now."

The sun was low enough in the sky to soak everything with a golden glow. There were two dozen women in their fifties, sixties, or seventies, most drinking chardonnay, wearing white jeans and brightly colored floral tops.

Abi kept thinking about Neysa Bures. She was likely the same age as many of the women here but looked far older. Haunted and ruined. Had she once mingled with them? Laughed and toasted a glass of rosé in this very place?

Abi's mind wandered but she maintained her smile as she was escorted around the patio. She had expected doctors and nurses, the women she would be working with; these women curated art galleries, ran foundations, or played around with real estate. None seemed to have any connection to the hospital, except as donors or board members or surgeon's wives.

Abi had grown up on a dairy farm, working forty hours a week as a waitress to pay her way through college. She had never had a pedicure in her life. Or bought a new car. Or shopped at Lululemon. This wasn't her crowd, but she did her best to make nice. She nodded sympathetically when someone complained about the housekeeper always misplacing the television remote. She tried to hide her yawn behind her hand when another woman talked about how acupuncture and her nutritionist had changed her life. And she tried not to spit out her wine when she overheard one woman say, "I'm thinking about leaving Harry. But only after he takes me to Rome for Christmas."

Ruth had her wineglass refilled and chimed it against Abi's goblet of Perrier. "Now, I heard you were at the Mustards Grill the other night when Mary Rizzio…" She didn't finish the sentence, as if it was too distasteful to say the word: *died*. "What dreadful timing."

"Did you know her?" Abi said.

"Oh, everybody *knew* her." Ruth explained that Mary had been an outspoken member of the city council. "A bit of a stick in the mud. Or thorn in the side. However you want to put it." Her voice had taken on a slurred edge. "To be honest, I don't think she'll be missed by many. She was *completely* opposed to development."

"Isn't that a good thing?" Abi said.

Ruth's voice was strangely loud when she said, "I'm sorry?"

"Just that…don't you want to protect a special place like this?"

"From McDonald's and Walmart, of course," Ruth said. "But not from real progress. The hospital, for instance, is on the brink of…" Her smile failed a little as she trailed off.

"What was that?" Abi said. "About the hospital?"

Ruth's smile returned, showing off teeth so white they appeared carved from porcelain. Before she could answer, her eyes wandered, focusing on something over Abi's shoulder. "Shit. Is nothing sacred?"

A woman had come through the gate from the street to the patio. Her long black hair was pulled back in a braid. Her jeans and shoes were grass- and mud-stained, and she wore a sweatshirt with the sleeves scissored off. It had been washed so many times that the YOSEMITE lettering across the breast had faded to a ghostly imprint, straining against her pregnant belly.

She held small-petaled roses in her hand, individually wrapped in plastic, each one no bigger than a baby's fist. She held them out and said, *"Floras, floras, floras,"* in a singsong voice. The night was cool, but she was sweating heavily. And the smile on her face appeared more like a grimace.

As she moved through the patio, more and more conversations died off, until everyone was staring at her and *"Floras, floras, floras,"* was the only sound.

When the woman stood before Abi and offered a rose, Abi could smell the hint of its perfume and could see the beads of sweat running down the woman's face. She noticed a bright pink Band-Aid on her shoulder.

Looking at the woman's pregnant belly, Ruth sighed audibly.

Abi knew what everyone was thinking—*She doesn't belong*—but Abi didn't belong either.

Ruth made a shooing motion with her hand and said, "Go away, please. We're trying to enjoy ourselves."

But Abi said, "It's all right." She reached into her purse and dug out a five-dollar bill, bunched up so that it looked like she was trading one flower for another.

"Are you feeling okay?" Abi said. "You look like you might be sick."

The woman said, *"Gracias,"* before twisting up her face in pain and slumping to the ground.

CHAPTER 10

ABI'S FATHER RAN a small farm. Seventy Holsteins, five hundred acres. He had a hired man who helped with the milking, but otherwise he handled most of the work himself. There weren't many small farms left. Not like his. Most had either closed down during the eighties or gone big.

The A Plus Dairy was big. A two-thousand-head operation outside of Stevens Point, Wisconsin, run by Abi's cousins. They milked day and night, rotating the cows through an automated carousel. Abi had toured the facility once. She remembered one of her cousins explaining, "We tried to hire local, but high school kids are always telling you they can't make it because of prom or a game or exams. Nobody wants to scrape cow manure and dip teats in iodine. Except illegals."

Undocumented workers, who lived in a trailer park outside of town. They weren't eligible for Medicare, Medicaid, or CHIP, so to avoid the cost of the emergency room, they relied on a team of doctors who scheduled home visits once a month. Abi remembered hearing stories about living room births and a man who broke, set, and splinted his own leg.

So she didn't call 911 now. She called Jeremy instead.

The woman—Sonora—sat in the passenger seat of the Subaru. Hunched over her stomach and hugging it. "No hospital, no hospital," she continued to say between gusting breaths. The roses sat on the dash, their petals fluttering with the air-conditioning.

"It's okay," Abi said. "Everything's going to be fine." Though she didn't feel certain at all. Maybe she should just drive straight to the emergency room? But then what? Would she have to volunteer to pay the medical fees? What if the woman died? Would Jeremy be furious at her? Should she have just stayed out of this altogether, like the women at the bistro, who scooted to the very edges of the patio when Sonora collapsed as if whatever she had might be catching?

On the sixth ring, Jeremy finally picked up. Sonora mewled in pain and Abi stomped down on the accelerator, saying, "I need your help."

The free clinic had closed for the night, but it was only a few miles away and Jeremy was still there.

"No hospital, no hospital," Sonora continued to chant.

"Yes. I mean *no*. *No* hospital," Abi said, echoing her. "It's okay. I'm taking you to the free clinic." She searched her brain for whatever specks of high school Spanish remained. *"Gratis? Libre?"*

The Stelling Free Clinic looked like a concrete bunker with windows cut into it. No beauty to it, only function. The brutalist architecture of the Cold War. Jeremy stood on the steps of it, waiting for her. He wore a rumpled gingham shirt and khakis and his forehead was wrinkled with concern.

By the time she parked crookedly out front and killed the ignition, he already had the passenger door open. He crouched down and blinked twice and touched the woman on the arm. "Sonora?"

Abi ran around to the other side of the car to join him. "You know her?"

"She was in here earlier today."

"Was she having trouble then? Is that why she came in?"

He always moved and spoke so slowly, calmly. As if an old calculator churned inside him and couldn't be rushed. She found this soothing most of the time, but at panicked moments like this, she found it maddening. "No," he said, and pinched Sonora's wrist to get at her pulse. "She was here for her son."

"How many months pregnant is she?"

"I can only guess. As I said, she was here for her son. I didn't examine her." He felt Sonora's forehead and then briefly touched the Band-Aid along her shoulder. "But my head nurse did…"

"Do you think it's preeclampsia?"

"Abi…why did you bring…" He opened his mouth to say something more, then seemed to think better of it. "She needs a hospital."

"No hospital!" Sonora said.

At that moment, Abi heard some footsteps padding down the front steps, and soon a nurse with a crooked nose stood between her and her husband. "Let's get her inside," she said.

Abi didn't help people. Her "patients" were past helping. She reverse-engineered. She analyzed and diagnosed. She found vomit in the lungs of the drowned, a bullet in the spine of the gunshot, someone else's skin beneath the fingernails of the strangled.

So she remained on the periphery of the exam room as Jeremy and the nurse, Stacie, did their best to help the woman.

They spoke in quiet voices, saying, "Blood pressure is one-eighty over one-ten," and "Her water has broken," and "She's dilated to four."

The air smelled like blood and the ammoniacal tang of embryonic fluid. Sonora's moans were punctuated by screams.

"Jeremy said you examined her earlier today," Abi said. "How was she then?"

Stacie glanced at her with a look of annoyance but did not respond.

"I assume, from the Band-Aid, you gave her a shot of some sort?"

"I'm sorry we didn't get a proper introduction earlier, but can we please talk later?" Stacie said.

"We should try to get a phone number for her husband."

"I don't see a wedding ring."

"Her family, then."

Abi took out her phone and tapped it against her chin and paced in a circle.

"I'm going to call nine-one-one, okay?" Abi said.

Stacie said, "Put that phone away!"

Her voice had a cutting edge to it. Maybe it was just the stress of the situation, but Abi felt an urgent dislike for Stacie and the way she otherwise ignored and dismissed her while standing shoulder to shoulder with Jeremy. "We'll help her."

Abi brought towels, latex gloves, gowns, and masks. She hooked the IV bag to the wall mount and untangled the line to hand to Jeremy. When she tried to peel open Sonora's clenched fist to hold her hand, pink rose petals fluttered to the floor. "Can you give us space, please?" Stacie asked.

The boy, delivered stillborn, was tiny. His skin was furiously red. He had a black thatch of hair and a tiny wrinkled face. Jeremy cut the cord and lay the child on Sonora's chest, and she fell asleep almost instantly holding him.

Jeremy remained by the table, stunned and quiet, but Stacie heaved a sigh and walked to the sink and gave Abi an assessing look, as if seeing her for the first time. "Sorry if I was sharp before."

"I'm—" Abi said, struggling to find the right words. "I'm sorry if I got in the way. I was only trying to help."

"So was I." Stacie peeled off her latex gloves and tossed them in the biohazard bin. "This is hard to understand, but we're kind of operating under the radar here. We have to if these people are going to come to us."

"I understand."

Stacie knobbed on the water and frothed her hands with soap. "Anyway. I know it's depressing as hell, but I always try to look on the bright side. What kind of life was that kid going to have anyway?" She shook the water off her hands. "Maybe we spared him."

It was then that Abi noticed the ring Stacie wore on her middle finger. The same as the CEO of the hospital, Matthew O'Neel. A black band.

CHAPTER 11

THE WEEK PASSED quickly. When Abi wasn't working, she was unpacking boxes, painting walls, running off to Home Depot for an edging brush or caulk or a new light fixture. She didn't really have time to think about anything other than her job and her home.

Occasionally she flashed on the image of Neysa Bures—drunk, with sleep-mussed hair—screeching, "They're killing people!" But then she'd shake it off and get back to whatever demanded her attention.

Abi and the morgue attendant hoisted frozen bodies onto carts and let them thaw in the refrigerator for a day or two before she began the external exam. It was a painstaking process: collecting hair and fibers, sampling fingernails, doing a UV sweep for any residue, maybe even X-raying the corpse to pinpoint a bullet's location.

Then Abi cleaned and measured and drained, scissored and sawed, peeled and detached, weighed and chemical tested. Here was a middle-aged man who died of cardiac arrest, the result of a cocaine overdose. A grandmother who had an aneurysm while swimming laps at the YMCA. And a young woman with a blood alcohol level of 0.3 who choked on her own vomit.

Four questions dominated her thinking: natural, accidental, homicide, or suicide? Every time she reached for the freezer door, every time she plopped a liver onto a scale. Natural, accidental, homicide, suicide. The four words looped through her mind so often they became a kind of dark nursery rhyme.

She came home every day exhausted and reeking of chemicals and blood. No matter how long she stood underneath the shower, she couldn't scrub or shampoo the smell away. She couldn't read, because her eyes ached from concentrating all day. She spent most of her workday alone—her only company a morgue attendant and the dead—yet her voice was hoarse from speaking, as she recorded her findings into a digital player.

Abi had scheduled and rescheduled an OB appointment but kept pushing it off. She believed she was twelve weeks, but it was difficult to tell, since her period had always been erratic. She had miscarried a half dozen times now; it didn't seem possible that she might actually carry a child to term, and even if she did, that was no guarantee. She couldn't help but remember Sonora, clutching her stillborn child so tightly, as if she could wish it back inside her.

And then Abi examined the body of a man named

Alexei Petrov, who had been in the fridge for a few days. Forty-three years old. Five foot five, one hundred fifty pounds. He'd died in a car accident after his truck crossed the median and struck an oncoming vehicle. When she unzipped the bag, she couldn't help but cringe. His face had ballooned and blackened on one side and was dented inward on the other. A shard of bone poked out of his collar. One of his legs was roughly severed.

At times like these she couldn't help but want to hurry the exam. Cause of death: crushed to a pulp. Wasn't it obvious? But she was a rule follower and a perfectionist. She would unpuzzle this body one piece at a time.

During the external exam, she almost missed the swollen index finger on his right hand, a red lump near the tip. It hardly stood out beside his other injuries, but she noted it in her recording before moving on.

It was another hour before Abi noticed the telltale signs of an asphyxia death—blood-deprived tissue, the buildup of lactic acid, tiny hemorrhages and veins over the heart and organs broken by intravascular pressure. Some liver necrosis. Discoloration of the skin separate from the injuries sustained in the accident.

It was as though Alexei had been strangled or suffered an asthma attack, without any other supporting evidence. He'd drowned on air.

Abi returned to the finger with a magnifying glass and noticed the pricked skin—a sting, or a bite. The longer you waited, the more things broke down. But she had blood, urine, and vitreous fluid from the one intact eyeball, as well as bile and lung samples for toxicology testing. She hoped to know by day's end what had killed him.

But first—she checked the clock on the wall and pulled off her face mask—she was expected to attend the dedication ceremony for the new ICU.

CHAPTER 12

EVERYONE GATHERED IN the windowed atrium of the new ICU. The sun warmed the room, as did all the nurses and doctors and orderlies and reporters and donors crammed together there. There was a table of refreshments, with a bowl of punch, urns of coffee, and tiny plates for cheese and desserts and fruit.

People milled about, talking through half-chewed bites of Gouda and strawberries dipped in chocolate. Cameras flashed. Abi always felt nervous and exposed in large gatherings, and she knew almost no one here. The best thing to do in situations like this, she believed, was to appear busy. So she was either filling her plate or moving along the edges of the crowd, smiling and nodding, always appearing like she was heading somewhere. She was relieved when one voice called out over the others and everyone went silent.

It was Matthew O'Neel. He wore a cream-colored sport jacket and a gingham shirt, his skin so tan it looked caramel. His bleached white teeth flashed when he spoke. "We're here to usher in a new era of healing here at the Queen of the Valley Medical Center."

He highlighted their expansion: not just twenty new beds, but twenty new rooms. Private care to reduce infection and make every child and family feel cared for uniquely. The ICU would be using the most advanced technology, including a new extracorporeal program for children who needed heart and lung support. He introduced three new pediatric specialists and pledged to hire twelve new nurses. Matthew spoke like a politician, emphasizing the final word of each sentence and pausing to provoke applause.

"And this achievement," he said, "would not have been possible without one man." He smiled and held out an arm, motioning for someone to join him.

It was difficult for Abi to see. Not only because of the wall of bodies, but also because the man who stepped forward was rather short and slight.

She could barely hear Matthew over the cheers and whistles when he said, "Thank you to one of the most generous men I've ever met, Eric Stelling."

Abi craned her neck, then edged forward to see the businessman, winemaker, and philanthropist. He was a giant by reputation, so she was surprised to observe him now.

He was pale by anyone's standards, but even more so beside Matthew. He wore a purple silk shirt and shiny slacks over tasseled leather loafers. Rosy blotches bloomed on his skin when he began to speak, his voice so quiet and gentle that everyone leaned forward to hear.

"I'm very pleased to be here today and to have helped make this possible. This is a donation close to my heart. You see, I was born prematurely. At five and a half months, my mother gave birth. I was so small I could have fit into a pocket. I wasn't expected to live." His voice had a flutelike quality, and his hand moved in such a way that he seemed to be conducting his own words. "But I did. Because of the attention I received from a place much like this. We must care for the next generation, especially in a location as special as Napa, where tomorrow's engineers and doctors and politicians and artists will rise."

Everyone brought their hands together in applause, and he nodded appreciatively and readied to speak again. But someone else called out then and made Stelling wrinkle his forehead with concern.

"It's ironic, right?" A woman lurched into view. "They work so hard to eliminate one life while trying to save another. Some people just aren't worth as much."

It took Abi a moment to place her out of context. Paul Bures's wife. Neysa. Her pajamas had been replaced by a summer dress, and she wore makeup now, but it looked like she had put it on in the dark, her mouth a red gash.

The crowd backed away from her. She pointed a finger at Stelling. Her words slurred and her eyes were wild with drunkenness. "I know better. I know what's really going on here!"

Matthew O'Neel overcame his initial shock and searched the crowd until his eyes settled on a broad-shouldered orderly. "You," he said, waving him over. "Help me out?"

Neysa took another step and stumbled, falling forward—into the arms of the orderly. He tried to speak to her comfortingly. "Let's get you some water and a chair, ma'am."

But she struck feebly at him and her voice rose to a high cackle. "You go ahead and eat your fancy cheese and you pat yourselves on the back and you feel good about the future. You go ahead. The louder you applaud, the harder it is to hear the knives they're sharpening."

"Please, ma'am," the orderly said.

"Leave me alone!" She clawed his face. He cried out and released her, and she charged forward a few uncertain steps before her eyes settled on Abi.

"You. You're one of them."

Abi felt the attention in the room swing suddenly toward her. "I…I'm sorry, Mrs. Bures. What are you talking about?"

All the energy seemed to drain out of Neysa then. Her face slackened and her volume lowered to a whisper. "Or maybe you're just pretty and dumb. Either way, you do what they want. Be their little pet. Or you'll be as dead as my husband."

The orderly was joined by a nurse, and the two men corralled Mrs. Bures and escorted her through the crowd and out of the atrium.

As they did so, Stelling lowered his gaze and shook his head sadly.

"I'm sorry, everyone," Matthew O'Neel said. "We still mourn for Paul Bures and we're all sad about the difficult time his wife is going through. Mrs. Bures is obviously not well and we'll be sure to get her some help."

But Neysa wasn't finished. She cried out, "Murderer!" just as she left the atrium. The word rang and tremored in the air like the aftermath of a church bell.

CHAPTER 13

WHEN ABI TOLD the doctor about her previous miscarriages, they decided on a more aggressive diagnostic screening than standard in the first trimester. In addition to the ultrasound, they would take blood and placenta samples. Her gynecologist, Jamet, spoke in a fast, friendly, chirpy voice that distracted Abi from the fact that her legs were stirruped apart.

"Here I am," Jamet said, popping up on the other side of the sheet to smile at her, "dealing with babies. And here you are, dealing with stiffs." Her earrings were long feathers and her purple-framed glasses sat on her nose a little crookedly. "Everybody's either coming or going, huh? Guess that's life."

Abi laughed, despite her discomfort. It seemed like everyone she had met so far in Napa was status-driven and fake friendly. By comparison, Jamet seemed so earthy and sincere. When the appointment ended, Abi nervously considered asking her out to coffee. Was that weird? Was she that lonely? Were you even allowed to be friends with your gynecologist?

But before she could ask, Jamet said, "Your predecessor was kind of an odd duck. Maybe that's a consequence of hanging out with dead people all the time."

"What do you mean?" Abi said.

"I remember people saying he was a conspiracy-theory type. And I know he stirred up some trouble when he sent out a hospital-wide email, asking everyone to resist the merger."

"What merger?"

"Oh, I don't really pay attention to any of that stuff. I'm too busy throwing babies around. But didn't they tell you about this when you took the job? There's basically some health care system that bought out— or merged with?—this one. Something like that. The wine guy is behind it all."

"Which wine guy? This place is crowded with wine guys."

"Somebody Stelling. He's on the hospital board. Major philanthropist."

"Eric Stelling." For such a slight man, he cast a long shadow. "He also founded the free clinic where my husband works."

"That's the one."

"I saw him yesterday. At the dedication ceremony for the new ICU."

"He dropped ten million on it, I heard."

Abi said, "But why was Paul Bures opposed to the merger?"

211

"I don't know. He was convinced there was something evil going on. Which is kind of fun to think about, yeah? Makes things more exciting. Anyway, I'm stacked with appointments, but as soon as I get these results, one of the nurses will call."

As Abi left the office, Jamet called out, "Oh, and congratulations again!" At first Abi didn't know what she meant; then she remembered. Yes. This was a good thing. The child growing inside her. The start of a new life.

Abi returned to her office to face another set of results, for Alexei Petrov. Toxicology had revealed the presence of venom, a conotoxin sourced from a marine gastropod mollusk. A cone snail. A quick Internet search revealed that cone snails are found the world over, but only in tropical areas are their stings potentially fatal. Abi read about the radula tooth—acting a little like a hypodermic needle—that stings the snail's prey and pumps out paralyzing venom.

It wasn't clear what had killed Alexei first: the bite or the car crash. But it was curious enough that Abi put in a call to the sheriff's department. She wasn't expected to do anything more than file a report, but she still hadn't met Sheriff Colton and figured this was as good an excuse as any to reach out. He wasn't available, so his secretary took a message.

Abi forgot all about it until a few hours later, when she dislocated a liver from a body and turned to set it on the scale, only to find a man standing a few feet away from her.

* * *

It was the deputy, Dean Poole, from the Mustards Grill. His boyish face was still dominated by the bad mustache.

Poole cocked his head and smiled. "How are the zombies treating you?"

She didn't respond except to set the liver down. She noted the weight and then shut off her recorder and peeled off her gloves and washed her hands. He had annoyed her before by dismissing her from the crime scene, and she liked him even less now, invading her work space.

"Got your message," he said.

"I left it for Sheriff Colton."

"And he passed it along to me. Said to swing by." He spoke to her, but his eyes were on the table, where an older man lay with his chest butterflied open. "What do you got?"

She pulled off her face mask and hung it on a hook. "Something curious."

She waved him into her office and showed him the photos and the toxicology results and he gave a little laugh and shook his head. "Okay."

"Okay what?"

"It's just kind of funny. You calling us on account of a snail."

"This *snail* is more dangerous than most of the people you arrest in a day. There's one species, the geography cone, that's nicknamed the cigarette snail. You know why?"

"No, I don't know why."

"Because if you get stung, you'll be dead in about the time it takes to finish a Marlboro Red."

The printer hummed to life and began to spit out the autopsy report, and she neatened the warm stack of paper and handed it to him.

Dean riffled through it and said, "Look. I dealt with two robberies, a beating, and a shooting last night. Earlier this morning, I busted a meth lab, and you know what I found there? A kid whose diaper probably hadn't been changed in a week."

"Oh." She was somewhat taken aback. "Here in Napa?"

"Yeah, here in Napa. And that's a normal twenty-four hours." He leaned against her doorframe and hooked a thumb in his holster belt. "There's a lot more trouble here than you might imagine."

"I'm sorry," she said, and immediately regretted it. Women were always apologizing for things they shouldn't apologize for. It wasn't her fault the baby had been neglected. It wasn't her fault he had come all the way down here.

"With all I have to deal with," he said, "I don't know that a *snail* is my top priority. Couldn't this guy have just pulled it out of a tide pool and got pricked?"

The more he spoke, the smaller and more ridiculous she felt. "No. No, not the kind that stung him," she said. "They're not native to this area. And the poison hit him when he was driving, so the bite must have come soon before. Meaning, it happened *here* in Napa."

"If you say so." Dean started out of her office and gave a backward wave and said, "Thanks, Nancy Drew. Like I said, I'll look into it."

CHAPTER 14

IT WAS HER father's fault that Abi was a perfectionist. He woke at exactly 4:30 every morning and went to bed at exactly 9:30. He scraped and swept down the barn floor after every milking. He waxed his tractors to a glow and navigated his combine in tidy turns, never missing a stalk of corn.

Jeremy thought she was the same way. When she rearranged a dishwasher he had already loaded, or refolded a shirt he had already put in a drawer, or remade the bed when he had simply roughed the sheets and quilt back over it.

Her encounter at the ICU reception with Mrs. Bures felt a little like that. Like a badly folded shirt or an unmade bed. She couldn't leave it alone.

So during her lunch break, she headed over to the sheriff's office. Dean Poole had pushed her out of the Mustards Grill and pushed his way into her office at the hospital. She would push back a little.

On the drive there she passed three Teslas, one

Jaguar, one Ferrari, three Mercedeses, and five BMWs. She and Jeremy had made this into a game, tallying luxury cars every time they went out.

You couldn't hurry anywhere here; the roads were clogged with traffic, every parking lot full, the door to every art gallery or oil and vinegar store swinging open to show someone smiling and tucking a receipt into their pocket.

She was stuck for a mile or more behind a limousine, likely filled with tourists on a marathon visit to Mondavi, Silverado, Coppola, Beringer, Kendall-Jackson—hiring a driver to save themselves from a DUI.

That really seemed like the only danger possible in a place like this: overindulgence. Dean had surprised her when he mentioned the robbery and the meth lab bust. She'd assumed, when she moved here, that the police existed more for pageantry. But she was slowly being cured of that illusion. Where there was sun, there were shadows.

The sheriff's office was newly built and perched on a small hill. With its wide walkways, tidy landscaping, sunlit windows, and stone-slabbed architecture, it more resembled a golf-course clubhouse than a police station.

At reception, she introduced herself and asked to meet with the sheriff. No, she didn't have a meeting. Yes, she realized he might be busy. But hopefully something could be arranged?

She sat in the waiting area for five minutes, before a

door buzzed and a big man stepped through it. Everything about him seemed squared off—his head, shoulders, fingertips, boots. His hair was a close-cropped, a white wire brush along his pink scalp. She guessed him seventy. He walked with a slight limp but looked like he could still do some damage on the football field. "Abi Brenner? Chase Colton." When he smiled, he showed off small teeth stained by coffee.

He waved her back and escorted her down several corridors until they arrived at his office. A flag hung on a pole in the corner. There were photos of him as a soldier, with his family, and at a winery, holding up purple bundles of grapes, toasting glasses of wine.

He saw her looking and touched the frame of one. "You should come up sometime."

"I'm sorry?" she said.

"To the winery. My family's winery. Colton Crossroads. You're officially invited. I'll give you the full tour, all the behind-the-scenes goodness."

"Oh. A winery? I didn't realize—I mean, *sure*, I'd like that very much."

He sat and motioned for her to do the same. A glass bowl of nuts sat on the desk and he scooped out a handful and munched them down. "You're surprised about the winery?"

"No," she said. "Maybe a little."

"Comes with the territory. Sheriff's a political position. Especially in a place like this. I'm not busting heads. I'm going to galas and giving the occasional press conference."

"Right."

He pushed the bowl of nuts toward her. "Want some? They're good. Costco."

"No. Thanks."

"Suit yourself. So it's good to meet you. Congrats on your new position. You settling in okay?"

"Fine so far. It's just…Neysa Bures."

"Oh, gosh. I'm sorry about that. I heard. The reception? Sounded like she had had a few."

"She appeared to be drunk, yes."

"She has a problem. A serious problem. We've pulled her off the road enough times that she's lost her license." He stood up and hitched his belt and stood by the window, taking in the hills in the near distance. He pointed with one of his giant fingers. "That's about where we're at—just tucked between those two hills. You see?"

"That's sad. About Neysa. But she seems convinced that someone killed her husband. That Eric Stelling…"

He looked back at her, as if trying to remember what they were talking about. "It is. Sad. And her mind is—not sure of the right word—warped? She's angry and she's looking for a target."

"Why blame Stelling of all people?"

He shrugged his heavy shoulders. "Remember that guy who killed John Lennon? He started off as a fan, then got it in his head that he was a blasphemer. Eric Stelling is a big name around here. He's in the papers a lot. Celebrity of sorts, all caught up in business and philanthropy. Sometimes weirdos get fixated on that type of person. A person bigger than they are."

"Her husband *was* opposed to Stelling's hospital merger..."

"Look. How he died was tragic. But it was a balloon disaster. The whole thing lit up like a torch. Paul Bures fell to his death. There are easier ways to murder someone—don't you think?"

His phone rang and he picked it up and listened and then said, "I've got to get this."

"That's fine. I should be going. I'm sorry if I've wasted your time."

"Not at all. Not at all." He pressed the phone to his chest. "Now, I meant it. You come on up to the winery. You'll love it."

On her way out the door, she said, "Just one last thing."

"Well, sure."

"Do you mind if I take a look at the file? Just so I can get this out of my head."

"Be my guest. Tell my secretary, Norma, to hook you up." As she closed the door behind her, he waved a hand as big as a catcher's mitt. "Bye now."

She sat on a swivel chair in the archives room. The autopsy report—processed by Millennium—revealed nothing she couldn't have guessed. Second-degree burns along his shoulders and the back of his head. Multiple lacerations, abrasions, and contusions from the explosion, including a full-thickness laceration to the bilateral, parietal scalp. Extensive skull fractures, with a hinge fracture of the skull base. A fractured pelvis. Multiple fractures in the cervical and thoracic spine. Extensive internal hemorrhaging.

She didn't know what she hoped to find. She should just go home. But Neysa's words kept echoing through her head, and she wanted to erase all doubt in her mind. As Jeremy said, she could leave no *t* uncrossed, no *i* undotted.

Colton hadn't specifically given her permission to do so, but she found the evidence locker and flopped the case file down on the desk. She gave the attendant her best smile and said, "The sheriff sent me down here."

A few minutes later she was handed a bin and a pair of latex gloves, and the attendant said, "Not much to see, I'm afraid. Hope this is what you're looking for."

Abi carried the bin over to a counter. In it were two plastic bags tagged and labeled. In one was a charred tennis shoe, size 12. And in the other a Nikon camera with a cracked lens.

She remembered the landscape shots in her office, the ones she had returned to Neysa. So he had been up in the balloon taking photos. She snapped on the gloves and removed the camera and tried powering it on, but the battery was dead. Of course.

She guessed there was nothing to see besides dawn-lit views of mist-swirled vineyards, nothing of interest. But when she popped open the storage compartment, she found the data card gone.

CHAPTER 15

ABI DROVE NEXT to the Del Sur development and parked on the street outside the Bures home. She sat there for more than a minute, the car idling, before she finally killed the ignition and climbed out into the dry heat of the day.

Her clogs clopped the driveway loudly, making her feel even more visible as a trespasser. What her plan was, she didn't know. Be kind. Stay patient. Don't run away, even if she was yelled at. Ask how Mrs. Bures was feeling, if she needed any help. Invite her over to dinner.

She wouldn't mention anything disturbing—not a single thing about the dedication ceremony or her husband or Abi's own concerns—until she had earned the woman's trust.

Like last time, the windows were dark and the porch was cluttered with forgotten newspapers. Like last time, she rang the doorbell, waited, then knocked.

But this time there was no response. She rang again, knocked again, then walked over to a window and peered inside. From here she could see the dining area and kitchen. Some takeout containers mucked with old chow mein sat on the table. Unwashed dishes were piled on the counter.

But it was the bottles that bothered her most. Dozens and dozens of empty wine bottles. If a hard wind came through the house and blew across their open tops, it would have made a ghostly chorus.

At the sound of an engine, Abi pulled back from the window. Why did she feel as if she was guilty of something? She was here to help.

A familiar white van rolled down the street and slowed as it approached. MILLENNIUM PROCESSING was stenciled across the side. The coroners.

Pete Rustad wore sunglasses, so his expression was hard to read, but only a few feet into the driveway, the van lurched to a stop. He had spotted her. She raised a hand, and he raised two fingers off the steering wheel in return.

The van continued forward until it nearly nosed the garage door and the engine died with a wheeze. The driver door opened and Pete said, "Didn't recognize you at first. Thought you were a Jehovah's Witness or something!"

"It's just me," she said. "Your friendly neighborhood medical examiner."

At this he laughed and reached out to shake her hand. She didn't squeeze as hard this time but pulled away when he held on to her an eerily long time. Then he started for the rear of the van.

"So," she said. "I'm confused. What are you doing here?"

"Doing here?" He unlatched the doors and unloaded a medical bag that he swung over his shoulder. "Same reason as you, I assume."

"I'm sorry?" The sun was at an angle that made her feel blind, even when she lifted a hand to shade her eyes.

"I'm here to collect the body."

"The body..."

He stared at her curiously and blinked a few times before saying, "She's dead. Neysa Bures is dead."

The front door was unlocked. Strange smells competed for her attention. Rotting garbage, sour milk, vinegary wine, body gas. Fruit flies clouded the air. Abi tried the lights, but the switches didn't respond. They passed a messy heap of mail in the kitchen and Pete said, "Looks like they shut off the electricity on her."

The hallway that led to the master bedroom seemed to keep extending as they walked. Pictures hung from the walls. Framed photos of Paul and Neysa. Among the redwoods. Along the coast. She paused to study one photo—of Neysa kissing Paul on the cheek, while he scrunched his face up with delight—that might have been taken on their honeymoon. Back when they were the same age as Abi and Jeremy...

Abi saw death every day. She thought she was immune to it. But that photo had the effect of a funhouse mirror: this dark, reeking house and dead marriage and drunk paranoid woman all added up to some cruel reflection, of what might befall Abi if she wasn't careful.

Neysa lay in bed, propped up crookedly by her pillows. Her eyes were half-lidded and her skin gray-green. She wore the same outfit as she did the day of the ICU ceremony, ruined by a purplish tide of vomit.

"A neighbor called it in. Came to check on her and found her like this," Pete said. "I thought you knew. I thought the wires got crossed at the department and they ended up calling us both."

"I just came by to check on her." Abi spoke quietly, as if she were in a library or church, the same tone of voice she used when speaking into her recorder at work. The dead quieted her. "I was worried—"

"Looks like you were right to be. Must have drank herself to death." He gestured to several empty bottles of red wine stacked on the night table.

She wanted to be suspicious, but it was hard to be around Pete. He seemed so blankly unassuming. Kind but empty. The sort of person who probably spent a lot of time fussing over his lawn and hummed Christmas carols year-round.

She took in a deep breath—to heave a sigh—but ended up inhaling a cluster of fruit flies. She coughed into her fist.

Pete unscrewed the lens from his camera and began shooting the room and the body. "You okay?"

"Yeah," she said, between coughs. "Just need…some water."

The camera flashed and strobed the room when she headed down the hall to the kitchen. The fruit flies were thicker here, amid the mess of mucked dishes, takeout containers, wine bottles. She ran the water and gulped directly from the faucet and tried to wash away the tickle in her throat.

As she did, her eyes settled on the unopened mound of mail. The corner of a manila envelope poked out of it. She knobbed off the faucet and wiped her mouth with the back of her hand. She knelt and pulled at the envelope until it loosed itself from the catalogues and unpaid bills.

BLACK WINE, it read. The envelope she had delivered here, the envelope she had found hidden in her office.

Pete's voice called out. "Everything okay?"

"Yes!" she said. "If you've got this, I'm going to take off." She tucked the envelope under her arm. "I've got work to do."

CHAPTER 16

AFTER WORK—AFTER Jeremy filled his final prescription and washed his hands for what must have been the three thousandth time that day, and gathered his backpack and rattled his keys—his head nurse, Stacie, appeared beside him with a smile brightening her face. "Hope you're not tired."

"More like exhausted."

"Nope." She shook her head and her smile widened. "Not allowed."

"Why not?"

She hooked an arm through his. "Because you're coming with me."

He couldn't help but laugh. "I can't. I've got to—I should really get home."

It was then that he noticed her lips were bright with fresh lipstick. Her blond hair was loose and brushed, though it still carried the crimp of her ponytail. She had changed out of her white sneakers and into leather flats.

"Oh no. You're not going to want to miss this."

* * *

He followed Stacie out of town and into Napa Valley, toward Yountville. She drove an ink-black Audi, and on straightaways he muscled the stick and ground the gears on his old Jeep Cherokee, trying to keep up with her. He wondered how she could afford such a car on a nurse's salary. Maybe she came from a rich family; maybe she divorced with a nice settlement—but he was mostly distracted by questions about what the evening held in store.

He'd first thought that Stacie had wanted to go out for a drink. He was a little embarrassed that he had wanted to believe it. Was he so weak that anyone who offered him a warm touch, a friendly smile, made him forget his marriage?

He remembered some statistic he had read: death, divorce, and moving were the three most stressful events someone could face in life. Abi had been distracted, on edge, exhausted for months now. She seemed thankful for him, but only as someone who could take care of what she couldn't handle, due to her burdened schedule. Maybe it was starting to wear his love thin?

No. He shook his head and concentrated on the road as it made a hard bend past a grove of aspens. All of these thoughts worming through his head were irrelevant. Because, in fact, Stacie was taking him to meet Eric Stelling.

His name was all over town. On the free clinic

where he worked. On the new wing of the library, the ICU of the hospital, the winery that was known especially for its reds.

The brake lights on the Audi flashed, and Stacie pulled into the parking lot of a two-story building with a vine-tangled balcony. THE FRENCH LAUNDRY, the sign read. He felt very aware of his rust-spotted Jeep when he parked it between her Audi and a white Bentley polished to a moon glow.

"French Laundry?" he said. "Isn't this supposed to be one of the hardest places to get reservations in the country? I heard it was closed. Aren't they renovating?"

"It is," Stacie said with a smile. "They are."

He ran his hand along the rough stonework of the wall, as if to test whether the place was real. Then he snorted out a laugh and said, "Well okay, then."

The front door was locked, but a woman in a purple shirt and an apron tied at the waist opened the door. She welcomed them in and led them to a table at the very center of the empty restaurant.

The man who waited for them was pale, small, delicate. His hair was somewhere between white and blond. He must have been in his sixties, but his skin was so untouched by the sun and his features so boyish that he appeared two decades younger. He wore a tan sports coat, a checkered shirt, and tortoiseshell glasses. He did not rise to meet them but smiled and motioned to chairs beside him.

"I'm very pleased to meet you, Jeremy," he said, his voice high, every word carefully enunciated.

"Mr. Stelling, sir—thanks so much for this treat. It's an honor."

Stelling didn't offer to shake, but Jeremy couldn't help himself. He thrust out his hand. It hung there for a long moment.

Stelling's smile trembled. But after a pause, he returned the gesture. It wasn't so much a handshake as a gentle clutch.

"Please." Again he motioned to the seats. "Join me." He removed a small bottle of sanitizer from his pocket and squirted out a dollop to massage into his hands.

There was a bottle of his own wine—a 2009 Stelling cabernet—already on the table, and the woman in the purple shirt uncorked it and presented it to Stelling before pouring a splash. He swirled it and sniffed it and tasted and nodded and said, "Excellent. But I'm prejudiced, of course."

She poured for the rest of the table and then left them.

"I hope you don't mind," Stelling said, "but we're guinea pigs. The chef wants to try out some new dishes on us."

Stacie raised her glass in a toast, her face warped on the other side of it. "Of course we don't mind."

"Wow," Jeremy said, and nearly knocked over his wineglass in his haste to reach for it. "Not at all!"

CHAPTER 17

JEREMY COULDN'T WAIT to tell her. "Abi," he said as soon as he opened the door, and then, not even a second later, "Abi!"

He would likely find her on a stepladder, in paint-splattered clothes, working a roller across the wall of the living room. Or maybe in a bubble bath, a candle lit beside her and Norah Jones playing on her phone.

"Abi!" he called again.

"In here," she said, and her voice was so strained and impatient he could almost see her gritted teeth.

He hesitated only a moment. Whatever was bothering her, his news would cheer her up. He hurried to the bedroom.

A few days ago, they had painted the walls the faint yellow of early morning sunshine, and the smell of the fresh coat still lingered. A mirror needed to be hung. So did the framed, dried bouquet from their wedding, which they kept in a rounded glass frame. A rod lay on the floor, beside a folded pile of curtains with a screwdriver set on top. But the room was otherwise in order, settled—more than any other space in the house.

Except it wasn't. The laundry hamper was now on its side and dirty clothes sprawled across the floor. The closet doors were flung open and the hangers rattled as Abi dug around. "Where are you?" she said.

"Right here," he said.

"Not you," she said.

"You're not going to believe this."

The hangers scraped as she shoved several skirts aside. "I haven't eaten since eleven. I was kind of hoping you'd have dinner ready." Her posture was rigid. And her expression, when she turned to face him, was clenched as if she had banged a shin. "Where are my pants?"

"What?" His excitement was draining. "Pants? Which ones?"

"The white ones. The ruined ones. The ones you were supposed to take to the cleaners." She was practically yelling.

When they tried to help the woman at the Mustards Grill—who fell from her table and lay choking on the floor—Abi had stained her pants when kneeling in the puddle of red wine.

"Shit," Jeremy said, and cringed. "I forgot. They're still in the back of the car."

He was expecting her to shake her head or sigh with irritation or even scold him. But instead her face brightened and she raced toward him and planted a full kiss on his mouth. "Yes! Oh, you're the best."

She hurried from the room, and he remained there a moment and licked his lips, before following her. "Abi!" he said. "Where are you going? Abi, hold up. You've got to hear this."

But she was already in the garage.

It wasn't just the meal he wanted to tell her about, though that was incredible. Ten courses, and three bottles of wine. They began with a bacon-wrapped date stuffed with chorizo and melted Gouda, and they ended with espresso and a sour cherry pie glazed with dark chocolate. He felt positively drugged from the goodness of it all.

But then, as they finished their dessert, Mr. Stelling had handed him an envelope. It was jammed in his back pocket now. "Thank you for your good work," Mr. Stelling had said. "I know it can be difficult, and I want it to be a rewarding experience for you."

He leaned forward confidentially, though there was no one else in the restaurant to hear them. "It's easier if this sort of thing is off the books. For us both. You won't have to pay taxes and I won't have to deal with the red tape."

Jeremy had counted it twice in the car. Ten thousand dollars in hundred-dollar bills—crisp, fresh from the bank.

The garage door rattled up. Abi opened the cargo door of the Jeep. Her pants were there, in a garbage sack that she snatched and examined and said, "Good, good, good." Then she hurried to her Subaru and yanked open the door and climbed behind the wheel.

"Where are you going?" Jeremy said. "I thought you said you were hungry. I can put together a salad, no problem."

"No time," she said, and cranked the ignition. "We'll talk soon, okay? Sorry. This is important."

CHAPTER 18

ABI HOPED IT wasn't too late. She hoped the continuity of the evidence hadn't been compromised by time, by messy handling, by the heat of the Jeep over so many days in the sun.

She was alone in her office. The sun had set, and she could almost feel the hospital emptying out all around her as visitors' hours ended and the desperately caffeinated, hollow-eyed nurses and orderlies took over for the night shift.

She collected a specimen from the stained pants and sent it off to toxicology with priority status. And then...and then what?

She had shut off her phone after messaging Jeremy: "Busy, will talk soon. Sorry to rush off." She almost thumbed on the power button now but didn't. She needed silence. And though she loved her husband, she didn't want any more men in her life advising her what to do. Pete Rustad, the coroner. Dean Poole, the deputy. Matthew O'Neel, the hospital CEO. All of them had made her second-guess herself—and she felt certain she was right on this. As crazy as it seemed, she was.

Her gaze floated to the manila envelope labeled BLACK WINE. Paul and Neysa Bures had felt certain they were right too. And maybe it had gotten them killed.

Caution was part of her training. She was never supposed to jump to a conclusion as a medical examiner. Just because you found a victim charred with third-degree burns didn't mean you weren't going to find a bullet in their brain.

It would be best if she carved out some space for herself, detached herself from the nerve-shredding panic that had seized her earlier, and approached the evidence clinically.

And quietly. Because if Paul and Neysa had indeed been killed, along with the councilwoman, Mary, then they all had this in common—they made noise. They called attention to themselves. Paul with his hospital-wide emails. Neysa with her drunken rant. The councilwoman with her outspoken agenda against development in Napa.

Abi needed to build a case without anyone knowing she was doing so.

She dug into the manila envelope and pulled out the three photocopied autopsy reports nested inside it. A quick Google search revealed the deceased were a high school principal, a Section 8 housing representative, and an ACLU lawyer. They all died from asphyxia. And toxicology indicated the presence of alcohol *and* poison in their systems. A conotoxin. From a cone snail.

"Looks like she drank herself to death," Pete Rustad had said earlier. In more ways than one, Abi suspected he was correct. And if her own wine-stained pants came back from the lab with a positive match, that meant the councilwoman had died as a result of a conotoxin as well.

"The thing about snails is," Abi said to herself, "they leave a trail."

She would pick up where Paul Bures left off. She was a detective of ruined bodies. She would simply expand her approach. Napa was her victim, and it was a corpse veined with grape vines that carried poison in them.

She started with Alexei Petrov, the car crash victim. The one who turned out to have died of conotoxin poisoning. She checked the phone book and found nothing. She plugged his name into Google and scrolled through thousands of hits that went nowhere, then Facebook and Twitter. Many of the results were in Cyrillic. Men from Russia. From Ukraine. From London. From New York and Houston. None seemed to be the man she was looking for.

Then she remembered something. It was a break-in that had happened to her neighbors in Milwaukee. They had gone to a movie, and when they came home, discovered they had been burglarized: part of a string of break-ins with a theater connection. When the police checked surveillance video in the multiplex parking lots, they spotted a man studying the license plates of cars as they pulled in. He had plugged the information into a public search database, pulling up the address of homes he knew would be empty for the next two hours.

Abi picked up her desk phone to call the police station and ask for the accident report and Alexei's license plate number. She hesitated, then hung up and instead searched the number for the primary tow company in town. She wondered if they would be closed, but they picked up on the first ring.

"Yeah?" A man's voice. Rough.

"Hi," she said. "I think you towed my brother's truck."

"Yeah? You going to pick it up? Cash only."

"No, it's totaled. He crossed the median and crashed head-on with another vehicle. About a week ago."

Silence…and then, "I think I know the one you mean. Your brother…He okay?"

"No."

"Oh. Damn. Sorry to hear that."

"He had something of mine in the glove box. Nothing valuable. Just a notebook. Could I come by and pick it up?"

"Sure, sure. Fine."

"You know what—sorry to be a bother, but I just want to make sure I'm going to the right place. There's probably more than a few totaled trucks in the lots around town. Can you just confirm the license plate for me?"

There was the sound of shuffling paper as the man

searched his desk. And then there it was—three letters, three numbers—that she plugged into the search engine.

And up came an address.

CHAPTER 19

THE ADDRESS BROUGHT her to a trailer park at the edge of town. When Abi drove slowly up and down the rows of mobile homes, she saw the asphalt was crumbled in places and gone altogether in others. Her wheels jutted through potholes. There were streetlights, but only some of them worked. Satellite dishes perched on roofs like gargoyles. Windows glowed with the watery light of televisions.

A shirtless man with a swollen potbelly sat in a lawn chair, while a grill smoked beside him. An old woman in a muumuu swept her porch. Three children rode bikes while shooting squirt guns. All of them stared at Abi when she passed.

Some of the mobile homes were well cared for, with a postage stamp of a lawn out front and pots of flowers on their porches. Others were sun-faded and rust-streaked with duct tape holding together broken windows and a scattered collection of crushed beer cans winking in the streetlights.

She finally found the lot number she was looking for, 163, and parked across the street from it. The single-wide trailer was striped brown and off-yellow, up on blocks with cheat grass skirting it. Four cars and a truck were parked in its driveway. The blinds were down, but light seeped through.

Abi climbed the splintery wooden steps, catching the sound of a television inside. There was a screen door, but no screen. She reached through the frame and knocked. The television muted. She heard voices whispering, the thump of footsteps that shook the trailer—and saw the blinds move as someone peered outside.

Then, silence.

She knocked again. Nothing. And again. "Hello! I'm here about Alexei Petrov?"

She stepped away from the trailer and tried to spot someone in the windows. Just then the children on bikes rolled past. One of them—a boy, maybe ten years old—braked with a squeak. "You ice?"

"What?" she said.

His shirtsleeves were cut off and his basketball shoes were three sizes too big. "You with ice? Gonna deport them?"

Only then did she know what he meant. ICE. Immigration and Customs Enforcement.

"No, I'm not with ICE," she said.

"You a cop, then?"

"Not a cop. Just a...doctor."

She looked back at the trailer, which had now gone dark, with a new perspective.

* * *

Fifteen minutes later, she was back, this time with a pie picked up from Safeway. The lights were on again, but when she stepped out of the car, she saw the blinds ripple again and the house go dark.

"I've got pie!" she said, loud enough to be heard through the door. "I'm not the police. I'm not with customs. I'm a doctor. I have some questions about Alexei, and I'm hoping you can help me."

In the Midwest, people showed up with food. If you had a baby, if you got sick, if someone you knew died. Hot dishes of beef and Velveeta, or egg noodles with gravy poured over the top. And pies. Especially pies.

Food made people feel better. Food opened doors.

"It's blackberry," she said. "I'm tempted to eat it myself, but I'd rather share."

At that, the knob turned, the door cracked, and a woman's broad, pale face peered out at her. "You are not with police?" she said with what Abi assumed was a Russian accent.

"No, I'm a friend," Abi said. "Can we talk?"

The door opened a little wider and the lights clicked on and the woman motioned for her to enter.

The woman, who introduced herself as Vera, wasn't alone. Ten others, maybe more, were crushed into the trailer. Some on the couch. Others on the floor. Others peered at her from down the hallway.

"I should have bought another pie," Abi said.

It wasn't until ten minutes later, after serving out

bleeding slivers of the pie onto paper plates, that Vera began to open up to Abi's questions.

Yes, Alexei was her husband. No, she hadn't gone to identify the body, because she was worried about being deported. They had lived here for three years now. No, they didn't have any enemies. They weren't involved in any protests. They had committed no crimes. They worked, sometimes eighty hours a week. She worked as a housekeeper, and he'd worked as a janitor and landscaper.

"He was on way back from work when crash happened," she said.

"Where?"

"On highway."

"But *where* did he work?"

"Stelling is name the boss," Vera said. "At Shellsong Estates."

CHAPTER 20

IT WAS AFTER midnight when Abi got home. The kitchen light was on, and she tossed her keys on the counter and poured a glass of water and gulped it down. Jeremy only snored when he drank too much, and the buzz of his breathing carried down the hall. She remembered the slurred rush of his voice earlier. And his lips, purpled by wine. He had wanted to tell her something...

She wanted to tell him something now. She entered the bedroom and found him half undressed, still wearing his pants and one shoe. The sheets had been shoved aside messily, except for one section that curiously shawled his head.

She freed his face from the sheet and he puffed his lips before letting out a fresh snore. She pulled off his shoe and let it *thunk* to the floor. She thought about nudging him awake. But he looked too peaceful. She wanted to allow him that peace; she knew that, come tomorrow, their lives might never be the same.

She wished she could take a sleeping pill or have a glass of wine. But her hand brushed her belly, remembering the baby. So she snapped off the lights, climbed into bed, stared at the ceiling, and listened to her heart pound in her ears, thinking, *I will never sleep,* until at last she did.

She woke to the smell of coffee and the scrape of a whiskery kiss at her cheek. For a moment, still lost in the fog of sleep, she felt happy. But only for a moment. She sprung up in bed so quickly that Jeremy splashed the mug on the sheets.

"Whoa," Jeremy said. "It's okay. It's me."

She looked around, at the sun-washed bedroom, which seemed so far from any threat.

"Bad dream?" he said.

"I wish."

"Sorry to startle you." He offered her the mug. "It's a few ounces lighter, but here."

She wrapped both hands around the mug, comforted by its warmth. She knew she should probably not drink caffeine, but she needed it. Needed every nerve alert and aware.

"Sorry I didn't wait up for you," he said. "I was kind of bombed."

"It's okay," she said.

"Are you finally going to let me tell you why I was in such a good mood?"

"I...," she said. "I need to tell you something."

He was smiling, but now the smile failed at its edges.

"Come on, Abi. You're not going to talk over the top of me like you did last night, are you?"

"This is important."

The smile was gone now altogether. "And what I have to say apparently isn't?"

"It's just…" She took a long gulp of the coffee, but it only made her chest feel full of acid, so she set it aside on the night table. "You're right. Go ahead."

He described the private dinner with Eric Stelling. Course after course after course—served to them alone. And then, the money. The ten thousand dollars he had gifted Jeremy in thanks for his service to the community.

Abi could feel herself stiffening further with every word, until she felt so rigid she might break. Jeremy sensed her reaction and slumped. "You're not happy, obviously. How can you not be happy?"

"I don't trust that man. I have reason to believe—"

Jeremy stood and swiped at the air, as though to knock away what she said. "Unbelievable," he said over his shoulder as he left the room. "Everything's about you, isn't it? *You're* the reason we moved here. *Your* job is the only one that matters. *Your* opinions are the only ones that matter. *Your* victories are the only ones that matter."

"That's not—" she said, but he had already turned on the shower and the hiss of water drowned her out. "True."

She should tell him. She should just lay it all out there, as crazy as it sounded. She had been ready to last night, but now his mood had stymied her. And the sun—the constant, yellow-gold glow of Napa—made the darkness of last night feel so distant and impossible.

A knock at the door rushed her out of bed. Abi pulled on a robe, hurried down the hall, and peered around the corner. She saw a shadowed profile in the frosted glass of the front door. Someone was out there.

She started forward, then paused. "Just a second," she said, and dashed into the kitchen and pulled a knife from the drawer. "Stupid," she muttered to herself. Probably she was being paranoid, but it felt reassuring to have some sort of defense. She slipped the blade into the robe's pocket, where she gripped it tightly.

On the front stoop waited the last person she expected to see. Jamet, her gyno. She wore her bird feather earrings and red-framed glasses and an earth-colored top woven with vines. "I'm sorry," she said. "Did I wake you? I hoped it wasn't too early."

"No. It's all right. I needed to be up anyway."

"I looked you up in the directory and saw you lived close, so I thought I'd just swing by."

"Oh. Well. Hi."

"Can we talk for a sec?"

It was only then that Abi realized she was barricading the doorway, holding it open only a crack. She released the knife, waved Jamet in, and said, "Excuse the mess. We're still moving in."

"From the looks of it, your version of mess is my version of clean."

"Can I get you coffee?"

"I don't have too long actually."

The way Jamet said it—and the way she pinched her mouth—made Abi realize she had bad news. She felt a sudden disappointment and wished some other terror had waited behind the door. As they moved into the living room, Abi said, "I assume this is the sort of news I should take sitting down?"

The expression on Jamet's face was warm, but worried. "Your baby is going to be okay. So are you."

They sat on the same couch and Jamet reached out to hold her hand.

There was a beat here, during which Abi *almost* allowed herself to breathe, and then Jamet continued. "But the diagnostics show that the child has Down syndrome."

The next five minutes passed in a daze. Abi nodded. She spoke—asking questions—but felt separate from her own voice. Jamet pulled out a white bottle of pills and handed it to her. "You're a doctor, so you might think I'm a bit crunchy. But I push a lot of natural supplements on my moms." She turned the bottle one way, then the other, making it rattle. "I think folic and gingko can help fight some of the developmental issues in your child. So start taking two pills twice a day ASAP."

Abi said thank you unthinkingly. She accepted a hug from Jamet when she showed her to the door. "Here's my card," Jamet said, digging it out of her purse. "That's my cell. Call me anytime. Seriously."

Abi thanked her and closed the door and leaned against it with all of her weight on the knob.

She had tried so hard to become a mother, and now she was finally pregnant, but...She had worked so hard to get a good job, and now she had one, but...

The situations felt entwined. Equally punishing. It would be so much easier not to acknowledge either of them.

She wasn't sure how long she stood there, gripping the doorknob as if deciding to stay or go. But eventually Jeremy appeared, buttoning his shirt, snatching a banana off the counter. "Did I hear someone?" he said as he headed to the garage.

"Yes," Abi said. "Just a friend. Stopping by to say hello." She wondered whether he was still mad, but her mind was too busy to care. She thought about saying more to him, try to explain. But no. A gnawing sense of doubt had taken over her.

Her body had failed her. Maybe her mind had too. She had proof...of what exactly? That several people (some of them in influential positions) had died of conotoxin poisoning. She suspected this came from wine and suspected a connection with the Stelling Estate, but this is where things got hazy. She had no source material. She was waiting on toxicology on the jeans. And she had no bottle.

"I'm out," he said. "Big day. We're doing a vaccination push at the clinic." He paused on his way to the garage. "Shouldn't you be getting to work?"

A bottle. She needed a bottle. She remembered then

the cluster of wine on the bedside table in Neysa's bedroom. Did one of them carry the Stelling label? She
would know for sure soon.

"Yes," she said as she hurried to the bedroom to get
dressed. "I'm going to work now."

CHAPTER 21

ABI DROVE BY the Bures's home twice before parking around the block and walking to it. She didn't know what to expect, perhaps to find it burned down or garlanded in crime scene tape and sprinkled with fingerprint dust. But the house was just as she had left it.

The door remained unlocked, and she moved through the cool, dark space quietly. She felt like she had to go through every room before she could get started, just to ascertain she was alone. Clouds of fruit flies remained, swarming out of the drains and the garbage and the wine bottles. The smell of the place was better, but a vinegary tang remained in the air.

Every wall of every room was adorned with photos. Paul and Neysa, in happier times, tracked Abi as she moved through the house. When she peeked through doorways, she couldn't help but feel that at any moment she might find Neysa seated on the couch or lying in the bathtub, green-skinned, saying, "They killed me. And they'll kill you too!"

Her body was gone, but the shape of it remained wrinkled and stained on the bedsheets. Abi stood over this impression for a time, uttering something between a prayer and a promise. Even if it was too little, too late, she would do what she could to help.

Two wine bottles stood on the night table. Neither of their labels read Stelling—she felt some sense of deflation—but Abi collected them anyway for testing. Had there been three before? Or even five? She couldn't remember. There were many red rings on the wood, dried scabs of wine, but that meant nothing.

Then something occurred to her. She checked the garage and found the garbage can and recycling bins alongside the sedan parked there. Abi was someone who always followed the rules: after working a scene, she bagged up all of her gear in a biohazard bag for disposal at the hospital.

But other people were sloppy. She was a doctor, and the coroners were administrators with a sliver of the training. And coroners working for companies like Millennium were valued more than anything for their speed and efficiency.

With one hand she crossed her fingers, and with the other she lifted the lid on the garbage can. Inside it she found the biohazard bag that contained a face mask, nose plugs, booties, and shed latex gloves. Nested beside it was a bottle of red wine that sloshed when she picked it up and read the label.

Kendall-Jackson. Merlot.

"No," she said aloud. That wasn't the puzzle piece she was searching for.

But then, with a flutter of her heart, Abi noticed the paper was loose. She scraped it back to reveal another label beneath...this one for Shellsong Estates, Black Wine.

Abi booted up the computer she found in Paul's office, and while it hummed and blipped, she went through his desk drawers and his filing cabinet. She found nothing there but old tax files, instruction manuals, contracts, mortgage information, and a few issues of *Playboy* dating back to the eighties.

The desktop was not password protected. She clicked through Word and Excel documents, hunting for something, anything. Here were old Christmas letters and even a half-finished novel. When she searched "Black Wine," the engine showed zero results. She called up Paul's email and found nothing relevant—except the curious fact that the final two months of his life seemed to be missing. There were eight weeks of no correspondence, as if his life during that time had simply been clipped away.

When Abi had moved into his office at the hospital, it was a mess, as if every drawer had been emptied and then smashed roughly back into place. If they—whoever *they* were—had indeed overturned his workplace, then they wouldn't have left his home unmolested. They would have come here. And they would have deleted or shredded anything seen as a threat.

She spun the desk chair, ready to stand from it, and her foot nudged the wicker trash can. She saw on top a receipt from Best Buy, listing a Wi-Fi–enabled 32 GB USB card. She tossed it aside, and beneath it was a torn piece of cardboard, the packaging for the device. She read the description, then read it again and said, "Oh, shit yes."

This could be—must be—the memory card pulled from Paul's camera. If it was Wi-Fi enabled, and if he had properly set up the software, it would have uploaded his photos as he took them. Her phone did that automatically, backing up all photos into the Google cloud.

She shook the mouse and the computer came alive again. She opened his email and this time selected the icon for Google photos. The computer chugged, slowing down momentarily, and she said, "Please, please, please."

And then the page finally materialized, and the photos began to blip to life, one after the other, the screen crowding, streaming with hundreds and then thousands of images.

She had only looked at a few before she put her hand over her mouth and said, "Oh my God."

CHAPTER 22

JEREMY'S PHONE WOULDN'T stop ringing. He had left it in his jacket pocket, which was hanging in the staff lounge, and had forgotten to silence it, so the ringtone carried down the hallway and through the door of the exam room. Over and over. Sometimes a minute of silence would make him think it was done—and then it started back up again.

Probably it was a telemarketer, some number he needed to block, offering him a credit report or auto insurance. But maybe it was his parents, who were getting older and had their share of health problems. It occurred to him, for a moment, that it might be Abi, calling to apologize; but no, she hated talking on the phone and preferred to text or speak face-to-face.

Regardless, he didn't have time to talk. The waiting room was crammed with people, every chair taken, with a crowd spilling outside onto the steps and sidewalk. They had advertised Vaccine Awareness Day throughout the community with posters and flyers and newspaper ads listing the health and societal benefits: "Don't Miss Your Shot."

Jeremy's head throbbed with a hangover. He hadn't found the time for a coffee break, and his thoughts were fuzzy. He tried to move as speedily as he could, introducing himself to the families, mostly mothers and their children, asking them to read and sign a waiver. They rolled up their sleeves and he stabbed them with a needle, or two, or three, or four; then slapped a Band-Aid on them, gave them some "magic" M&M's, and sent them on their way. He had done it so many times that their faces were starting to blur and his thumb was developing a tender spot from the plunger on the syringe.

And now the phone. The damn phone. It wouldn't stop, but he couldn't answer it.

Despite the incessant ringing, despite the headache, despite his annoyance with Abi, he felt good. The dinner last night had given him a strong sense of purpose, of professional worth, personal pride.

Abi was the reason they moved here, but since their very first night in Napa, she had been stressed and dark-mooded. It was as though all her hope and excitement about their new life had died with that woman in the restaurant.

She wanted to hang up a painting of a barn and cow in their bedroom. She wanted to check on the scores from the teams back home. Rarely an hour seemed to go by when she didn't mention something about Wisconsin.

One of the things Abi loved about her home state was how everyone took so much pride in it. They cheered for the Packers and Brewers and Badgers, yes, but also for polka and cheese and brats and beer and corn and ice fishing and cranberries. Everyone who lived in Wisconsin loved the hell out of the state, and that gave the people there a sense of connection and identity.

But Jeremy had a different mind-set. Wisconsin was what people settled for, while Napa was what people dreamed about. The luxury cars, the mansions perched on hillsides, the tasting rooms and rowed vineyards and Michelin-starred restaurants. Everything they had left behind seemed so small and drab and trashy by comparison. He took pride in living in a place most could only hope to vacation. People sometimes used the word *elite* as an insult, but he was happy to be among the elite. He was worthy of jealousy.

Now that they were here, Abi didn't seem to appreciate it, and it was cheapening his experience.

In the exam room, Jeremy spoke quietly and assuredly to a boy who whimpered and shook his head. "It's okay," Jeremy said, hiding the needle from him. "It's only a little poke. A tickle-pinch. You'll only feel it for a second. I promise."

There was a knock on the door and Stacie popped her head in. "Thought you were probably ready for a refill." She hefted a container of vaccines and set it on the counter beside the sink. "You have enough M&M's?"

"For another few hours anyway."

"You're pushing the HPV vax on all the girls and moms, right?"

She had been especially adamant about this, mentioning it several times this morning. He said, "Don't worry. Everybody's getting dosed."

"Good work," she said. "Is that your phone, by the way? It's driving me crazy."

With the door open, the ringtone was even more obnoxious, its volume rising and falling like a siren.

"Sorry about that. Could you shut it off for me, next time you're near the lounge? It's in my jacket."

"Happily." Stacie smiled at the boy and the boy smiled back. Jeremy used that distracted moment to plunge the syringe into his shoulder.

The boy let out a shriek, and Jeremy said, "All done. That was easy, right?"

Two hours and two dozen patients later, Stacie poked her head into the exam room again. "Knock, knock."

"What's up?"

"Time for a quick break."

"I can't."

"Sure you can." She waved for him to follow. "It will only take a minute."

He washed his hands—which had gone raw from the soap—and followed her down the hallway and then out the back door. "What's up?" he said, and blinked painfully in the sunlight.

It took him a second to process what she was motioning toward.

Beside the Dumpster, in the alley, an egg-white Bentley idled. Its rear door open. He couldn't be certain, because the windows were tinted, but he thought it was the same car from yesterday. At The French Laundry. Mr. Stelling's.

"I don't understand."

"Eric wants to talk to you about something."

"About what?"

"Something." Stacie always smiled, but she wasn't smiling now when she put a hand to his back and led him toward the car. "About your future."

"Is something wrong?" He remembered the phone then. "Did you happen to see who was calling me earlier? Was it my wife?"

She scooped an arm through his elbow, as she had done the night before, and led him toward the car. "No need to worry."

"But was it her?"

"It was. But like I said, there's no need to worry."

When they reached the car, she released him and he leaned toward the vehicle to say hello, to fold his body into the rear seat. At that moment he felt a prick at his neck, and he swatted his hand there, thinking he had been stung. But instead of a wasp, he found Stacie's hand. She gripped a syringe.

It didn't take long—only a few seconds—for the

drugs to flood his system. The sensation was a little like a black blanket drawn over him, the promise of a deep, terrible sleep.

"Don't worry," she said as she lowered him into the backseat. "It will only hurt for a second. And when you wake up, I'll give you a magic M&M."

CHAPTER 23

ABI DIDN'T REALIZE she was being followed. Not at first.

It felt important to move. Her thoughts were stopping and starting and turning and merging, and so was she as she drove through Napa—first the city, then the valley itself.

Abi's parents had a routine of Sunday drives. After church and their noon dinner, they all climbed in the station wagon for a drive around Chippewa Valley. Not saying much, except to point out foliage or a new combine or a house being torn down. Otherwise, they rode in silence, maybe with the radio playing old country. It was a time for reflection, to process the week prior and ready for the week ahead.

Abi felt calmer as she followed the roads that twisted through the blond hills and green clusters of trees. She passed bicyclists with picnic baskets lashed to their handlebars and limos with people laughing out the open windows. Here was a spa, a cedar lodge with a mineral-water pool, a stony inn advertising organic sheets, a resident masseuse, and a lamb shoulder dinner. Here were solar panels flashing on hillsides beside rows and rows of knotty vines.

She called the hospital first, confirming the toxicology report with her assistant, which established the trace presence of conotoxins in the sample taken from her pants. She asked the assistant to scan and send the file to her email. "Now, please, as soon as we hang up."

The news was one more piece of a jigsaw puzzle that was coming together. It didn't surprise or excite her. Not much could, after seeing Paul Bures's photos.

Paul Bures had done his homework. His photos captured vehicles, locations, and people; they made explicit the connections he must have suspected.

The coroner, Pete Rustad, walking through a vineyard with Sheriff Chase Colton, tasting a grape plucked off the vine. Chase Colton climbing out of his Range Rover at The French Laundry, then sitting down at a table with Eric Stelling and Matthew O'Neel, in photos taken through vine-tangled windows. The dead councilwoman, Mary Rizzio, in a heated argument with Matthew O'Neel at a park in Yountville. The photos were taken rapid-fire enough to appear filmic: Abi watched O'Neel handing Mary a leather satchel, which spilled money when she refused it, knocking it over and walking away.

There were other photos too. Some highlighted well-known wineries and restaurants and spas. Handshakes. Hugs. Whispers. Toasts. Some included women she recognized from the Ladies' Night Out.

How many of these people were actually connected? How widely did this conspiracy spiral outward?

But the photos, along with the toxicology report, cemented Abi's understanding that something murderous was indeed happening here. She had inherited the work of her predecessor in more ways than one.

Two series of photos in particular made her feel as if she might unravel with panic. They were the reason she was driving now, trying to outrun her shredded nerves, while taking deep calming breaths, blowing them out until her lungs were empty.

The first series showed Matthew O'Neel unloading boxes at the Stelling Free Clinic. He was parked in the alleyway and assisted by the blond-ponytailed nurse— Sarah? Stacie? Abi had forgotten her name.

The telephoto lens focused on the box's label as Matthew hefted it into Stacie's arms, and Abi could make out a word: *cyclophosphamide*. This was a chemo drug, she knew. Cyclophosphamide had shown up in a wrongful death lawsuit she had been involved with in Milwaukee.

Why would O'Neel be the one delivering it, given his rank? And why would the free clinic distribute it, given their limited resources?

For the lawsuit, Abi had performed a heartbreaking autopsy on a baby whose father accused the mother of killing the child. She had downed a chemo cocktail known to cause miscarriage, or a "ninth-month abortion" as the newspaper had said.

The memory brought Abi to the woman selling

flowers, who had collapsed at the Ladies' Night Out. Who had miscarried her child at the Stelling Clinic after having been "vaccinated" at the very same place, the very same day.

Abi hurriedly thumbed her phone, calling Jeremy. Waiting for the voice mail to pick up, then trying again. Waiting for voice mail, redialing. He had to answer eventually. He might be ignoring her, still sore from their fight from this morning, or he might be too busy. But he had to answer. Had to. She texted as she drove, trying to explain what was happening, knowing it would sound crazy or alarmist, but at least then he would call her back.

The second series of photos that had caught Abi's attention depicted the hot air balloon's ascent. A dawn-pinkened sky over mist-smoked vineyards. The red and white stitching of the balloon itself, swollen with the heat of the burner. The thick wicker basket that hauled Paul Bures into the sky.

And then…image after image of a winery. One with several cars she recognized parked in its lot, despite the early hour. The Range Rover, the white Bentley, a squad car, among others.

The facility was not an old mansion or a Spanish revival or a steel-roofed, sharply geometric modern design, like so many of the other wineries here. Instead it was built into a hill, mounded with dirt that created a giant conical shape. Bushes were planted in diagonal patterns, curling from one side to the other, giving it the grain and form of a shell. The shell of a cone snail.

And then the photos zoomed in on a car parked outside. The squad car. Zooming closer. And closer still. There was a man beside the car. He was holding something: a rifle. The rifle was aimed at the camera. His face was half hidden behind the scope. But she could see the mustache. She could see that it was Dean Poole. And then the black bore of the muzzle blurred. The gun fired.

A tear streaked down Abi's cheek as she imagined Paul's last moments, and she roughed it away with her hand. Then she blew out another steadying breath and checked herself in the rearview mirror.

That was when she noticed the vehicle behind her. A forest-green Range Rover. Could it be the same one from the photographs?

Abi took her foot off the gas and the vehicle closed in. She knew it was him. The sheriff, Chase Colton, his broad silhouette just visible through the sun-smeared windshield.

Some small part of Abi hoped it was a coincidence, but when she picked up speed, he did too. She took several turns and still he followed. She pushed the accelerator to sixty, to seventy on a straightaway, and he growled up behind her until he filled the mirror.

She braced herself, gripping the wheel two-handed, certain he was about to crunch her bumper and shove her off the road. But he only nudged her, a test, or a warning.

She thought about reaching for her phone to dial 911, but what could she possibly tell them? *I need the police—to rescue me from the police?*

Then Colton gained speed again, and she cringed as his lights flashed and his grill loomed.

But then he backed off by ten yards.

A short stream of traffic flowed by—a Mustang, a Viper, a Mercedes convertible—and she realized her only hope was to stay seen, to find someplace public and surround herself with people.

So when Abi saw a sign for the Francis Ford Coppola Winery, she crushed the brake, spun the wheel hard, and skidded slightly as she sped into its parking lot.

CHAPTER 24

THE PARKING LOT already held a hundred cars, maybe more, but Abi managed to shove into a space near the entrance. She stepped out and felt the heat of the day. The air tasted like dust.

Abi shouldered her purse and rushed down the sidewalk, pushing past visitors who were snapping photos or taking in the grounds. At picnic tables staggered across a sunlit patio, people snacked on cheese and crackers and clinked their wineglasses together.

Pulling the door open, Abi overheard someone say, "I hear Nicolas Cage sometimes hangs out here. He's the nephew, you know."

She looked back to see Colton starting up the pathway, maybe fifty yards back. He leaned forward like a linebacker moving in for a tackle, his eyes on her. She considered hiding in the bathroom, but if he had followed her this far, he wasn't going anywhere. She was better off hiding in plain sight.

The building was dedicated as much to Hollywood history as to wine, perfectly capturing the aspirational but exclusionary quality of Napa. Here was the desk from *The Godfather*, the red armor striated with muscle from *Dracula*, the hat and boots Robert Duvall wore in *Apocalypse Now*, a gleaming row of Francis Ford Coppola's Oscars.

Abi found the tasting room and pushed up against the busy counter, wondering if the people around her could hear the slamming of her heart. She tried not to look for Colton, but she could feel him coming. Her back felt exposed, vulnerable. As if he could reach out with one of those big hands and rip the spine from her body.

A bartender—young, with a choppy, gelled haircut—approached her with a smile. He pointed out the list of wines available to sample and asked her what she was in the mood for. She couldn't tell whether his slight British accent was real.

Abi's voice seemed separate from her as she requested the chardonnay. "Of course," he said. "A good choice for a hot day." He poured a splash into a glass, gave it a swirl, and said, "It's got a nice buttery finish, from the French oak barrels. Let me know what you think."

When she reached for the glass, her hand was shaking so badly that she almost knocked it over.

She heard his voice before she saw him. "You two mind if I sneak in here?" he said to the couple beside her. "Need to chat with my friend here."

The couple scooted over and made room for him and he laid his arms on the bar and leaned forward with a happy sigh. "This place is a circus," he said, turning toward her with a smile. "But the wine isn't bad. Not bad at all."

Colton was close enough that she could smell the mint on his breath. His face was broad and pink, his body hulking. He must weigh twice as much as her, if not more.

The shiver in her hand took over her whole body, a surge of adrenaline that made her teeth chatter in her mouth. Abi concentrated on remaining still.

He knocked his knuckles on the counter. "How about the claret?" he called out to the bartender, who hurried over with a bottle and glass.

"This is a full-bodied wine," the man said in his lilting, singsong voice. "Packed with fruit. You might notice some black cherries. And a certain plumminess. It's heavy with tannins, so that ripeness will give way to an interesting dry, acidic zing. Now forgive me for making assumptions, but you look like a man who knows his way around a grill."

"I am!" Colton said. "Charcoal all the way."

"Well, this claret would go *perfectly* with a steak. Try to imagine following up each sip with a rare bite of dry-rubbed porterhouse."

"Hey, that sounds great." He nudged Abi with his elbow, and she nearly cried out. "This guy's good at what he does. Thanks, buddy."

"Cheers," the bartender said, and left them to attend

to a woman down the counter, wondering if they had any sweet wines.

Colton swirled the wine. "Good legs." He sniffed deeply from the glass. "Nice stink to it." And then he slurped a drink and smacked his lips. "That's pretty all right."

"So," Abi said, barely a whisper.

"So?" he said.

Abi turned to face him and was able to maintain a steady gaze, but her eyes kept blinking, and she felt like she had forgotten how to breathe. "Why?" was the only word she could manage.

"That's a complicated question."

"Maybe I should rephrase it. How *could* you?" This came out as a scolding whisper.

But he only chuckled and took another sip of his wine, the redness clinging to his lips. "We were really hoping to have this conversation with you down the line. After we all got to know each other a little better."

The words were coming easier now, the fear giving way to anger. "Oh, and how were you planning on doing that? Make me feel special? Invite me out to French Laundry, slip me a fat envelope?"

"Worked on your husband."

She spit more than said, "He didn't know what you were offering."

"From what I heard, he seemed open to anything."

She focused on her glass, staring through the wine, studying the way it warped the wood grain of the bar top. "By the time he understood what was going on, he'd be in too deep. Was that what you hoped?"

"Oh, he's already there. Deep enough that he's already drowning in it."

"Because of what's happening at the clinic."

"You said it."

"You're sterilizing poor people."

"I'm not doing anything except keeping my county safe and happy."

"How many people have you killed?"

"Me? I've never killed anyone. Sheriff is an elected position, remember? I'm more of a politician, a deal-maker."

"So what's the *deal* you're proposing?"

"It's a pretty lucrative one."

"I don't care about—"

"You care about your husband's life? Because that's what's on the table."

"Liar."

He dug into his pocket then, and though she knew it was ridiculous to think he might draw a weapon here, that was where her brain went. It took her a moment to recognize what he held: a cell phone, not a gun or blade. He pulled up a photo to show her.

Jeremy. In some shadowed space. His eyes half lidded, his gaze uncertain, drugged. His hands cuffed. She thought she could make out some wine barrels in the background.

Colton set down the phone on the bar and slugged back most of his wine. "There's a way out of this."

Before she could respond, a bright voice called out to them. "Well, hey there, stranger!"

Chase's eyes tracked away from her and his expression shifted in an instant, suddenly warm and expansive. He shifted off his stool to shake the hand of a man in a golf shirt and sharply creased khakis. "What do you know, Bob? Haven't seen you in months."

Colton stood close, but turned his back against her, blocking the man off from any contact with Abi while walling her in.

The bartender came over, seeing that Colton's glass had only a tiny puddle of wine at its bottom. "Another pour? Or is he done?"

Abi said, "Go ahead."

Then she thought better of it, grabbed the glass, and said to him in a rush, "Actually no! Leave it. Thanks."

Abi waited until the bartender slid away to another customer, then reached into her purse, her hand closing around the neck of a bottle.

It was another three minutes before Colton slapped his friend on the back and promised to arrange a nine-hole outing one of these afternoons. Then he settled back onto his stool and picked up his glass. He toasted it against Abi's, downed the wine in a gulp, and said, "Make a decision yet?"

"Can I have a little more time?"

He gave a little snort. "How long do you need?"

"About a minute, I think."

Less than that, actually. He was already beginning to wheeze. A vein forked at his temple. His eyes began to bulge. He slammed his hand against the counter, trying to maintain his balance.

But before he fell to the floor, his body shuddering, she pulled the bottle out of her purse, showing off the logo of Shellsong Estates. "It's like you said. There's a way out of this."

He would be somebody else's autopsy.

CHAPTER 25

IT WAS POSSIBLE Colton would live. She hadn't poured much wine into the glass. But even if he did, she didn't feel as bothered as she probably should. Maybe that would change. Or maybe she had encountered enough death in her profession that it felt like a common enough currency. She was able to see his body failing him, tracking the poison through his system, imagining the tissues swelling in his throat, the tiny hemorrhages occurring all through his body, bursting like fireworks from the intravascular pressure.

She had no sympathy. Right now Abi cared only about her husband. And she didn't have much time to save him.

So when Colton fell to the ground, she snatched his phone off the counter and slid it into her purse. Then she knelt beside him and feigned worry, shaking his shoulders, calling out, "Somebody call 911! Is anybody here a doctor? Please!"

Nobody noticed when she slipped the keys out of his

pocket. Just as nobody noticed when she slipped away after a man announced, "I'm a doctor. Please. Make room," and knelt beside Colton's shuddering slab of a body.

In the parking lot, Abi held up the key fob and hit the button. A horn chirped and she found the Range Rover hurriedly parked diagonally, taking up two spaces. She climbed in and checked the glove box. Nothing but registration papers. Then she reached beneath the seat and found what was she was looking for: a spring-loaded holster containing a Desert Eagle.

Abi popped the clip out and found it full. She nudged off the safety. She was no stranger to guns; she had grown up hunting deer every fall. Her parents had a gravel pit on the edge of their property where they had set up a target range, using coffee cans and pop bottles to shoot with .22s and .357s.

Abi set the pistol on the passenger seat and cranked the ignition. She wasn't even a mile down the road before an ambulance came flashing by her, its siren wailing.

Abi parked a mile away from Shellsong Estates at a cheese shop in St. Helena. Not because she was having second thoughts, but because she knew she needed some insurance.

Earlier that day, in the tomblike stillness of the Bures's home, it had been easy for Abi to remember she could end up like Paul and Neysa. Dead because of what she knew. So she had emailed all of the cloud photos to herself and then downloaded them onto her phone.

She balanced Jamet's business card on the dash and thumbed out a series of emails, attaching the photos along with the toxicology reports she had gathered and the very best summation of what had happened that she could manage in the short time afforded to her.

They barely knew each other, yet Jamet felt like the only person in Napa that Abi could trust. Who would grasp the horror of what was happening here—a kind of eugenics program. Jamet brought life into the world, after all. She was the mother. A baby catcher, she had called herself.

"I need your help," Abi wrote. "If you don't hear from me by tonight, it's safe to assume I'm dead. In which case, I need you to share this information with the city police, the *Napa Valley Register*, the *San Francisco Chronicle*, whoever you think can help."

When she hit send, it made her feel less alone.

CHAPTER 26

CLASSICAL MUSIC PLAYED constantly through the tunnel system at Shellsong Estates. Violins flowed and pianos trembled. And sometimes, because of the arrangement of the chambers, choral compositions would echo so that the underground winery sounded like it was full of choirs calling back and forth to each other. This soothed Eric Stelling, and he believed it as essential to enology as the timing of the grape harvest, the malolactic conversion of the tanks, the oak of the aging barrels.

This was what he cared about most. Improving quality. Removing impurities.

It informed his interest in wine, as he carefully curated vintages that won awards of excellence and rated in the 90s for *Wine Spectator*. It encouraged his investment in medicine, as he built and expanded a private hospital system that would benefit those who could pay for the care they deserved.

And it's what made him call Napa home. A perfect dose of naturalism and protectionism and experimentation had made Napa into *the* premier wine region in the world. *Terroir*, the myriad environmental and cultural influences when growing grapes and making wine. The sense of place. The geographic *identity*. The somewhereness, you might say, of a region.

The same terroir mind-set could be applied to its people as well. Protectionism was his goal. Refinement. The natural gifts of this place, aided by law, politics, and science, could create a stronger, more elite population.

Jeremy was handcuffed to a chair in the innermost chamber. The heart of the ocean ballroom. Seated at the head of a large stone-topped table as if he were awaiting a meal. When he finally woke up, he cried out in a wobbly voice, saying, "I don't understand."

"And you don't need to," Stelling said. Any more than the grape pickers need to understand fermentation.

They had stationed him at the free clinic because he seemed vacant and eager to please. They had hired his wife because she was young and inexperienced. Jeremy wasn't the problem. She was. But maybe they could still move forward. Money changed minds. So did blackmail. Jeremy's culpability in the vaccination program put him at risk. And if none of that worked, they would simply be eliminated and replaced.

Jeremy said, "I don't understand" again, his words louder this time. He blinked his bleary eyes. He smacked his cottony mouth. He yanked at the cuffs. "What—why am I here?"

"Everything will be fine," Stelling said. "Don't you worry. Your wife will make the right decision."

The rough-hewn rock walls framed brightly lit salt-water aquariums cut into them. When Stelling paced the room, his reflection slid across them like a pale blue ghost. The tanks were home to fish and coral, but also limpets and whelks and cone snails. Hundreds of snails, their rounded and spiked shells threaded with reds and pinks and purples. They were pets, mascots, weapons. Their venom was the final ingredient in what he called black wine: a small batch that could be found in the cellars of several local restaurants and basements. An arsenal on standby that they used to quiet those whose goals didn't align with their own.

Many would find his position horrifying. He understood that point of view, and the limits of it. But here was the simple truth: geographically, economically, genetically—the world was not equal. California had Muir Woods, Mount Shasta, Yosemite, Death Valley, the redwood forests, the Pacific coastline. California had Hollywood, Silicon Valley, and the agriculture industry—and thus the seventh largest economy in the world. Dreamers moved here, innovators—the talented and the beautiful. It was superior in every way.

And Napa was its crown jewel, its gated community, its inland island. And it was worthy of protection from undesirables.

Jeremy rattled the cuffs. "Please let me out. Let me out please."

"I'd appreciate it if you were quiet," Stelling said,

making his voice as gentle as possible, and Jeremy stared at him, confused but obedient. "Your wife will be here soon. Then we'll all talk."

He checked his phone for what must have been the twentieth time in as many minutes. He had received a text from Colton, alerting him that he had cornered the Brenner woman, but more than an hour had passed since. He typed out a message: "Still nothing?"

Stelling was standing before a hundred-gallon aquarium and humming along with a Chopin sonata when it happened.

A gunshot sounded, and the same acoustics that carried classical music through the winery sent the report booming and rippling into the chamber where he waited.

CHAPTER 27

THERE WAS NO tasting room at Shellsong Estates. No grape-to-glass tours. Aside from the occasional private event, the gates were closed to the public. But this was September, and the harvest was under way. The hot August weather had transitioned the grapes from veraison to full ripeness.

So the vineyard was full of workers, snipping clusters into buckets, loading them onto the backs of Gators. And the gates—silver and blacksmithed to look like crashing waves, bordered by rough stony pillars—were open. For one short moment, when Abi passed through them, she thought this might be easier than expected.

Then she spotted the squad car, parked back in the brush.

She guessed Dean Poole hadn't seen her. She hoped. She drove the Range Rover down the long crushed shell driveway. It was flanked by gnarled oak trees, the setting sun in red flashes between them. She was halfway to the winery when the squad car pulled out, following—slowly, not in any rush. Whether because he was biding his time or because he believed her to be Colton, she didn't know.

A half dozen trucks and sedans were parked in the pebbled lot. A few with primer gray doors. Another missing its bumper. The same sort of vehicles she saw in the trailer park. The same sort of vehicle driven by Alexei Petrov, who she assumed at this point had been a random casualty, stung by one of the cone snails Stelling must keep inside the facility. She could see the men and women working, distant figures moving among the vines.

From Paul's aerial photos, the winery had appeared as a conical shell, but from the ground it looked like something out of *The Hobbit*, a large grassy mound with two double doors built into it.

Abi pulled up as close as she could. And waited. A faint trail of dust hung in the air, coughed up by the Range Rover, and she saw the squad car following it.

She curled a hand around the pistol. Checked, then double-checked the safety. Pressed her body into the seat, making herself as small as possible.

She had parked in such a way that he wouldn't pull up alongside her, but she could see him. She heard the engine to the squad car cut and the door open, and saw Dean step out. She thought he was reaching for his gun, but he was just hitching his belt. He ran a hand along his mustache, neatening it, as he moved closer.

When she swung the door open, he called, "Well? You got her?"

She swiftly aimed down the line of her arm, trained the Desert Eagle on him, and said, "Yes."

CHAPTER 28

SALTWATER AQUARIUMS, TWO hundred gallons each, flanked the foyer of Shellsong Estates. They bubbled faintly. Fish flitted through pale blue water. Eels curled lazily. Coral bloomed. Cone snails spiked the white sand bottom.

Dean walked a few yards ahead of her, his hands up. She knew she ought to reach out, yank the gun from his holster, toss it aside, but she didn't want to risk getting that close. Or risk his finger on the trigger if she asked him to do it himself.

"We wanted to talk to you," he said. "You don't have to be on the outside of this."

"I don't want anything from you," she said. "Except my husband."

She stood in the doorway, holding it open, and a wedge of sunlight lit up a mosaic on the floor. It was ten feet in circumference, a multicolored rendering of the winery's shell logo. Dean stood in the center of it. "That's far enough."

"Where's Colton?"

"Probably the ER."

The doors closed behind her and choked off the sun. There was no light beyond that of the aquariums, and it took her eyes a moment to adjust to the shadowy space.

That was when Dean made his move, dodging to the side and reaching for his own pistol.

His shot hit the door behind her, lodging in it with a splintering crack. Hers hit the aquarium behind him. The gunshots were drowned out by the sound of glass shattering. The water released from the tank with a shushing boom.

Dean was hit by the surging wave, jeweled with thousands of pieces of broken glass. He got off one more shot, aimed wildly at the ceiling, before he collapsed and rolled over with the tide.

Instantly the air smelled of brine. The wave hit her knees, and she stumbled but did not fall. The water subsided after only a second, hissing down the curving hallway. The broken aquarium dribbled and plopped. And Dean sputtered and coughed on the floor, climbing up on his hands and knees, searching among the shells for his lost pistol.

Abi didn't hesitate. She shot him twice—once in each leg—incapacitating him.

While he screamed, cursing her, she kicked through the coral and shells until she found the gun. Then tucked it into her waistband and started down the hallway, splashing her way through puddles as she jogged.

* * *

She could hear her husband calling out—"Help! Anybody? Let me out!"—and she tried to follow his voice. But Dean's screaming and the orchestral music interrupted Jeremy's echoing plea, and the curved, interlocking hallways and chambers confused the sound. Sometimes he sounded ahead of her and sometimes he sounded behind.

She didn't dare respond to Jeremy, not wanting to reveal herself. But she couldn't help but cry out when the phone in her pocket buzzed. It was Colton's. She had snatched it off the counter, back at the Coppola Winery, hoping it might house some evidence. Someone was trying to reach him now, and when she pulled out the phone, she saw that the screen listed the caller as Eric Stelling.

She answered without saying hello.

And there was that voice. "Chase?" The one from the ICU dedication ceremony. "Chase?" The one she would have mistaken for an old woman's, if she didn't know better. "Chase, is that you? I heard gunshots. I hear screaming. What happened? Do you know what's happening?"

He sounded so fragile. She imagined him somewhere deep in the winery, pale and frightened and retreating into his shell.

She hung up. Not knowing what kind of danger her husband might be in, but not wanting to give away her advantage. Stelling sounded afraid and uncertain and she wanted him to stay that way. For all he knew, a SWAT team might be swarming toward him.

The ever-curving space was lit by the occasional shell-shaped sconce or aquarium. Abi had no idea where she was, lost in the coil of hallways. Wine barrels were stacked along the walls and among them were so many shadowed spaces to hide. She turned in constant circles, looking ahead and behind and to all sides of her. For all she knew she was covering the same fifty yards repeatedly.

She heard a clattering thud—like something heavy and wooden falling over. Jeremy's voice had gone silent, and she worried what might have happened to him.

Abi had felt nauseous with fear for some time, but now her stomach cramped and her vision wheeled and she had to lean against a wine barrel for a moment before the feeling passed.

Then she took a deep breath and approached an archway that opened up into a wider space. She could see a stone-topped table with more than twenty high-backed chairs surrounding it. An event space. She edged through the doorway, her eyes sweeping the space, seeing nothing.

And then she heard her name—"Abi?"—and swung the pistol toward the source of the sound.

One of the chairs was on the ground, and her husband remained seated in it, his wrists and ankles handcuffed. While tipping himself over, one of the arms had splintered, and he reached out to her with his free hand. "Abi!"

"Where is he?"

Jeremy motioned toward an archway on the other side of the room. "He took off. Just a few minutes ago. He hung up the phone and ran through there."

She hurried over to Jeremy and put her hands on him. His cheeks rough with stubble. Just to feel him. To make it real that he was still alive.

"Will you help me?" she said.

"First you need to help me," he said, and rattled the chains of his handcuffs for emphasis.

CHAPTER 29

JEREMY HAD SO many questions, but she didn't have time for answers. People were dying. That's all he needed to know right now. People were dying and Stelling was behind it.

From the look on his face, he clearly wanted to say, "This is crazy." Only the gun in her hand—and the Glock she handed him, Dean's—made the situation inarguable.

He rattled as he moved beside her. They had broken him free of the chair, but the handcuffs still dangled off him. They ran a few paces, then paused to listen. Then ran farther before pausing again.

"Do you know where you're going?" Jeremy said.

"No clue," she said. "Out."

The chamber where she'd found Jeremy was not only at the center of the winery, but also at its deepest point. The corridors all had a slope to them, Jeremy pointed out; if they wanted to get out, they had to go up.

They heard a noise up ahead, down the bend of the passage. A scrape. A groan. Then the *boom-boom-boom* of ten or so barrels collapsing from their stack and rolling toward them.

They both fired, stupidly, shocked by the sudden motion up ahead. A small crater opened in one barrel and a geyser of red wine frothed from it as it turned over and over, rushing toward them.

Jeremy scooped an arm around Abi's waist and pulled her off to the side as some of the barrels rolled past, others crashing into stacks and collapsing, a domino effect that continued down the corridor.

"Thanks," she said to Jeremy. "But I don't need you saving me."

"I know you don't," he said.

Abi eyed the tunnel ahead and bashed the grip of the pistol against her forehead. "I don't know what to do."

"Maybe we should go back," Jeremy said. "Maybe we should go back and try to circle around another way."

"No," she said. "No. We're not running. We're chasing."

They clambered over the barrels jamming up the tunnel. Up ahead the air grew brighter—and when they rounded the bend, they saw a doorway exiting into a high-ceilinged, fluorescent-lit room.

The floor was concrete and staggered with drains. A dozen stainless steel fermentation tanks rose around them like bunkered missiles. The air was thick with the sour tang of tannins.

A figure stood at the end of the room. Stelling. His

hair flaxen. His skin pale. He wore a sweater vest, robin's-egg blue. He hardly looked like someone capable of murder—until he looked at them. His mouth was arranged in a grimace and his teeth showing in a serrated line. "Do you know one of the downfalls of modern medicine?" he said. "Everyone's living."

"Please get down on the floor," Abi said.

But he continued on as if he hadn't heard her. "There are too many of us. And too few are actually benefiting the world. People complain that health care is too expensive, but it's not expensive enough. What this country needs is a good cleansing."

He didn't carry a weapon, and she let her own lower to her side. The threat seemed over. "Please get down on the floor," she said again.

She took another step and then another step toward him, and Jeremy paced her.

"You think you've got me cornered," Stelling said. "But you're wrong." His voice was a fluttering whisper.

She did her best to sound like someone in a cop show, shouting at him. "Down on the floor!"

"Do as she says, Mr. Stelling," Jeremy said.

"And then what?" Stelling said. "Are you going to call the police?"

She and Jeremy continued their steady march toward him.

"There are too many of us to contend with," Stelling said. "And too little evidence. All it takes is a phone call and a bottle goes down the drain. All it takes is an envelope full of money and I make another friend."

With that, he reached his hands toward a lever. One that opened the hatch to one of the wide-bellied tanks.

"Stop," she said, knowing what it must contain. His latest batch of black wine.

Stelling yanked at it twice, before it budged. And then the door swung open violently and released a tide of wine. Even over the splash, she heard the *crack* of the door's metal corner striking his temple.

Only then did Stelling do as she told him, finally falling to the floor. His body was limp and moved only because of the wine pouring over him. It flopped his body over, shoved him one way, then another, before pinwheeling him toward the drain, where the wine swirled downward in a bloodred whirlpool.

CHAPTER 30

ABI HAD BEEN hollowed and soured with worry before, but now her body felt carved out by a jagged spoon. She was at once too hot and too cold. Her belly stabbed through with cramping pains.

"What's wrong?" Jeremy said when she dropped the pistol and leaned heavily against him.

"Everything."

"How can I help?"

"Just...get me outside," she said. Thinking the sun might help. Thinking it would do her good to escape the wine-soaked body of Eric Stelling, who was staring blankly upward while the emptied tank dripped and the floor drain gurgled.

The sun had set, and the evening gloom felt like it matched her mood. Out in the vineyard, lights glowed and the harvest continued.

She made it only a few paces before falling to her knees, completely overcome. She retched and some bile splattered the shell driveway.

Jeremy rubbed her back and said, "I'm worried you're going into shock."

"I'm pregnant," she said, the words coming out as a coughing gasp.

He took a moment to respond. "What?"

She spit and wiped her mouth with the back of her hand. "I was going to tell you, but—"

"You're…Jesus."

"I'm sorry."

"Don't be sorry. You're hurt—and you think it's the baby?" He patted his pocket, hunting for the phone that wasn't there. "I need to call an ambulance."

"No calls. No." She was speaking without really thinking. The pain was such that she felt distanced from her body. Someone else might as well be saying to Jeremy, "We don't know who might come."

He tried to help her stand, to hoist her up, but she couldn't just yet.

"No calls," she said. "No ambulance."

"Okay," he said. "Just tell me what to do. We need to do something."

"Take me to the hospital," she said, and hugged her belly. "Take me to the hospital, please." She gritted her teeth and pushed herself upward and into his waiting arms. "Take me to Jamet."

The next hour passed in a haze as she slipped in and out of wakefulness. A traffic light glowed red. A hand squeezed hers. The moon rose and silvered the hills. A voice whispered to her, "Abi? Abi?"

And then she snapped open her eyes and everything came suddenly into focus. She was wearing a hospital gown and lying on an exam table, her feet in stirrups. Her belly throbbed like an open wound.

A woman stood nearby. In a white lab coat. Jamet. She was studying her phone, the screen lighting up her glasses. She wore feather earrings that dangled to either side of her downturned face.

"Jamet?" Abi said, her voice a croak.

Jamet looked up suddenly but didn't offer her a comforting smile. Just a dead gaze.

"Where's...my husband?" she said. "Where's Jeremy?"

"He's being taken care of. The same as you." Jamet held the phone as if weighing it in her hand. It had a polka-dot cover...the same as Abi's.

"Is that...?" Abi said.

"Your phone?" Jamet said, and held it out as if to hand it over. Instead she dropped it on the floor. It hit the tile with a crack.

And then Jamet stomped on it—once, twice, three times—until it broke open and its electronic guts spilled everywhere.

"Why...What's happening?" Abi didn't feel lucid. Everything seemed to be happening too slowly and her words came out in a mushy slur. "What are you doing?"

"You took those pills I gave you, like a good patient," Jamet said. "And they did the trick."

"No," Abi said, and then lurched toward Jamet, only to discover she was lashed to the table. "No!"

"This is for the best, Abi. The last thing this world needs is another undesirable."

"Where's Jeremy?" she said.

Jamet's eyes tracked across the room, and it was only then that Abi realized they weren't alone. Matthew O'Neel and Stacie Parsons stood there, watching Abi with grim expressions.

"What are you doing here?" Abi said. "Where's my husband?"

"He's at the winery," Matthew said. "It's a shame. A murder-suicide. The motives are unclear, but it appears Jeremy had diverted some funds from the clinic, and when Stelling confronted him about it, he flipped."

"No," Abi said, and kept repeating the word, faster and faster, until it matched her pounding pulse.

"Peter Rustad will be collecting the bodies and performing the autopsies. He'll swing by here afterward. Pick you up."

"No."

"Though you could probably do him a favor and fill out your own autopsy report, Abi. Did you know you died in childbirth? A tragedy."

"No."

"We were sloppy before," Jamet said. "We'll be more careful this time." She moved toward Abi, holding a syringe. On the middle finger of her other hand was a black band.

THE SHUT-IN

JAMES PATTERSON
WITH DUANE SWIERCZYNSKI

CHAPTER 1

COME, FLY WITH ME.

That's it—up, up and away. Don't be afraid. I've got you. Everything's going to be all right.

We float up one story...two stories...three stories...and there, we've just cleared the edge of the rooftops.

If you're nervous, don't look down. Just look *out*...at the skyline of Philadelphia, my adopted hometown. Falling away below us is my neighborhood, Spring Garden, just on the fringes of Center City.

Let's soar a little higher, shall we?

(Don't worry. I'm not going to drop you.)

It's just after eight, which means lots of people will be making their way downtown for work. Prime people-watching time.

An endless variety of people—millennials with their gelled hair and too-tight jeans, probably off to work at some start-up with exposed beams, reclaimed wood, and a foosball table. Lawyer-types in their fine suits and even more expensive shoes who will spend their days in air-conditioned conference rooms. Ordinary Philly dudes in jeans and button-down shirts, trying to make it to 6 p.m. as fast as they possibly can.

Or take a look at the middle-aged woman just below us. She's probably in her late forties or early fifties, wearing business attire that's at least a decade out of style. Maybe she moved to Spring Garden full of excitement twenty years ago and never quite figured out how to leave. She walks like her feet hurt. The last thing she wants to do is shuffle downtown to an office where she's ignored or undermined at every turn.

She stops at the corner of 19th and Brandywine, looking up at the bus route sign, then seems to think better of it. Instead, she continues down 19th.

Go, girl, I want to tell her. *Fight the good fight.*

But all too soon, our time is up. We must glide back home. Which is a sad proposition as much as it is a delicate one.

Because if we don't stick the landing in just the right way, we're going to end up splattered all over the side of this building.

CHAPTER 2

NO, YOU WEREN'T just floating along with a friendly neighborhood guardian angel. I'm not dead, and you're not a ghost.

Those glorious city views are courtesy of my personal drone, *Amelia*. I send her out every morning and evening to see a bit of the world that I can't.

I pilot *Amelia* using an app on my smartphone. The controls are super sensitive, so getting her to zoom back in through my rear window without knocking off a propeller takes a bit of finesse. When I first bought *Amelia,* she bumped into the side of my brownstone building so many times I'm surprised she's still in one piece.

Some lucky drone owners are able to go outside into an empty field and launch their quadcopters straight up into the air.

But not me.

My name is Tricia Celano. Call me "Trish" at your own peril. I'm twenty-five years old, live in a small but sweet studio apartment at 20th and Green, and if I step outside, the sun will kill me.

No, for real.

I have a condition called *solar urticaria,* which is a rare allergy to the sun. Yes, the same ball of swirling gas ninety-three million miles away that gives everything else the gift of life wants to give me a severe case of death.

My symptoms were minor back in college—hives, itching, burning. But soon I was breaking out in severe body rashes that made me look like a lobster–human mutant hybrid. By senior year, the condition was so severe that I stayed in my room to finish classes remotely and even had to sit out my graduation.

All of which turned me into a twenty-five-year-old shut-in—confined to my apartment all day, every day.

But you'd be surprised how easy it is to live your entire life indoors. Before the Internet, I'm sure I would have withered away and died. But now I can order pretty much *everything* online—food, clothing, entertainment—and have it delivered, downloaded, or streamed straight into my apartment.

As for other forms of entertainment…well, sometimes I'll pull a Jimmy Stewart and spy on the people coming and going from my building. I especially like to watch the hot dark-haired guy who lives upstairs in 3-D. I've gotten to the point where I recognize the way he clomps down the stairs toward the entrance of the building just a few feet from my door. Usually it's a mad scramble to the peephole to catch even a tiny glimpse of him, and I don't think I've ever seen his entire face. But the parts that I have seen...

Anyway. You might say, *But Tricia, if you're allergic to the sun, why don't you just go out at night?*

Because...well, life really likes to stick it in and twist sometimes.

In the three years since graduation, I've also developed this oh-so-charming phobia of the dark. The very thought of stepping out into the night paralyzes me with raw, naked fear. Logically I know I'd be fine. But try telling my subconscious that.

Friends from college will try to coax me out for a drink, but...I just can't. Once I was even showered and dressed, makeup and hair done...and then broke down sobbing in the vestibule of my building.

I miss the outside world so very, very badly. Chatting through social media or even Skype doesn't quite fill the void. I yearn to be out in the world again, eating it, drinking it, bathing in it.

So, as I did with my other challenges, I came up with a technological solution.

Amelia—named after legendary aviatrix Amelia Earhart—is a ready-to-fly quadcopter with a built-in camera and absolutely no problems with the sun. She cost me a shade under three hundred bucks, but who can put a price tag on the feeling of being part of the world?

I can fly *Amelia* within a half-mile radius of my apartment, and her camera feed is sent straight to my cell phone in real time. She's my amazing, soaring window on the world. Or at least my tiny sliver of it.

Technically, I'm breaking the law. There's this thing in drone culture called "line of sight," or LOS, which basically means that you're supposed to keep visual contact with your drone at all times.

But the Philadelphia Police Department has bigger fish to fry than tracking a lonely girl's renegade drone. Which is a good thing. Because what started as a hobby has turned into a bit of an obsession. And now I'm not sure how I'd live without it.

I work as a marketing associate for an entertainment company with offices in California, Scotland, and Germany, so I find myself working at odd hours anyway. My day is broken up by *Amelia* flights, at least three per day. They span eleven minutes each, which is exactly how long her batteries last.

First flight is usually during the morning rush, when there's a lot of people to watch. Same goes for the evening commute. But lunchtime has become fun, too. I like to take *Amelia* downtown, just beyond the tightly packed rows of Victorian homes, where you can make out the Benjamin Franklin Parkway. It's modeled after the Champs-Élysées in Paris and is usually full of a mix of tourists and homeless people.

When darkness falls, however, it's game over. It's too risky to fly *Amelia* in the dark, and not just because of my phobia. The images on my phone are too dim to help me avoid the obstacles out there.

Night is when I feel most like a prisoner.

CHAPTER 3

BUT THIS IS a bright Thursday morning in early September, and it's time to send *Amelia* out into the world to see what's up.

Or down, as it were.

If you've ever used an app on your phone, you already know how to pilot a drone like *Amelia*. There's a little gray circle on the lower left that controls her altitude, and a bigger gray button on the right that controls her horizontal movements. If you hold the right button down, you can spin her around. Working all these buttons in tandem, however, is the tricky part.

I tap the green Fly button at the bottom of the screen, and we're up, up and away.

I send *Amelia* zipping down Green Street, then tweak the controls so she makes a smooth, gliding right onto 19th Street. Turns are the hardest thing to master. Play with the buttons too much, and *whammo,* you're kissing a brick wall.

When I want to play it safe, I take *Amelia* over the

rooftops. But up there, it's too hard to see what all the people with real lives are doing. So I try to keep her no more than two stories above the sidewalk.

Amelia zooms down 19th Street, toward the Free Library. Along this path there's a stunning amount of new construction—condos and restaurants, mostly. It's crazy how fast this stuff goes up. Sometimes I send *Amelia* out and I really have to study the images on my phone to figure out where the heck we are.

But instead of checking out the cranes and the construction guys—who don't catcall or wolf-whistle at a drone, by the way—I steer *Amelia* to one of my favorite places in the neighborhood: the old Philadelphia & Reading Viaduct that's currently under construction.

Most Philadelphians have no idea this thing is in progress. That's because its only access point is an unmarked opening on the block between Hamilton and Callowhill on 19th Street. But go past the caution signs...and it's basically a wonderland up there. And in the daytime, it's all mine.

I only happened upon it last month, and it took me a few weeks to work up the courage to fly *Amelia* directly above it. Even now, the very idea sends a flutter through my nervous system. Back in the late 1800s, it was a bustling railway that would carry steel to the Baldwin Locomotive factory. But then the twentieth century happened and it was no longer used. By the 1990s, the tracks were torn up for scrap. A few years ago, a group petitioned the Reading Railroad to turn the area into a public green space. In the meantime, however, they've sealed it off.

Too bad they can't seal it off from *Amelia*…

From above the abandoned space, I watch the sunlight cast its rays through the sidewalk grates. It's dim in the early morning light, but the space is brightened by the wild plant life that's already started to grow here. Some quick googling helped me identify the goldenrod, foxglove trees, and even a weird Southern magnolia that sprouted up in a lonely corner, as if in defiance of the northern climate. It's amazing.

Each time I visit, I push *Amelia* a bit further. I move her along the viaduct, hoping to catch a glimpse of something new.

Today does not disappoint.

Shockingly, there are two people here, right off the main chasm in clear violation of SEPTA rules. Now I'm sure urban spelunkers explore this place all the time, but I've never seen anyone here in the daylight hours. What could they be doing?

I pilot *Amelia* into a kind of hover mode up in the sky. I don't want to get too close and spook the people.

Keeping *Amelia* steady, I zoom in with her camera to take a better look. Are they punks, here to tag the construction signs along the viaduct? Or perhaps they're lovers who have snuck away for an early morning tryst?

Standing on the rock-strewn ground is a woman in business attire…and a few feet away, there's a man on his knees. If this is a tryst, it's clear who's boss in this relationship.

"Steady, girl," I tell *Amelia,* as if she can hear me. I zoom in closer, which pixelates the image a little. "I promise, if things get racy, I'll pull you out of there. Don't want you scandalized."

But things do not get racy.

Instead the man lifts his hands, as if he's pleading with the business woman. The woman walks toward him, lifting her left arm like she's pointing a remote control at a TV set.

Then something flies from her hand so quickly, it barely registers on the camera. But a second later, I see it clearly, because it is sticking out of the man's chest.

An arrow.

And the man keels over.

CHAPTER 4

Target Diary—Day 7

SUBJECT NUMBER FOUR falls down quickly.

But when I press my fingers to the side of his grimy, disgusting neck I find a weak but insistent pulse.

Disappointing.

Of my four in-field experiments thus far, only two have died immediately with a single shot—subjects Two and Three.

Death for Number One, like Four here, required a bit of extra effort.

I pull up my sleeve and load another arrow into my gauntlet. The wires bite into my fingertips as I pull them taut. I ignore the pain and enjoy the callusing effect. There's a sharp click.

I'm ready to go.

Number Four's eyes flutter open. At best, he's probably sixty seconds away from death. But you never know. Some human beings have been known to survive extreme body trauma for shockingly long periods of time. Number Four may be an indigent in poor health, but there's no accounting for his genetic stock. He may be one of those people who survive.

"Please," he's stammering now, his voice hushed. One of his lungs has most likely collapsed. "You don't have to do this, I'm a nobody, lady, nobody..."

"Shhhh," I tell him.

"I thought you wanted to help me!"

I take careful aim, again, wondering how I'd miscalculated the first shot. The tip of the arrow is supposed to slip past the protective rib cage and strike the portion of the heart that will cause the organ to fail within seconds. I've done my homework. Had consultations with three different cardiovascular surgeons. Used a half-dozen cadavers from a black market medical supply concern for target practice early in the mission.

There is no substitute, however, for a live target.

"Please please please...."

Especially one who is squirming around like a maggot.

"Shhhh," I tell him, then take a few steps back. I want to perfect this shot at the proper distance. No sense cheating it now. The more practice I can log, the better my chances of success for the Big Day.

Now that he sees that I'm aiming, his writhing becomes even more erratic, as if he can somehow twist himself out of harm's way. This amuses me. A laugh bubbles up out of my throat, much to my own surprise. Number Four gawks at me, insulted, and stops twisting for a moment.

And that is exactly when I take my shot.

This time it's a perfect hit. A second after impact, the life visibly fades away from his rheumy eyes.

I take a moment in the silence to allow the last few seconds to imprint themselves onto my nervous system. So much of this profession is about the visualization and coordination of my muscles and brain.

Dilettantes waste those glorious moments after a successful hit. To me, they're everything.

But nevertheless, I am distracted. Because there's something out of place. A sound.

A buzzing sound.

CHAPTER 5

OKAY, NOW I'M freaking out.

Don't get me wrong, I was pretty much freaking out the moment I watched a business lady shoot *a freakin' arrow* into the chest of a poor homeless man.

But then, just as the guy was begging for his life and wriggling around like a worm on a fish hook…she shot him again! With another arrow!

And this time, it worked. He stopped wriggling.

Part of me is praying that what I've watched is some kind of elaborate form of street theater, a pretend assassination for the delight and amusement of commuters. Then I remember that no one can possibly see these two people, except if you happen to be flying a drone at a specific angle, high above the blocked-off viaduct.

This is no street theater. I've just witnessed a murder.

I'm frozen in place, my thumbs trembling as they hover above my phone screen. *Amelia* hovers, too— almost impatiently. *What are we going to do next, boss?*

"We're going to retreat, Amelia."

I pilot her straight up into the air, not wanting to bang her on the railings of the viaduct. But at the same moment, the business lady turns around, and for a fleeting moment, it's as if we've locked eyes.

Oh no.

She saw me.

Go go go go go, Amelia!

My thumbs do a desperate dance and poor *Amelia* is spinning and the image on the screen is chaotic and confusing.

Don't flake out now, Tricia, says a voice in my head. *Not when it counts.*

Because even in my panic, I'm formulating a plan. And the plan is this: take *Amelia* to a safe height, and then wait for this business lady and her arrows to emerge from the viaduct. There are very few ways in and out. Once I have a fix on her at street level, I call the police, and they can go scoop her up. As long as she stays in the quarter-mile range, I can follow her and lead the cops directly to her.

Miraculously, I'm able to stabilize *Amelia*. She's hovering above 20th Street, just up the block from those safe and familiar bastions of urban life—the hipster coffee shop, the organic grocery store. You know, civilized places, where people don't go around *shooting other people with arrows*.

But when I hold down the right button and spin *Amelia* around, I see a large white object coming right at us at approximately sixty-five miles per hour...

...and it's the top of a white delivery truck.

My thumbs go ballistic as I struggle to put as much distance between *Amelia* and the speeding truck as possible.

And I would have been successful, had it not been for this pesky building nearby.

Amelia crashes on the edge of the roof, right smack into an old metal frame that used to hold an ancient sign.

"No no no," I murmur as I futz with the controls. "Please don't be stuck..."

Good luck with that.

And the voice inside my head is right; it's no use. In my haste to escape, I somehow impaled poor *Amelia* on that old, rusty sign. She's pinned like a butterfly in a collection.

"I'm so sorry, honey," I say as I give up and power her down.

I'll have to mourn her later, though. I close out the app, then push 911 on my cell. This is the first time I've ever done such a thing in my life.

It's also the first time I've ever said the words:

"Hello? Um, I think I've just witnessed a murder..."

CHAPTER 6

Target Diary—Day 7 (continued)

I TURN TO look, but the sun temporarily blinds me. After shielding my eyes I'm able to make out a blurry shape rising out of view. The buzzing sound fades away.

It's entirely possible the two are unrelated. The buzzing may have been an echo of nearby traffic. The humming of a motorbike, for instance.

But I don't think so. My senses are finely tuned to notice any sights or noises that don't fit the usual patterns. This is also something a dilettante will ignore. But if something is coming for you, the environment will give you plenty of warning.

From my perspective, however, all seems normal.

I slip on a pair of latex gloves and prepare for the grunt work.

There's a fairly deep pit approximately a hundred yards from my current location. It is the current resting place of Numbers One through Three.

I grab Number Four by his wrists and begin to drag him toward it. I would usually pull the legs, but he's not wearing any shoes and the stench is already disgusting enough.

Yet, the disadvantaged are perfect for my needs, and abundant here in Philadelphia, especially near the Parkway. Many of them are wary, but it's easy enough to find the few who are willing to believe a perfect stranger is offering a hand up.

Some are even willing to believe that there might be more than a warm meal on offer.

Perhaps even a real personal connection, and a way out of a desperate situation.

I can spot the tiny flicker of hope in their eyes, and I'm just the person to fan it into a proper flame.

It helps, too, that my appearance is homely. This works to my advantage, because nobody trusts a gorgeous face.

Finally, I reach the edge of the pit. I can smell the others, decaying there. I crouch down and roll Number Four into the darkness with the rest of his kind. Thank you for your services.

Still, when I ascend back to street level, the mysterious buzzing sound that I heard continues to vex me. I walk around the neighborhood, searching for its possible source. I'd like to be able to put this out of my mind.

I head down Hamilton Street and watch the construction crews assemble yet another condominium. I stroll toward the Parkway, where tourists blindly flock to the museums, pay their entrance fees, and look at objects they are told are beautiful.

But they have no real appreciation for beauty. They

possess neither the mental capacity nor the imagination for it.

The bodies in the pit. They are beautiful.

Nobody pays me any particular mind as I wander around. My garments are that of any workaday Philadelphian, on her way downtown for a pointless office job.

Which, frankly, is the whole point.

CHAPTER 7

THE KNOCKING IS so loud that I think my door's going to pop off its hinges.

I'm not surprised the cops have shown up, but I am a little disappointed. Aren't phoned-in murder tips supposed to be, you know, *anonymous*?

Because I don't want to be involved. I don't want my name in a report. I just want to be a good citizen, even if I spend my days locked away from the general population.

"Ms. Celano?" one of them asks, butchering my surname. It's *sell-AHH-no,* but this one, weirdly, is asking for "Miss Kell-AYE-no."

I look through the peephole at both cops, and the glass morphs their bodies in carnival funhouse dimensions. Big heads, little legs and feet.

"We're here about your phone call," one of them says. "Can you open the door, please?"

My hand rests on the lock and I take a deep breath. I can't remember the last time someone's actually set foot in my apartment. Whenever there's a delivery, I accept it in the relative safety of the building's hallway. If I look through the security doors and feel uneasy, I simply head back inside my apartment.

But where can I hide from these guys? My tiny bathroom?

"Miss Kell-AYE-no?"

"Uh, one minute please!"

I take another deep breath then flip the lock and open the door. The two cops slowly make their way inside, their eyes expertly scanning the interior of my apartment. I wonder what they are thinking. Perhaps they're looking for telltale signs of crazy?

"You're Miss Kell-AYE-no?"

"It's Celano," I say.

"I'm sorry?" the taller of them says.

"Apology accepted."

My peephole view didn't prepare me for the sight of these two land monsters in the flesh. The tall one is seriously tall. He's at least six three, but has a baby face that he tries to hide with a little chin scruff. He would be sort of adorable if I weren't terrified of him and everything he represented.

His partner is almost as tall, and is also nearly double his width. He had to practically step through my doorway sideways.

All of which makes my studio apartment feel all the more claustrophobic. As they look around, I see the place through their eyes and I'm ashamed. My entire world is a dark box subdivided into a tiny galley kitchen, a bathroom, a messy living room with a desk shoved into the corner, and a loft space where I sleep on a single twin mattress. One look at this place and you'd agree: I'm pretty much failing at being an adult.

Baby Face, whose name tag reads YATES, tries to hide his amusement. "Can you tell us what you saw?"

"There was a lady who shot an arrow at a man down by the old viaduct," I say. "And now he's dead."

I basically sound exactly like Dr. Seuss. All I can say, in my defense, is speaking to a person in real life, with my actual voice, is not something I do very often.

"Exactly where was this, ma'am?"

"You know, the viaduct, by Callowhill Street. The old train tracks?"

Yates glances over at his partner, whose nametag reads SEARS, just like the company that makes huge appliances. In fact, this guy reminds me of one of them. I wonder if he comes with a warranty.

"So you were over there with them?" Yates asks. "Or were you just walking by?"

"Neither, I…uh…." And here's what I was dreading. The part where I incriminate myself in the process of trying to do the right thing. I force myself to spit it out. "I saw them from the camera feed from my drone."

"Your camera on *what*?" Sears asks, speaking at last.

"Um, my drone. I use it to look at the city. I was flying it down by the library when I saw two people on the viaduct, which you never see—"

"A drone?" Sears asks.

Yates taps his partner on the shoulder. "You know, man, those flying things kids send up by remote control, to shoot videos from the sky."

Sears finally gets it, which only makes things worse. "So basically, you spy on people?" he asks, leveling a frosty glare at me.

"No, I don't—I swear, I just look at the city."

The cops look at each other with a "get a load of this" expression on their faces. Even *I* know I'm lying. So I give them a brief rundown of my medical history, which is none of their business. They look at me like I'm crazy, and then, as if I hadn't said anything, they continue.

"Those things are a public nuisance," Sears says. "I'm sure your neighbors don't appreciate you looking through their windows or into their backyards."

"I think my neighbors would be more concerned about the crazy lady who's been walking around killing people with arrows!"

Officer Yates sighs. "Look, we checked the viaduct. There's nobody over there. No signs of anything."

"I'm telling you, I saw a woman. She was maybe in her late forties or early fifties. She pulled up her sleeve and…"

"A lot of homeless congregate there. You're looking down at the scene through your computer—"

"Through my cell phone."

"Yeah? Even worse. I think your eyes were playing tricks on you."

Sears interrupts. "Where's this camera drone now?"

"It crashed."

"Into what?"

"Um, it impaled itself on a sign on top of a building."

"So," Yates says, "if we pull the camera out of it, we should be able to see what you saw, right?"

"No," I tell them. "It only transmits live."

"Look, lady," Yates says, handing me his card. "Take my information. If you have something concrete to give us, give me a call. Because unless you have some sort of tape…"

"But my drone doesn't have any recorded footage."

"So in other words," Sears says, "you don't have any proof."

CHAPTER 8

Target Diary—Day 8

IN THE EARLY dawn hours Friday morning I patrol the length of the Parkway, searching for Subject Number Five.

"Would you like some lunch?" I ask. "Blessings to you."

I pull a rolling suitcase behind me. It is full of dry socks, bottled water, soap, toothpaste, and other sundries. Each item is gathered in an individual plastic Ziploc bag to make them easier to dispense.

I also have packed individual lunches. Turkey and cheese on wheat, as well as tuna salad for the individuals who are missing too many teeth. Each sandwich is paired with condiment packets and a small treat, such as a shortbread cookie.

"Are you hungry? Blessings to you."

I am posing as the Ultimate Do-Gooder, selflessly giving up her busy morning to tend to the needs of the less fortunate here in the nation's birthplace.

It only took me a few days to establish this pattern

and achieve a level of acceptance among the indigent population.

The police have an unofficial understanding with the homeless here on the Parkway. You can stay after 10 p.m., when the museums are closed, but you have to move to somewhere that's out of sight by 7 a.m.

So I do my hunting on the tail end of that curfew, as the unwashed masses stretch out the stiffness in their limbs and seek their daytime shelter.

"Would you like a lunch bag? Can I give you some clean socks?"

All morning long.

As I pull my bag, I match their pace and try to engage them in conversation so I can look them in the eye. This is vital to my operation. I'm looking for that flicker of hope, that small spark of intelligence. Any small amount of fuel that I can use.

That said, I also don't want someone who can look directly into my eyes. Some of the sheep are very adept at spotting a wolf, and those are the ones to be avoided at all costs.

But as I search and hand out gifts this morning, I can't help but be distracted. The mysterious buzzing sound from yesterday continues to trouble me. I find my eyes flicking skyward at odd moments, as if expecting judgment from somewhere above.

When my eyes were squinting at the sun—did I see something moving through the air? Or was that a figment of my imagination? Or was it simply a benign floater in my field of vision?

"Yo, can I have a tuna?"

"Yes, of course."

My instant kill rate, only fifty percent, also concerns me. I thought I'd have the technique to my wrist apparatus more finely tuned at this point in my mission. Ordinarily I would go days between experiments, because nothing draws the attention of law enforcement like a pattern.

All of these thoughts are leaving me anxious. I need to perfect my art as soon as possible. I expected the practice period to require no more than five subjects, but I might be forced to go as high as nine or ten.

"Are you hungry? Blessings to you."

CHAPTER 9

I WAKE UP early Friday morning and instantly feel depressed.

There's no more *Amelia* to fly around. No way to fly next to my neighbors during their Friday morning commute. No way to check in on my city. I'm trapped in this box of an apartment. I have nothing to look forward to except an email from my German bosses, telling me to restructure my current marketing campaign. Then I'll probably get one from the California bosses that tells me to ignore the Germans, while the Scottish bosses tell me *Aye, ignore the both of them.*

Even when I hear the telltale *clomp-clomp-clomp* of the hot guy from 3-D coming down the stairs, I can barely rouse myself from my mattress and go spy on him through the peephole.

But yeah. I'm *that* depressed.

As much as I hate to admit it, *Amelia* is a goner. I can't very well venture out to pry her off that rusty sign. Nor can I ask any friends (not that I have any of those left, anyway) to go up there and retrieve her for me. That'll result in too many questions and too much awkwardness.

I've come to accept that friends are best kept in the virtual world. The ones I used to have in real life pushed too hard. They didn't understand. I suspect that deep down, they thought I was making all of this up.

Pity party, table for one? Right this way, Ms. Celano!

Geez, even my inner voice feels sorry for me.

There's only one thing that will get me out of this funk this morning. And that's going online and searching for a replacement drone.

Amelia would have wanted it that way.

After about an hour of surfing and browsing and comparing clips on YouTube, I fall in love all over again.

Hello, *Amelia II,* you gorgeous thing.

The new girl is a bit more expensive. Okay, a *lot* more expensive: six hundred bucks. But my would-be *Amelia II* has a better flying range—up to a mile!—and twenty-three glorious minutes of flying time. Best of all, the camera comes with about an hour's worth of on-board memory. When I hit Record, she'll make a movie and then fly it back home to me.

You were looking for proof? I've got your proof *right here,* Officer Sears.

Ordering her with same day delivery will also be a minor shock to the bank account. But what am I supposed to do? Wait until midday tomorrow? By that time, who knows how many other victims "Mrs.

Archer" (yeah, that's what I've started calling her) will have racked up. With any luck, *Amelia II* will arrive before sundown, and if set her up quickly, I might be able to squeeze in a quick lap of dusk patrol.

I click BUY NOW.

While I wait for *Amelia II* to show up, I try to do some honest-to-goodness detective work. If I don't know the identity of the killer, maybe I can work an angle from the side of the victim—the one who doesn't even exist, according to Officers Yates and Sears.

One thing I've learned living life online is that there's an advocacy group for everything. And sure enough, there's a Facebook group of concerned neighbors who look out for the homeless around Spring Garden and along the Parkway. I join the group and begin to type:

> Hi everyone! I'm a fellow Spring Garden resident (20th and Green) and I'm worried about a gentleman I used to see along the Parkway.

Already I'm lying. But I don't want to invent too much detail, lest I rule someone out. For instance, I can't say that he's someone I used to joke with, because what if the murder victim had no sense of humor? What if he never spoke at all? So I stick to physical description.

> He's in his late 50s, with longish blond/gray hair and a very long beard. Last time I saw him he

(Had an arrow sticking out of his chest, and was pleading for his life.)

was wearing a tweed jacket, chinos and wasn't wearing any shoes. I'm worried something may have happened to him. If anyone knows his name

(Because that's what I'm really after.)

or knows where he might be,

(Even though, sadly, I already know this.)

please let me know? Many thanks!

I hit POST and wait for the glorious Internet to help me fill in the blanks.

CHAPTER 10

IT'S HARD TO stay focused on work because I can't take my mind off the poor homeless guy, especially now that I've conjured him up in my mind again. Maybe he's someone's missing parent, brother, or husband, and no one in the world (well, except for me) knows what happened to him. Worst of all, I have a feeling that crazy Mrs. Archer has probably killed people many times before, and is preparing to do it again...

Come on, FedEx guy, bring me the goods! The website promises delivery by 8 p.m., but surely you can do better than that?

The afternoon moves forward in a slow, languid crawl. I struggle to check the FedEx tracking site every half hour, instead of every ten minutes. I put on a pair of dark sunglasses and peek out at Green Street from behind my thick drapes. My mom used to say that a watched pot never boils, but that was before the Internet. I'm sure there's an app out there that will calculate exactly how many seconds until your water reaches 212 degrees Fahrenheit.

And then finally, at 6:57 p.m., the front door buzzer sounds!

I almost trip as I scramble to the front windows to confirm that the big gorgeous FedEx truck is parked out front on Green, with its blinkers going and all. I know it's probably seriously angering everybody behind him already.

But...no truck?

My usual MO is to have visual confirmation and then buzz the delivery guy all the way in so that he can walk right up to my door and hand over the package— groceries or whatever—while he remains standing in the hallway. But that initial visual confirmation is key.

Oh man. What do I do? Who else could it be, buzzing at me?

I tiptoe over to my door, take a deep breath, then flip the lock and open it the thinnest of cracks so that I can peer through both sets of front doors, scanning for that familiar black and purple uniform of my usual FedEx guy, Gene.

But instead, I see the red baseball cap of Andre, the main delivery guy from Fairmount Pizza, which is a few blocks away. It's weird to see him, because I didn't order pizza...

But then a shadowy form passes my line of sight. I see the tufts of thick black hair as well as a set of broad shoulders sitting squarely under a fitted gray T-shirt. I'd recognize the back of that head and shoulders anywhere.

Seems the guy from 3-D ordered pizza tonight.

"Sorry, man—I hit the wrong buzzer," Andre says. "For a second there I thought I was bringing this to Tricia."

"Who?"

"Your neighbor? Tricia? The girl right over there in 1-B? Anyway, that's $22.95, buddy."

I die a million deaths pushing my door shut as quietly as I can. Granted, I've never met the guy from 3-D, never introduced myself. But still it hurts that he's so totally unaware of my existence. *Oh, there's someone living in 1-B?*

After that, time slows to a stop. Somehow, the sun sinks below the horizon, which means that even if my package arrives in the next three seconds, there will be no drone flying tonight. I check the FedEx tracking site obsessively now, hitting refresh every minute or so, as I simultaneously check the local traffic news to see if there's, oh, a FedEx truck on fire on the Vine Street Expressway.

Then, after what seems like an eternity...and at ten minutes until eight exactly...the front buzzer finally rings.

This time it's Gene, and he's here for me.

CHAPTER 11

ON SATURDAY MORNING, *Amelia II* is prepped and ready for liftoff.

Okay, so maybe I was up all night getting her ready. Don't judge me.

She's a lot bigger than I imagined. The photos online made her seem like a stealth predator—but in real life, she's as bulky as a flying *Terminator* robot that hunts and kills human beings.

If the first *Amelia* was a sleek dragonfly, her replacement is a fat armored cicada. Maybe that's the price you pay for the extended battery life, expanded range, and camera with memory.

There's no time to break a mini bottle of champagne over her nose by way of christening, though. She needs to be up and patrolling the streets as soon as possible. I push down my sleeves, pull on gloves, open the rear window, then gingerly place *Amelia II* on the sill.

The first thing I notice after liftoff is that *Amelia II* is a bit slower all around. She doesn't maneuver as flawlessly as her predecessor did, nor can she go zooming down the block like her pants are on fire. But that's okay. I'll just have to learn to compensate with the controls on my phone.

As it turns out, I have plenty of time to learn. Because on that first day, I can't seem to locate Mrs. Archer anywhere, even though I sent *Amelia II* out on a record eight daytime patrols.

Sunday doesn't warrant results, either. I don't even want to tell you how many times I flew my poor girl.

But then on Monday morning...

I almost jump out of my own skin when I see the familiar body shape of Mrs. Archer making her way up 19th Street, right next to Baldwin Park.

"Now where have you been, psycho lady?" I murmur excitedly, tweaking the controls so that *Amelia II* can float down for a closer look.

But that's when the weird thing happens.

Mrs. Archer stops in her tracks *and looks up at me,* and it's as if she's heard me talking.

CHAPTER 12

Target Diary—Day 11

AFTER A WEEKEND of thinking that I've been unduly para-noid, I heard the buzzing sound again. Directly overhead.

At first, I was relieved that I hadn't been imagining things. But immediately after that, I became furious at the intrusion of privacy.

Who, exactly, has been keeping tabs on me?

I am prepared for this encounter. For the past ten days I have taken to wearing my wrist apparatus all day long. I want my body movement to look natural at all times so even the most experienced antiterrorism agents won't look twice at me. I keep an arrow spring-loaded and ready for launch at any given second.

Over the weekend, I have perfected my aim. Sub-jects Five and Six can attest to that. Well, technically, now they're unable to do just that.

I don't even think Six saw her doom coming. Which I suppose was a small mercy for her.

I was thinking about the vacant look in her eyes when I first heard the buzzing.

I glanced up at the source of the sound and immediately realized what I've been dealing with: an unmanned aerial vehicle. Also known as a personal drone.

Presumably, it's equipped with a camera.

The movements are so hardwired into my nervous system that I'm barely aware I'm making them. I lift my sleeve. Raise my arm. Point my finger at the exact location where I want the arrow to make contact. With the drone, I presume that the main body is its electrical center, and a direct strike will take it out of play.

I squeeze the trigger.

CHAPTER 13

THE SKIN ON my arms suddenly turns to gooseflesh. My phone might as well be a brick in my hands for all the good it's doing.

No! Move! Move! Move!

Amelia II is depending on me to steer her out of harm's way. She is equipped with an emergency button that will instruct her built-in GPS to send her back home immediately. The moment I hit that button, however...

She was struck with an arrow.

I didn't actually see it coming at me, though I did see a vague, fluttery blur. And then the image on my screen rocks, and suddenly we're descending down toward the park. No amount of furious screen-tapping is able to control her altitude nor her pitch.

We're going down—hard.

Amelia II bounces, and suddenly I have a view of the perfect September sky, complete with little fluffy clouds. My poor drone is resting on her propellers, which means that liftoff will be impossible.

"No!" I scream, thumbing the buttons anyway.

Then a face fills the screen. Mrs. Archer. She's even uglier up close and personal. And I swear, it's as if she can see me through *Amelia II*'s camera, and she's scowling at me.

She reaches down with thin, reedy fingers and the video stream goes dead a second later, leaving me to stare at a blank screen.

Then a thought occurs to me.

Oh no…

Can she trace *Amelia II* back to me?

CHAPTER 14

Target Diary—Day 11 (continued)

IF ONLY I could dispatch human beings with the same precision that I take out toy drones.

The pathetic little machine sputtered, and then nose-dived into the green grass lawn. I cleared the distance swiftly, before its owner could dart out from the shadows and reclaim it. If I'm to discover who's been spying on me, I need to trace him through his plastic flying machine.

The camera was staring up at me, so I reached down, covered the lens with my palm, and twisted it until I heard a satisfying snap.

Before I scoop up the machine, however, I check my surroundings. Is my nemesis hiding somewhere behind the bushes? Hobbyist drones do not have too great a range. The controller of this one might be very close, or at the most, only a few blocks away.

No matter. I will unmask my spy soon enough.

I hoist the machine from the ground. It is surprisingly light. The only part of this drone that interests me is the "brain"——the neural center that controls low and high speed settings, along with its GPS unit. Everything else runs on rudimentary mechanics.

I snap off the propellers, limbs, and motors, and then I deposit them into a nearby trash receptacle. They land at the bottom with heavy clunks.

The drone's brain goes into a deep pocket in my jacket.

I take in my surroundings one last time, tempted to shout a taunt to my unseen spy. But such a thing would only gratify my ego, and wouldn't serve the greater mission. As I walk away from the park, the drone's brain knocks against my thigh from inside my pocket.

What if that were my job—to take down human beings and steal their brains? That would add an entirely new level of joy and skill to the process. I think I would relish cracking open their skulls and carefully removing their thinking organs.

Civil War soldiers became quite skilled at trepanning in a battlefield. I'm sure that with the resources available to me, I could develop a technique that would leave law enforcement and other agents of justice utterly befuddled.

Human brains, however, are nothing like a computerized brain. We don't yet have the technology to stimulate the dead synapses and recover the intelligence within.

But this is not a human brain. And with a little bit of probing, the drone's brain will give me everything.

It won't be difficult, especially with my level of expertise. If a device was designed to transmit, then it has no choice but to give up its secrets—namely, the Internet protocol address of its user.

Ordinary citizens do not realize how much of themselves they surrender to their little smartphones and tablets and other miracle devices. They happily trade their souls for a tiny bit of convenience. Or worse, a meaningless distraction.

I do not own a cell phone or a computer so I can never be traced. Besides, why would I need my own personal version of such devices when there are so many available for the taking?

The central branch of the Free Library of Philadelphia offers everything I need. It only takes a few minutes of surveillance to pinpoint my target: a doughy man in his midforties who is poring over historical tomes with his thin laptop off to his left.

History bores me almost as much as old sporting matches. You already know the outcome. Why not focus your attention on making history? That's my objective here in Philadelphia.

I use a classic distraction technique, bumping into his table with just enough force to send those historical tomes a-tumbling. While the doughy man tries to catch them, I scoop his laptop from the table and immediately make a hairpin turn into the stacks. By the time he realizes what has happened and is shouting for a librarian, who tells him to shush out of reflex, I am already safely hidden in a labyrinth of books.

In another room, I help myself to a stray USB cable.

This is as easy as breathing! Then, in another room after that, I connect the drone's hardware to my new laptop and start the hunt.

The owner of this drone hasn't entered any of his personal information yet, but that's fine. The IP address is still in its memory, and I log on to a service I frequently use in order to trace it back to its user.

And that's when I find it.

How nice to meet you, Miss Patricia Celano, of 1919 Green Street, Apartment 1-B. I look forward to making your acquaintance in person.

CHAPTER 15

AFTER I'VE GONE through just about the craziest Monday I've ever had, I'm surprised I'm able to sleep at all.

Following the crash of *Amelia II,* I spent the rest of the day in a horrifyingly manic state, checking the peephole through my front door and putting sunglasses on to take a peek through my front windows.

I'm not saying I was stupid enough to tape my name and address to the body of *Amelia II*—IN CASE I'M SHOT WITH AN ARROW PLEASE RETURN TO PATRICIA CELANO, 1919 GREEN STREET, APT. 1-B. HUGE THANKS!—but a smart creep could, like, trace the serial number or something to find out who bought her. Heck, I'll bet someone who's especially determined could go on the so-called dark web and find out how many times I've ordered toilet paper in the last year. Why someone would do this, of course, boggles the mind…but you get my point.

And if Mrs. Archer figures out who I am, then

what's to stop her from showing up at my door, knocking, and politely putting an arrow through my eye?

Now you might be saying to yourself, *But Tricia, why don't you call those nice tall policemen and tell them what happened?*

Oh, you mean Yates and Sears, the cops who already think I'm a nutcase? I can imagine that exchange already.

Okay, Ms. Celano, first you tell me that this crazy lady shot a homeless guy with an arrow, and now you're telling me she shot your toy drone? Why would she do that?

Seriously, was it *homeless, too?*

And what if they decided that I needed to be put under a twenty-four-hour psychiatric watch or something? I can just see it now—the rest of the cops in the squad room will snicker and roll their eyes as they watch me attempt to function through the tinted glass.

She says she's allergic to the sun, too—I'm tellin' ya, ya can't make this stuff up!

No, thank you.

It is much preferable to spend the rest of my day in a state of extreme paranoia.

Which I do.

Needless to say, not much work gets done today, either. I seem to be jumping at every single noise outside and checking the peephole and windows every fifteen minutes.

So at bedtime, I find myself on my mattress in the loft, staring at the ceiling and trying to calm myself down. With every noise comes the urge to climb down the ladder and check the peephole and windows, but I command myself to stay put. And let me tell you, there are a *lot* of noises at night.

Eventually, though, I do drift off. At least I think I do. That, or I'm so crazy I'm losing whole chunks of my memory because the next thing I know there's a very loud *CRACK!* at my front window.

If my eyes weren't already open, you can bet they're open now.

What the heck was *that*?!

As if in mocking reply to my panicked mental question, there's another *CRACK!*

And yep, there I am, suddenly sitting up in bed (or, er, on my mattress), doing my best impression of a bat as I try to do some echolocation to pinpoint the origin of that sound.

For a blessed number of moments, there is no sound at all. All of Philadelphia seems to be absolutely quiet. It's as if someone hit the Mute button on the entire world.

And then—

CRACK!

My head spins toward the exact location. The god-awful cracking sound is coming from my front windows.

Could be worse, Tricia. It could be coming from inside *the house…*

I crawl off the mattress and somehow force my trembling hands and feet to navigate the ladder all the way down to the floor. As quietly as possible, I make my way across my apartment in the dark. The glow-in-the-dark clock on my wall tells me it's ten after midnight. Ambient light from outside slices through the edges of my curtains. I would appreciate the spooky *film noir* ambience of it all if I weren't so freaking terrified.

I embark on the same circuit I've done what feels like hundreds of times today: I look through the peephole. Then, I push the curtains aside to check out the empty sidewalk on Green Street.

Only…

It's not empty.

Mrs. Archer is standing there, near the curb, hands in her pockets, looking up at me.

CHAPTER 16

Target Diary—Day 12

HELLO, MISS PATRICIA CELANO.

So good to finally put a face to the name.

I spent the better part of my afternoon reading up on you. You seem to live your entire life online, revealing yourself in bits and pieces through Facebook, Twitter, Instagram, Snapchat, Tumblr, and the like.

So why are you being so shy now, ducking behind the window like a frightened child? When you reveal yourself to the world, you can't be shocked when someone like me looks back at you.

But it's not only the information you willingly gave up to the Internet. With a little simple digging, I was able to flesh out a fairly detailed biography. I know it all—your work record, your shopping habits, your tax records. I know all of your friends. Your family. Your neighbors.

I know about your medical condition.

Oh yes, I know all about your poor skin, my dear. Such a pity, being cooped up in that $1,350 a month studio apartment all day long.

I almost feel sorry for you.

But alas, you've stuck the nose of your drone in my business, so now it's time to return the favor.

Don't worry, Miss Celano. You won't really see me again until the very end. And by then, it will be too late to do anything about it.

CHAPTER 17

MY ENTIRE BODY freezes. I squeeze my eyes shut, hoping that this is just my mind playing tricks on me. Perhaps the image of Mrs. Archer outside my window is just some kind of bizarre hallucination because I've completely tired myself out today.

But no. When I dare to look again, Mrs. Archer is still standing there, her beady eyes staring *right up into mine*.

Then she cocks her head slightly, slowly removes a hand from her pocket, and makes a little *tsk-tsk* motion with her thick index finger. As if I've been naughty.

Nope nope nope nope…

I choke back a scream, fall to the floor, and duck my head under the windowsill like a small child who's hiding from the bogeyman. How on Earth did she find me so quickly? And how did she know I'd be looking out of my front windows at this exact moment in the middle of the night?

Calm down, I tell myself.

No, YOU calm down, shouts my inner voice.

Then I remember: those cracking sounds. They were from her! She must have been throwing tiny rocks at my window like a lovesick schoolboy. She was trying to wake me up, draw me to my window so she could get a look at my face...

And now she's seen you.

I feel my heart pound the inside of my rib cage. The muscles in my neck tighten. I'm dizzy and I can't breathe. For a horrible moment I think I'm having a heart attack, and wonder how long it will take for the police to find my dead body. Days? Weeks, even?

Then I realize what I'm actually experiencing, and recognize that it's not cardiac arrest. No, I'm having a good old-fashioned panic attack.

I used to get them a lot back in college, when my condition first appeared, albeit in tiny doses. I used to be the kind of kid who loved being outdoors, playing and cavorting from pretty much the crack of dawn until the sun finally went down for the count. So when I found myself unable to enjoy the fresh air on a regular basis, my subconscious took it very, very badly. Or so said my therapist. *Deep down,* she explained, *you feel like you're being buried alive*. It took many expensive sessions in cool, dark rooms to work my way past that feeling.

And now it was back, big time. Thank you, Mrs. Archer.

My brain splits in two: one half tries to push back the sheer panic, and the other focuses on what to do about the murderous stalker outside. What does she want? Is she just frightening me into silence? If so, then I might as well give her the big thumbs-up as I hold up a sign in my front window: MISSION ACCOMPLISHED.

And that's when I hear the front door of my building open. The sound is unmistakable—the creak of the hinges, the echo through the hall.

Someone is entering my building.

CHAPTER 18

AFTER A FEW deep, collected breaths, I force myself to crawl across the hardwood floor. My heart is still pounding like it's trying to launch itself out of my chest. My throat is constricted so tightly that I might as well be wearing a noose.

Halfway to the door of my apartment, I realize that I'm on the ground because subconsciously I'm afraid Mrs. Archer is going to shoot one of those arrows straight through my window and into my skull.

My target: my front door. Because as difficult as it will be to look through that peephole (hello, arrow!), I can't just hide in my apartment, waiting for death to come knocking.

I *have* to know if it's her out there.

As quietly as I can, I place my palms on the door to steady myself as I get my legs up under me. Then, I rise.

And place my eye to the hole.

And...

It's not Mrs. Archer.

Alert the media! Tricia Celano catches a break!

Instead, it's my handsome dark-haired guy from apartment 3-D, just standing there by the mailboxes, lingering, looking down at his cell phone.

He's probably just returned from a night out with his bros, hoisting a bunch of craft beers over artisanal tacos while listening to some indie band over in Northern Liberties or whatever the heck else it is normal people my age do on a Monday night. And now he's probably checking his texts to see if anyone is still up and carousing about before he decides whether it's worth it to call it quits.

I've fantasized a thousand times about opening the door, propping my elbow on the frame and saying, *Hey, there, how's it going?* But a desire to save myself from a case of terminal embarrassment has prevented me from doing so.

This time, though, I have a very good reason to talk to him.

Before I can talk myself out of it, I yank open the door.

Handsome Guy from 3-D looks up from his phone.

"Hi," I say.

"Hey," he says, with a curious expression on his face. It's hovering somewhere between bewilderment and confusion.

"I have a weird favor to ask," I say.

"Okay..."

"No, I mean it. This is seriously going to sound weird."

The Guy smiles. "No worries. What do you need?"

"Um, when you came in did you see someone stand-ing outside, watching the window to my apartment?"

The look on Handsome Guy's face now turns to complete confusion, which makes my thudding heart slam to a halt. There, I've gone and done it. I've freaked him out.

But he quickly recovers and flashes a smile that re-suscitates me. "Let me go take another look. I'll be right back."

As he moves back through the vestibule, I pray that I haven't just sent him to his death. That would be one hell of a story to share with the police.

Girl meets boy, boy meets girl, boy gets an arrow in the eye socket for his trouble.

CHAPTER 19

"THE COAST IS clear," he says. "Who did you think was out there?"

"Nobody," I say out of reflex.

"So you wanted me to look outside for you on the off-chance that someone *might* be watching your front windows?"

"I don't know...maybe I was dreaming it, but I thought I saw someone out there. I'm really sorry to have bothered you."

But of course I know this isn't the truth. At this point, I'm sure my eyes weren't lying.

Handsome Guy gives me the same kind of smile you'd give a lost toddler. "You sure you're okay?"

My nerves are so fried at this point that I say a few words that I immediately want to suck back into my mouth and swallow. "No, I really don't think so."

Argh, what are you doing, Tricia?

But Handsome Guy turns out to be the extremely chivalrous type. He gently steers me back into my own apartment and closes the door and guides me to the couch and sits me down and then places himself a friendly, yet respectful, distance away.

"It's okay. Everything's going to be fine," he says. "Look, my name's Jackson—"

"Dolan," I blurt out, because of course I know his name. The moment I realized he lived in 3-D, I took a peek at a package waiting for him in the hallway one time. *Jackson Dolan.* Of course he'd have a cool name like Jackson Dolan. (And don't think I didn't try that surname on for size. Tricia Dolan. It has a nice ring to it, don't you think?)

Jackson raises his eyebrows in surprise.

"Sorry," I say. "I'm a bit of a snoop. Anyway, I'm Tricia…"

"Celano," he says with a grin. "Guess that makes us both snoops."

No, that makes my heart swell three times its normal size. Jackson Dolan actually knows who I am! That means, at one point, he wondered who I was, and peeked at my mail, too. Or maybe he even asked around.…

"Tell me what's going on," Jackson says. "I'm a big boy, I can take it."

I want to gush and tell him everything. My *Amelia*s. Mrs. Archer and her killer arrows. The homeless people she's probably killed. And the fact that she learned my name and address, all thanks to *Amelia II.*

But…I can't. I mean, I can't even believe I'm talking to him! That he's actually here, sitting right on my couch. It's almost surreal, as if a leading man in a movie just removed himself from his two-dimensional prison and stepped down through the television screen to speak to...*me*.

I guess that's what happens when you look out at life through peepholes and computers. The few things you actually encounter in life feel glaringly real.

"It's okay," he says, reaching out and taking my hand. Geez, even his hands are warm and large. They're like no other hands I've seen before. Then again, I haven't been touched by another human being in years, so...

So I tell him.

Everything.

My *Amelia*s. Mrs. Archer and her killer arrows. The homeless people she's probably murdered—and so on, and so on. The events of the past few days tumble out of my mouth in non sequiturs. I'm positive they only make sense to me—and that's the problem, right? I'm the only one in the world who believes that Mrs. Archer exists, and that she's doing horrible things to people.

Jackson, to his credit, takes it all in like a perfect gentleman. And when he's finished processing everything, an excited look washes over his face.

"So...you're hunting a killer?"

"I guess that's one way of putting it."

"That. Is. Awesome."

CHAPTER 20

HELLO, *AMELIA III.*

I shouldn't be dropping this kind of money on you, but as Jackson said... I *am* hunting a killer. And what is an amateur housebound sleuth without her magical flying machine?

(I wonder if Nero Wolfe would have kicked Archie Goodwin to the curb if he had an *Amelia* in his life.)

I have to say, it was Jackson's enthusiasm last night that inspired me to keep up with this investigation. Not only did he convince me that I wasn't crazy, but he said that I could actually do something about Mrs. Archer. Like, catch her doing her creepy things with her arrow-shooting device. Maybe even record it this time.

Hence, *Amelia III.* Unlike her older sisters, this sprightly young thing has better maneuvering capabilities in order to avoid those lethal arrows. And I'm going to be able to record everything she sees right on my phone, including (hopefully) Mrs. Archer stalking those poor homeless guys.

How's *that* for proof, Officers Yates and Sears?

Such advances come with a hefty price—not counting the extra money I'm spending for same-day (by 5 p.m. guaranteed!) delivery. But the second fee is also for a good reason: Jackson said he'd stop by right after work so he could learn how to pilot her, too.

Only *I* could turn the hunt for a serial killer into a…*date*.

With all of the dough I'm spending, you'd think I'd be putting my nose to the grindstone at work. *Au contraire, mon frère.* All I can think about is the image of Mrs. Archer, looking up at me from the sidewalk. And Jackson, of course. The one person who doesn't think I'm completely bonkers. Yet.

Somehow I resist the urge to don sunglasses and a knit cap to take a peek out from behind my curtains every seventeen seconds. No good could possibly come of that. (Especially if she's standing out there…*waiting*…and *tsk-tsking* at me.) Maybe that's why the afternoon drags on like a small eternity. Seriously, no day has ever lasted this long before.

And then, finally, both things I've been waiting for happen almost at once.

Amelia III arrives in the afternoon, and she's barely out of the box before there's a knock at my door.

"Is that her?" Jackson asks, excitedly.

"Well, she's indisposed at the moment," I tell him,

"but yeah, it's her. Jackson, meet Amelia the Third. Amelia, meet our upstairs neighbor, Jackson."

We dig into the scattered pieces of *Amelia III* like kids on Christmas morning who've received a new Lego set. Jackson reads me the instructions, while I do the snapping and screwing and connecting, all of which is cake for me now. The two of us have the easy groove of a married couple putting together a crib.

The whole evening is shocking to me because I've known Jackson less than twenty-four hours, and I rarely have contact with other human beings. Especially startling is my ability to banter with him.

"I hope you're not afraid of heights."

"Why?"

"Because if I crash *Amelia III* on a roof, I'm going to need somebody to climb up and get her for me."

Jackson chuckles. "Well, how about we don't crash her then?"

"We? You think I'm actually going to put my girl in the hands of a complete stranger?"

"C'mon, we're neighbors."

"Stranger danger, stranger danger…"

But after a brief tutorial, I *do* let Jackson pilot *Amelia III* around the neighborhood. He's quite agile with the controls. ("Years of wasting my life with a PlayStation controller in my hands," he explains.) I love watching his hands. They are lean and strong.

Of course, I'm splitting my attention with the image on my laptop. Jackson helped me figure out how to beam it from my phone to the laptop so I'd have a bigger image of the neighborhood as we go speeding by.

"Any sign of her?"

"Not yet," I say. "Just keep her steady, Captain."

"I'd better bring her back. Amelia's almost run out of her battery life."

"That's because we rushed her out before she had a full charge."

"We were excited."

I'll say we were excited.

Jackson is the first person in a long time who doesn't think I'm a freak. What's he going to think, then, when I'm forced to explain my medical condition to him? Sooner or later, it'll come up. It always comes up.

Only, I'm hoping it doesn't happen too quickly.

That is, until he asks, "After we bring her in for a landing, how about we grab a quick bite? I'm starving."

"Oh, right," I say, clearing my throat nervously. "I guess it is getting late. But you know, I'd better get back to work. I'm kind of behind on a few things, with all of this excitement."

"Are you sure?" Jackson asks. "I know this great café just a block away, on the corner of Green and 21st. My treat, since you let me fly Amelia the Third and everything."

Argh, this is killing me.

"Maybe we could go some other time? I'm really sorry."

Jackson is quiet for a moment, as if he's trying to figure out whether I'm really swamped with work or just not into him. I want to scream, *TRUST ME, I AM TO-TALLY INTO YOU!* But of course, I say nothing.

"Sure, maybe some other time," he says.

And it *kills* me.

CHAPTER 21

BUT AFTER JACKSON leaves, I don't throw myself into my actual job. Instead, I resume my online hunt for the name of the murdered homeless man while *Amelia III* recharges. (Unfortunately, her battery's so low that I won't get the chance to fly her again tonight; the sun is already setting.)

I try not to think about the hurt puppy-dog look on Jackson's face as he excused himself from my apartment. Why couldn't I have said something vaguely romantic like, *Hey, why don't I whip up something here for the two of us?* Because I'm an idiot, that's why. We could have shared a meal together, maybe even kept up with some more of that playful banter we had been exchanging.

But no. I had to tell him *maybe some other time*.

Anyway…that's why I'm distracting myself, looking for some news on the homeless advocacy front. I check Facebook, and there's a single message waiting for me from an older hippyish-looking guy named John Burke:

Hello, Tricia. There's a fellow named Allen Moyer who hasn't been seen around the Parkway in a while. (But I also hear that he might be up visiting a cousin in Wilkes-Barre.)

Things are a little chaotic down at the Parkway anyway; they're preparing for the senator's visit on Wednesday, so they've been shooing people away and putting up barricades like it's a goddamn police state. Chances are, your missing guy was probably one of the unfortunate ones to be shooed away first.

Hope this helps. Blessings to you.

Right back at ya, Mr. Burke.

Of course, this is no lead at all. I was hoping for...I don't know, a set of *actual clues* to go on. It's not as if I can fly *Amelia III* up to Wilkes-Barre (wherever the heck that is) to snoop around the Moyer family. If that's even the right guy at all.

I do a search for "Allen Moyer," but there are no hits anywhere near Philadelphia. An image search brings up a bunch of white dudes, mostly in goatees, who look nothing like the man I saw that day.

So I type Mr. Burke a reply:

Thanks so much for your help, Mr. Burke! At the risk of pressing my luck...do any of your contacts have a description of Mr. Moyer? Or, by chance, a photograph? I want to be sure I'm thinking of the same man. Huge thanks, and blessings to

My message is interrupted by a knock at the door.

First thought: it's Jackson, with flowers and take-out because he couldn't stand the idea of dining without me.

Hah.

Second thought: aside from *Amelia III,* I didn't have any deliveries scheduled for today. (And when you're stuck inside, your life kind of revolves around deliveries.)

Weird.

But then comes my third, and most chilling thought: *Mrs. Archer has returned.*

And now she knows that I'm alone.

Instantly, my heart is pounding and my throat is tightening and my brain feels like it's swimming in my head. No. Not again. I refuse to turn into a basket case for the second time in a twenty-four-hour period. I go to the front door and look through the peephole and—

Nobody's there.

But there is movement behind the shades of my front window. I quickly put on my sunglasses and knit cap and peek outside, just in time to see a bright green Fresh Grub Now truck parked outside, near the corner. Which is one of my delivery services. Did I have something scheduled for today? Could I have simply forgotten?

Back at the door, I take a deep breath, then flip the lock and twist the knob. Sure enough, there's an insulated Fresh Grub Now bag waiting for me.

The bag is small, but heavy. Why would I have

placed such a small order? That's just a waste of the delivery fee.

I bring the bag to the kitchen, drop it on the counter, and pull out the contents. They seem to be a dense squishy mass of...*something*. Then the odor hits me. It takes me a while to place, because I'm vegetarian. And even when I was a preteen and still eating meat, my parents always opted for the fresh stuff.

But that's not what this is.

This is rotten meat.

CHAPTER 22

IT'S NOT A THREAT.

It's not a threat.

It's not a threat.

I tell myself.

But honestly, what else could it be? *Oops, looks like I clicked on the wrong box at the website. I meant to check "rhubarb treat," not "rotten meat"!* I check my order history, and discover that, of course, I didn't order any food from Fresh Grub Now in the past few days.

No, this little package must have been a gift from you-know-who.

I know I'll have fat luck, though, convincing Officers Yates and Sears that this huge chunk of fetid meat was from my friendly neighborhood murderer. It's not like my track record is working in my favor in that department.

I hastily rewrap the meat in the Fresh Grub Now bag and consider walking it straight to the Dumpster behind the building...except, I *never* walk to the

Dumpster. (My landlord takes pity on me and allows me to leave my lonely little trash and recycling outside my door every Monday, and he takes it out from there.)

So I have no choice but to leave this disgusting chunk of decaying meat in my trash bin all week. Which is going to be awesome.

Maybe it's psychosomatic, but as the evening goes on, the smell of that meat becomes even more intense. For a moment, I consider putting it out in the hallway anyway. But then the odor would waft throughout the building. I'm sure that'd turn me into everyone's least favorite tenant in about two hours flat.

Even if Jackson were to come knocking at my door right now, flowers in hand, I'd have to turn him away before he started gagging.

I spray the living daylights out of the interior of my trash bin with a bathroom deodorizer before I go to bed. If I had a hundred of those pine tree car fresheners, I'd hang them all over my apartment, just like that crazy guy did in the movie *Se7en*. Honestly, anything would be better than this.

My mind is too agitated to allow itself to sleep. I keep thinking about the meat. And *why* meat? It's kind of a juvenile prank, along the lines of leaving a flaming bag of doggie doo on your doorstep.

Unless...

Unless Mrs. Archer somehow *knew* about my condition. And that I'd essentially be trapped inside this one-room apartment with rotten meat for an entire week. Which makes it downright diabolical.

Crazy Arrow Lady: 1
Tricia: 0

Sometime after midnight I finally drift off, which is a nice break from the stench. I dream about walking around outside. It's a common recurring dream for me. There's fresh-cut grass under my feet, and warm sun on my face, and it isn't covering my skin with blisters or turning it to ash. Maybe my subconscious mind is starved for this experience and recreates it when I'm in my most defenseless state. Or maybe my subconscious just likes to torture me with what I can't have.

But for the moment, it's all so wonderfully real and vivid that I forget about my troubles. Do you remember those carefree days as a kid during the summer, when time seemed to stretch into forever? No homework, no responsibilities whatsoever? That's what this dream felt like, right up until the moment—

My front door slams shut.

CHAPTER 23

I'M SCRAMBLING DOWN from my sleeping loft before I'm even fully awake, slamming my elbows into walls and banging my knees on the ladder. I'm in such a hurry that I don't realize that I'm doing something very stupid.

What if the slamming door was meant to wake me up, and right now I'm rushing into the waiting, murderous arms of Mrs. Archer?

I skid to a halt in the middle of my apartment and attempt to see in the near dark. Is there someone in here with me?

If there were an intruder, Tricia, what exactly would you do about it?

The heart, the throat, the brain—they all start up again with the pounding, the tightening, the dizziness. Instead of paralyzing me, though, the panic attack seems to spark the opposite effect. I'm suddenly furious.

"Is there somebody here?" I say. "Look, if there's

someone in this apartment, stop being a coward and show your face!"

There is no reply. The gloomy dark keeps its own counsel.

One by one, I flip on the lights, illuminating every square inch of my place. One by one, potential hiding spots are eliminated. After a good fifteen minutes of searching (it's not a big place—but I searched everything five times anyway), I'm reasonably sure I am alone.

But I am definitely awake. There will be no more sleeping tonight.

I consider calling Jackson, who's probably sleeping just two floors above me. But no, he doesn't need my brand of crazy in his life right now. I'll just have to deal.

I spray the inside of the trash bin with deodorizer again, but it doesn't seem to do anything. I don't think the fetid stench will ever get out of my nostrils.

I'm still angry. So, somewhere around 4 a.m. on Wednesday morning, I silently tell Mrs. Archer:

You psycho—it's time for me to take the fight to you.

CHAPTER 24

I'M READY BEFORE the crack of dawn on Wednesday morning. *Amelia III* is perched on my windowsill and ready for active duty. Let's do this thing.

Amelia III flies up, up, up, and over the edges of my rooftop. Then she zooms toward the city proper. This is my first time piloting her, since Jackson had the honors of making the maiden voyage. And *wow,* is she a thing of beauty. No offense to the previous *Amelia*s, but they were basically just radio-controlled helicopters when compared to this fighter jet of a drone.

I swoop around the Parkway. Today there are wooden barricades, all up and down the sides of the street, which means Philly will be hosting some kind of important visitor this afternoon. Then I remember: it's the senator that Mr. Burke mentioned. That's the reason the authorities shooed all of those homeless people away.

But never mind that. I need to focus on my target.

I check Mrs. Archer's last known locations, hoping she's returned to the scene of the crime. I start in the park, but there's no sign of her there. So I guide *Amelia III* down 19th Street and I'm about to enter the viaduct when I see . . .

Flashing lights.

Police—and they're like, *everywhere*.

What's going on?

The tricky thing here is getting a good view without the police knowing that I'm watching. Fortunately, they're so busy keeping onlookers on the fringes of the scene that none of them even bother to look up. (Besides, it definitely helps that *Amelia III* is much quieter than her sisters.)

I tweak the controls until I'm at the best vantage point possible, allowing me to see right down into the viaduct, where there is a lot of activity and uniforms and detectives and forensic-type people.

My blood freezes as I realize what the police are doing.

They're carrying dead bodies away from the scene.

The urge to vomit almost overpowers me—and not just because there's a stench of rotten meat in my apartment.

I struggle to keep *Amelia III* steady as I count the bodies under the tarps.

There are *six* of them.

Apparently, Mrs. Archer has killed many people.

Was the murder I saw the first one? Do I share the blame for those five other poor souls? Did they die because I'm such a freak and wasn't able to convince two police officers that what I saw was real?

This isn't happening. This can't be happening...

My view of the crime scene is interrupted by a ding on my cell phone—a Facebook message is waiting for me.

It's from John Burke, the homeless advocate who messaged me last night. No doubt he's heard about the bodies being discovered and checking in to see if I know anything.

I know more than you could ever guess, Mr. Burke...

I hesitate clicking on the message, though—what am I supposed to say? That I knew what was happening all along and wasn't able to stand up and do anything about it?

Stop being a baby. Answer the man's message.

But it's not a Facebook message from John Burke at all. Instead, it's a dark, slightly blurry photograph from an unknown account. What the hell?

I use my thumb and middle finger to pinch it open.

And I see it's an image of me.

Sleeping in bed, nearly eight hours ago.

CHAPTER 25

Target Diary—Day 13 (The Big Day)

SOMETIMES YOU THINK a mission is all nailed down. You've planned every detail to perfection. Every possible scenario is conjured and considered.

And then along comes a wrench. Or in this case, a nosy little *wench,* who throws herself into the works. Now a dilettante would react to such a complication with panic or, at least, fear of discovery. Most likely, the final result would be a cowardly abandonment of the mission.

But, as I've explained before, I am no dilettante.

The mark of a truly gifted operative is to take those frustrating little complications and work them into the very fabric of your mission. Not only will your antagonist never see it coming, but if you're smart enough, it will seem like the complication was part of the mission all along.

And how exciting, this new adjustment to the mission!

The first thing I did was shake Miss Patricia with a

special delivery. I couldn't have her get too cocky and comfortable.

The police discovered the bodies of Subjects One through Six exactly as I'd planned. It happened the day after I visited the pit, taking the piece that I needed with me. Then I phoned in the anonymous tip myself.

And then, posing as "John Burke," I reached out to my dear Patricia so I could give her a little bit of comfort about her mysterious homeless man. After all, for my plan to work, I can't have her become too unhinged. Now, I need her to fall asleep.

Patricia Celano, I hope you understand. We were meant to be joined together on this wonderful day. It's almost as if you and your particular affliction were crafted by some brilliant deity for this singular purpose. My purpose.

Blessings to you.

CHAPTER 26

THERE'S NO TIME for a panic attack. I barely have time to pilot *Amelia III* back home safely before there's a sharp *knock-knock-knock* at my door.

Please don't be Mrs. Archer, come to finish me off...

But no. The view through the peephole reveals the burly frames of Officers Yates and Sears. And this time, I couldn't be happier to see them. I fling open the door, feeling like my soul has just lost three hundred pounds.

"If you're here to apologize, then you're in luck. Because I'm taking apologies all morning long."

Yates, the babyface, says, "I'm sorry?"

"Ms. Celano, we're here to ask you a few questions," Sears says. "May we step inside?" He asks the question without really requesting my permission.

"Sure, come on in. Want me to put on some coffee?"

Yates wrinkles up his nose. "Ugh, what is that smell?"

"The garbage. Which is part of the reason I'm so happy to see you guys. You won't believe what's been going on the past couple of days."

"So you've been inside your apartment this whole time?" Sears asks. "You never left once?"

"No. I haven't," I say. "Like I explained to you the other day, I have this…"

"Sun allergy, right," Sears says. "I did some looking into that. It's extremely rare. I mean, like, you'd have a better chance of being struck by lightning while winning the lottery."

"I guess that's me," I say. "Lady Luck."

Yates and Sears give each other a knowing look. What is going on with these two?

"Look, I'm not the type to say I told you so, but I saw the news about all the bodies you guys found."

"You did?" Yates asks.

"Yeah. I swear to God, though, I only knew about the one! The one I told you about. I don't know if she's been at this a while, or racked up a few more since I last saw you guys, but—"

Sears interrupts, "How many bodies did you hear we found?"

"Six."

"And how, exactly, did you hear about them?"

"What do you mean?"

"TV? The radio?" Yates asks. "Maybe online?"

And that's when I realize I've been caught in a lie.

"Because, you know, the department hasn't released any details to the media yet," Sears says.

"Okay, I admit it," I say, huffing out a breath. "I flew my drone over the scene and saw what was going on. And I swear, I was about to call you guys when I heard from the killer again. She was here! Inside my apartment last night!"

"Hold on—what drone?" Sears asks. "I thought you said you crashed that drone after you saw this supposed killer."

"Unless you left the apartment at night to take the drone you crashed off the roof," Yates says. "Is that what happened? Were you able to get it back and fix it?"

They're both trying to catch me in a lie. I already said I hadn't left the apartment in days—so why would I admit to slipping out at night (which I haven't)? Why would they do such a thing?

Oh no, I realize.

They think I did it.

CHAPTER 27

"LOOK," I TELL THEM. "I know how this is going to sound, but I need you guys to believe me."

Sears gives me this super-patronizing smile. "Why don't you tell us what happened, and we'll let you know how your story sounds?"

Thing is, I know *exactly* how it sounds. But I try to clear my name anyway.

"So I bought another drone—you know, because I crashed the first one."

"We remember," Yates says. "And like I said, did you ever manage to pull it down from the roof?"

"No, dummy, she *can't,* because she's allergic to *the sun,*" Sears says, with all of the conviction of a man telling another man that the Easter Bunny is real.

"Anyway," I say, "this drone had recording capabilities. That way, if I found Mrs. Archer—"

"Who?" Sears asks.

"That's what I've been calling the suspect. You know, because of the arrow thing? I wanted to capture

Mrs. Archer on film so I'd finally have proof for you guys."

"That's very nice of you," says Yates. "So did you find her?"

"Um, yes and no. I definitely caught her, in the park down on 19th Street."

"So let's see the footage."

"Well...I can't because she shot my drone out of the sky with an arrow."

Both tough guy cops blink at that one.

"I'm sorry?" Yates asks.

"I don't know what to tell you, other than the fact that she has amazing aim. But yeah, she took down my drone with an arrow, then presumably destroyed it, which is why I don't have any footage of her."

"You said she shot it down...with an arrow?"

This is getting annoying. "Can we move past the arrow? Please? Because the really scary thing is that I think she traced my address and online identity through the drone. And now some really weird things have been happening to me over the past couple of days..."

Then I start to gush, telling them about everything— the rocks against my window pane in the middle of the night and the delivery of rotten meat. Everything except my new visits with Jackson Dolan, because the last thing I want to do is send these two lugs to his front door. I may be a freak who has to hide indoors all the time, but I'm not the girl who brings trouble into someone else's home.

And that's when I suddenly remember the creepy sleeping photo.

"Oh, wait! I do have proof."

Officer Yates makes this grand sweeping gesture as if to say, *Well, then lead us to it, my fair lady.*

I open my laptop then call up Facebook. There it is—the message, and the photo of me taking forty winks. "See? Clearly I couldn't have taken this."

I sense the sheer presence of their bodies as they both lean around me to take a look at the image. Not only do I not come in close proximity to any other human beings 99 percent of the time, but I never have this kind of personal space violation. My heart begins to do its jackrabbit thing and my throat tightens.

"You know, a friend could have easily taken that," Yates says.

"What kind of friend would sneak into my place and snap a photo of me while I'm sleeping?"

"The kind of friend who wants to help you create an alibi," Sears says.

There's a truly awful moment where I think the handcuffs are going to come out. I'll be read my Miranda rights, but it won't matter, because the moment they drag me outside this building will be the moment my heart explodes, and my skin disintegrates to nothing.

CHAPTER 28

HELP ME, *AMELIA III*, you're my only hope.

Up she goes, clearing my rooftop and gliding over Spring Garden, making a beeline for the Parkway. Even though my girl has enough battery power to last for a long and leisurely flight, my own clock is ticking. I need proof of Mrs. Archer's existence, and I need it now.

Otherwise, I might be facing a long stretch of time in an even smaller room.

The image on my cell phone—beamed straight from *Amelia III*'s camera—reveals a strangely busy Parkway. There are throngs of people lining the sidewalks, with police vehicles and ambulances and concessions and oh crap…that's when I remember. The political rally!

Being the completely self-absorbed millennial I am, I don't follow politics like I should. But after that weird email from Mr. Burke (blessings, indeed) I looked up an article about this senator and his visit to Philadelphia. Turns out he's not just a senator from Utah—he's the vice-presidential nominee after the guy they had announced over the summer suffered from a complete meltdown and had an embarrassing flame-out (as they sometimes do).

So now Senator Dude from Utah is making the lightning rounds around the country, trying to introduce himself to everyone in enough time for the November election. This afternoon, he's making a stop in the City of Brotherly Love.

And *Amelia III* has the perfect point of view to watch the main event.

There's no hiding from me, Mrs. Archer.

That is, until *Amelia III* reaches the fringes of the Parkway. The view on my phone goes all jittery, as if she's had a pre-flight shot of vodka.

"What are you doing?" I mutter.

The controls under my thumbs are suddenly useless. I can't adjust the pitch or altitude or *anything*. This doesn't make any sense! Come on, girl—what are you doing up there?

Suddenly *Amelia III* turns to show me the crowd below, and then we're rushing toward it. Like, at supersonic speed. No, no, no—not toward the people! My thumbs pound on my cell phone so hard I'm shocked the screen doesn't shatter.

Thankfully, *Amelia III* rights herself at the last minute and swoops right over the rally-goers, heading for an expanse of green. And then, rather unceremoniously, she crashes into a line of trees near the Barnes Foundation.

My screen is full of swirling leaves and branches as she tumbles down through the thick trees. I have no idea what the heck just happened. Did Mrs. Archer spot my girl before I spotted *her*, felling my poor drone with another arrow? But that would be crazy, right?

Finally, the leaves clear a bit as *Amelia III* comes to a halt. Her camera is pointed down at the sidewalk, where a group of rally-goers are gawking up at us.

Hi, hello, nothing to see here, folks.

But then the crowd parts and men in dark suits with plastic earpieces come running up. One of them is holding a device that looks like one of those radar guns the police use to catch speeders on the highway. Another one is pointing up at us—that is to say, at my poor *Amelia III*.

The radar gun looks familiar, but where have I seen it before?

I scramble to my coffee table where there's a messy pile of magazines (don't judge—even a housebound, sun-allergic girl needs her hits of high fashion). Under a stack of *Vogues*, I find it—a UK magazine called *Drone Life*. That could actually be the title of my autobiography. But I digress...

Flipping through the pages like a maniac, I finally find it. That wasn't a radar gun, and it wasn't meant to track speed. The thing is an anti-drone gun, designed to disable an aircraft like *Amelia III*.

Holy cats—*Amelia III* must have been taken down by the US Secret Service!

I guess they have a zero tolerance policy when it comes to visiting senators and private flying aircrafts.

Meanwhile, onscreen, I'm treated to the sight of a G-man climbing the tree toward *Amelia III,* as if she's a frightened kitten in need of rescue. This would ordinarily amuse me, except for a few sad truths:

I'm no closer to finding Mrs. Archer or proving she exists.

That was just $1,500—i.e., more than a rent payment—down the drain.

Soon *Amelia III* will be in the possession of the Secret Service, and soon they'll know my name, and soon I should expect the attention (and comic stylings) of Officers Yates and Sears—or worse, the FBI or CIA.

I am so screwed.

CHAPTER 29

LOCATE YOUR CHILL.

That's what my online friends tell me when I freak out about something they feel is trivial. (Like, say, never being able to feel the warm sun on your skin.) *It's going to be okay, Tricia,* they say. *Locate your chill.*

Most of the time, I absolutely *hate it* when my friends tell me to locate my chill.

It kind of makes me want to locate my inner rage and drop it on them like a nuclear bomb.

Nonetheless, I try to follow that advice now and locate my chill. And I do that by trying once again to locate my nemesis—Mrs. Archer.

I hit the homeless advocacy boards on Facebook, seeing if anyone has a fresh lead on my murder victim. (Well, not *my* victim…ah, you know what I mean.) I repost my original description, hoping to catch different pairs of eyes this time. I add a bit more pathos, telling everyone how worried I am about this guy, especially with all of the crowds down by the Parkway.

About a microsecond after I hit the Post button, one of the homeless advocates sends me an instant message:

Why are you asking about this NOW? Haven't you heard what happened?

I blink. What is that supposed to mean? Then, a second later:

It's all over the news!!!

I open a new browser tab and check my favorite local news site (*The Philly Post*) and holy crackers and cheese—I can't believe what I'm reading.

That visiting senator from Utah? That guy who is trying to become our nation's vice-president?

He was just assassinated.

CHAPTER 30

I READ THE breaking news article in a kind of stunned haze, feeling like I was just involved in a car accident. Nonetheless, certain words jump out at me.

woman in crowd.
vanished without a trace.
killed with what appears to be an arrow...

No.
No no no no...
But that's what's being reported. In the middle of cheers and handshakes and a marching band performance of a Sousa march, a middle-aged woman fired an arrow straight into the heart of the good senator from Utah, killing him almost instantly.

Eyewitnesses differ on the description of the assassin, who is said to have disappeared into the throngs gathered on the Parkway...

It all makes sense.

Perfectly horrible sense.

Only now do I realize what Mrs. Archer has been up to this whole time. She's not a serial killer hunting homeless people. They were just *practice* for her main goal. She's been gearing up for something far, far worse...

And I could have stopped her days ago.

I pick up my cell and dial Jackson. All of those rules about waiting a certain number of days before calling a guy have gone right out the window. I'm pretty sure there's a clause about being involved in a political assassination, right?

"Hey! Tricia! How are you?"

He's huffing and puffing, as if he's out of breath.

"Not good, to be perfectly honest, but...I'm sorry, is this a bad time?"

"No, it's fine. Why?"

"You sound like you're climbing the Rocky steps at the Art Museum."

Jackson laughs. "Ah, you caught me. I was just squeezing in a little exercise, and I guess I got winded faster than I thought. Kind of embarrassing. But what's up?"

"You haven't heard the news?" I ask, but then realize that I was very recently accused of not watching the news, either. "Never mind. Mrs. Archer has done something really, seriously horrible, and I think she's trying to pin it on me!"

"Whoa, take it easy."

Girl, if he tells you to locate your chill, you hang up on him.

I choke back my frustration and try to remain calm. "If you saw the news, you'd know that pretty much the last thing on my to-do list right now would be to *take it easy.*"

"Then come on upstairs."

The suggestion, simple as it is, stuns me.

"To...your apartment?"

"Yes," Jackson says with a chuckle. "You know the one, right? 3-D. Like the movies."

"I thought you were exercising."

"Yeah, in my apartment. But I just stopped. Look, I'm still panting because I'm not exactly in optimal shape. There, are you happy?"

"I didn't mean to...look, I'm sorry. I should probably go."

"Come on, don't be silly, and just come upstairs. We'll figure this out together."

Together. He says it so casually it makes me fall for him all over again. And before I can protest any further, he hangs up.

But upstairs?

Me?

He's got to be kidding. I haven't even been all the way down my hallway in a couple of years.

Then I remember my predicament. The last place I want to be is in my own apartment, alone, with the Philadelphia Police Department already suspicious of me. Plus the Secret Service about one Internet search

away from discovering Patricia Celano, the woman behind the drone they've shot down.

I've toughed it out alone all of these years.

Maybe it's time I actually ask for a little help.

CHAPTER 31

I SLIP ON a light jacket and pull the hood up over my head. My hand grabs the knob and turns it. The door creaks open. The hallway looks about a thousand feet long. And beyond them, the ornate wooden staircase looks so foreign to me that it might as well be a detail in an alien spaceship in a sci-fi movie.

Years ago, this was one big brownstone mansion before they divided it up into a bunch of apartments. My prison cell of an apartment was probably only a study or something. I live in a big house and have never seen 95 percent of it.

"Come on Tricia," I say aloud, trying to psych myself up. "There's no reason you can't do this."

Oh yeah? How about the crippling panic attack that will shut down your heart in about ten seconds?

"That's not real. The only thing preventing you from walking upstairs is a delusion."

I'll be sure to mention that to the coroner when he shows up.

This is the debate I have with myself—half out loud,

half in my head. At this point, I'm freaking out so much that I'm not even sure which parts are which.

But it's good, because the banter distracts me while my body steps out into the hallway and moves slowly toward the staircase. My feet follow a perfect line, as if someone had laid a tightrope across the floor.

The whole experience—moving down the hallway and ascending the two flights of stairs—is sort of dreamlike. I keep my head down, with my hands in my pockets, my right hand clutching my cell phone like it's something that can protect me during this dangerous journey.

I hear the stairs creak beneath my feet and avoid the rays of sunlight that blast in through side windows. It's a good thing that I'm wearing the hoodie.

The feeling is so bizarre that I wonder if I *am* dreaming all of this, the whole thing. Maybe I'll wake up any minute now in my sad little apartment with my toy drones and realize I've been so starved for human contact that I conjured it all up. Mrs. Archer. The dead homeless guy. The cops. The senator.

Even cute Jackson Dolan. Because in real life, why would a guy like him even bother with a freak like me?

I snap out of my reverie when I reach his door— 3-D. The fact I'm actually standing here is unreal.

"Jackson?"

I knock timidly at first, then a little harder. The door opens—just a crack—with the same creaking noise as mine. He left it open for me.

"It's me… Tricia."

I push open the door a little farther and a strange odor fills my nostrils. Ugh. What is that? Post-workout sweat gone horribly wrong? And to think, I was self-conscious about the *eau de rotten meat* in my own apartment.

"Jackson, um, are you still here?"

Brazenly, I push open the door a bit more so I can see the layout of his apartment.

It's just as small and dark as mine, but laid out in a different way. The shades are drawn, so it's hard to make out much detail.

From my vantage point in the hallway, however, I can see all the way through his living room and into his shadowy bathroom, where there is an arm dangling over the edge of a bathtub.

The arm is not moving, and it doesn't appear to be alive.

CHAPTER 32

Target Diary—Day 13 (The Big Day, continued)

THE HARD PART is over. I lean back against a parked car, pull a candy bar from my jacket pocket, carefully rip open one end of its wrapper. Then I peel the plastic back halfway down the bar like it's a banana skin.

The candy bar is a Snickers. I love the combination of nougat and caramel and peanuts, enrobed in a thin shell of chocolate. I take a long leisurely bite, chewing slowly, savoring the sugar rush and marveling at how something that looks so unappetizing on the outside can pack so much delicious flavor inside.

There's only one thing that gives me more pleasure than this Snickers bar. And that's the fact that right about now, Miss Tricia Celano will most likely be doing one of two things.

The first option is that she's cowering in her apartment, waiting for law enforcement to arrive. This would, of course, be a satisfactory way to bring my mission to a successful—albeit humdrum—conclusion. My expectation is that the government investigators haven't considered Miss Celano seriously as a suspect. But her strange condition will inject plenty of doubt into the case, completely obfuscating my involvement in the matter of the slaughtered senator. Even if the government *were* to believe her story, they'd be scouring the country for a middle-aged woman. Which I, certainly, am not.

On the other hand, Miss Tricia Celano could be making her way up to apartment 3-D, where I left the door unlocked. Will she be bold enough to venture inside?

And if so, will she find the present I left her in the bathroom?

Will it make her scream?

Especially when she sees the arrow in the eye, which killed the poor fellow almost instantly?

There's a good chance she'll scream.

But there is a small chance she'll summon some inner strength previously unknown to her and take a good look at the face of the corpse in said bathroom.

And oh, I very much hope she will.

Because upon closer inspection, she may notice that while the details of his face generally resemble the man she's come to know as "Jackson Dolan," they won't exactly match his. I was working off hastily made reconnaissance photographs, and even though I am quite skilled at the art of impersonation, there are some limits to my abilities.

And Miss Celano, if you *do* notice the small discrepancies, what will you do then?

Will you run to the police with your discovery?

Perhaps.

But I'm hoping not.

Because you're special. Because you amuse me.

I realized that the moment you stepped into my life and I learned everything I could about you. Your skin allergy. Your habits. Even your girlish crushes. You really shouldn't openly fawn over the "handsome guy from 3-D" if you don't want someone like me taking advantage of that particular emotion.

So no, I do not believe you will run to law enforcement.

And besides, I've already called them.

You'll soon realize how inescapable the trap is that I've assembled around you. That you're much like a lab rat who realizes that—if it is to survive—it must abandon the one habitat it has known all of its short, miserable life.

You're a rat, Miss Celano. And you're about to gnaw your way out of your own cage. Which is a good thing.

Because I'll be outside waiting for you.

CHAPTER 33

THERE IS AN arrow sticking out of my dead boyfriend's eye socket.

Yes, I know he's not *technically* my boyfriend, but he's not exactly alive, either. Right now, I just need a minute to come to my senses.

I'm still in shock.

Somehow I find the strength to touch his neck, just to make sure, but his flesh is cold. Very horribly cold. He's been dead a long time. I look at his skin and at the congealed, partially dried blood at the bottom of the tub.

That's when I realize I can't look at him anymore. I take a deep breath and it's a huge mistake. The stench is horrible. Clearly, this happened more than a few hours ago. Most likely, it's been days.

So how did he answer his cell phone just five minutes ago?

Duh, Tricia—this is not the man who talked to you five minutes ago.

So then who the hell is he?

Downstairs, on the first floor, there's a loud banging

sound that reverberates like gunfire up the stairwell. It startles the hell out of me. This is followed by the baritone voice of Officer Sears, which startles me even more.

"Ms. Celano! Open up. It's Officer Sears. We need to talk to you."

KNOCK KNOCK KNOCK.

The pounding sounds again.

"We have a warrant, Tricia." This is Yates now. "You don't open up, we're going to come in anyway."

"Come on," Sears bellows. "We *know* you're in there. Where else could you be—right?"

Ha-ha, the joke's on you, Sears! I'm not in my apartment. I'm crouching down next to a corpse and feeling the peculiar sensation of my entire world caving in on me.

I very much need to get out of this apartment with the corpse of the stranger who kind of resembles my almost-boyfriend.

But clearly, I can't return to my apartment, either.

And that's when the panic attack that I've been able to keep at bay these past few minutes comes roaring back. An invisible hand of steel seizes my throat, determined to squeeze the life right out of me. My heart flutters, and it feels like there are bird wings flapping wildly against my rib cage.

Logically, I know it's the classic fight or flight response—a physiological response to a grave threat. And I also know that trying to "fight" or even reason with Sears and Yates would be futile.

Which leaves only one option.

The unthinkable one.

CHAPTER 34

I'M TREMBLING VIOLENTLY as I peek outside the front hallway windows in the third floor stairwell.

I'm half-expecting to see an entire SWAT team assembled, along with a battalion of Secret Service guys, each one of them ready to take me down.

But the corner of 20th and Green is more or less deserted. There are sirens in the distance, most coming from the Parkway. The sun has already slipped behind the buildings of University City, casting the whole block in a sinister shade of darkness.

Downstairs, Yates calls out, and this time his voice is almost pleading with me. "Come on, Tricia. You don't want us busting down your door. Your landlord's gonna make you pay for it."

"Enough of this," Sears says. "Open up this door now!"

But I'd be okay with them destroying my property. Because if Yates and Sears are busy trying to break down my door, I might be able to sneak down the stairs, through the hallway and out the front door before they realize I'm not home.

Did you just hear yourself, Tricia? You? Go outside?

Shut up.

So you can what—die of sunlight and fear in the fresh air?

Seriously, I don't have time for this. My apartment is tiny. Once they're in, Yates and Sears are going to realize I'm not there in about 2.3 seconds. If I'm going to make a break for it, I need to start running *now*.

I steal another glance outside, just to make sure nobody's watching, and then I—

Wait.

Somebody *is* watching.

More precisely…a skinny man, leaning against a parked car, eating—with relish—what looks like a candy bar, is staring at my apartment window three floors below. He might as well be seated in a theater, waiting for the main attraction to begin.

I squint in the near darkness to see if I recognize him. And honestly, I don't. He's kind of a plain-looking guy. Middle-aged. Thin, but otherwise perfectly unremarkable.

But you do recognize him, Tricia. Because you called him just a few minutes ago.

No I didn't. I called Jackson!

The real Jackson is lying dead in the apartment down the hall.

Then who's this creepy stranger?

Come on, Tricia. You're smarter than this. You've got all of the pieces of the puzzle. Now put it together.

And that's when I do.

This is him. No matter what this guy looks like, he's the one who's been misdirecting me from the beginning.

The whole dowdy, middle-aged lady thing? That was a disguise.

He wasn't killing out of boredom or because he just stepped off a train from Crazytown. He specifically created the Mrs. Archer persona so that he could blend in with a crowd of political rally-goers and take out the senator with the arrow. Then he must have shed his disguise like a snake, sloughing off a skin to blend right back into the crowd once again.

And that night, when "Mrs. Archer" was pinging pebbles off your front window? That was just another test, wasn't it?

If you remember, I looked out my window and saw Mrs. Archer, giving me the *tsk-tsk* thing with her finger. Which freaked me out.

And then a minute later, I heard the front door open. I thought it was Mrs. Archer, that she had come to kill me. Instead, it was the man I *thought* was my neighbor—a man I thought was Jackson Dolan.

But that man wasn't really my neighbor.

He was the killer, who used some sort of disguise to *look like* my neighbor—a neighbor whom I'd barely seen, and wouldn't recognize except by the broadest details.

Even thinking back on the features of the dead guy in the bathtub, it becomes clear. That wasn't the same man who helped me build *Amelia III* in my apartment last night.

It was someone else.

It was Mrs. Archer, in yet another disguise.

So how did this killer know about my crush on my neighbor? Well, if he was smart enough to track me down through my fallen drone, he's certainly smart enough to check my Facebook page.

I can't believe it.

For the past couple days, I've been making goo-goo eyes at a *professional assassin*.

CHAPTER 35

Target Diary—Day 13 (The Big Day, continued)

I UNWRAP THE second half of my Snickers bar and finish it while the two police officers force open Miss Patricia Celano's apartment door.

I fold up the wrapper neatly and tuck it back in my pocket. That was a very delicious treat. Definitely worth waiting for. I'm eager for my next assignment to get under way so that I'll have another candy bar to look forward to. Vices, after all, must be kept in check.

If the cops are any good, they'll quickly find what they're looking for: a handmade wrist apparatus, complete with spring-loaded arrow. I quickly slipped through Miss Celano's window, and then tucked it away in a kitchen cabinet once I watched her work up the courage to enter apartment 3-D.

They'll also later realize that Patricia's browser history is full of links to sites that provide detailed instructions on how to make such an apparatus. As well as the usual political paranoia/conspiracy theory blogs, message boards, and social media networks.

And the apparatus, of course, will be analyzed in great detail. Eventually, a group of specialists will prove the weapon to be the one that killed the senator. As well as the young man in apartment 3-D.

But right now, the two cops will call it in, of course, and this block will be swarmed by enough government agents to take down a dictator in a small Latin American country.

Which means I don't have much time.

There are only two ways out of that apartment building. One is through the front door, which I am watching carefully. The other is through a back entrance with an alley that leads out to 20th Street, which I also can see. The rest of the block is dense with brownstones, so there is no way out. Even the cockroaches have to scuttle sideways to make their way from building to building.

Where will you go scurrying, Patricia?

CHAPTER 36

NORMALLY, I'D BE proud of my Sherlock Holmes–like powers of deduction. I mean, gimme some credit here. This is a complicated conspiracy, something that has apparently eluded the US Secret Service, and I've solved it. Go, me!

But there's no time to celebrate, because Yates and Sears have just kicked in my front door, and I have to make my move. Like, right now.

Well, you can forget the front entrance and the back door, because either one will put you in plain view of the assassin.

It's a good point.

And that's assuming you could even make it out either of those doors without losing your mind completely.

It's dark out. The sun has set. I'll be fine. Theoretically…

Just like you were fine last year when you got all dolled up and tried to join your friends for dinner?

I can handle it. I just need an escape plan.

Hmmm. How about you pretend you're a drone?

And what—fly away from here? Very funny.

Do it. You need to survive.

CHAPTER 37

Target Diary—Day 13 (The Big Day, continued)

SIRENS ARE APPROACHING. The police officers have made their call, and I'm sure the cavalry is on its way.

So where is Patricia Celano?

It could be that she's curled up in the fetal position next to her dead "boyfriend," just waiting for a lawyer so that she can plead insanity. Or maybe she tucked herself away in a closet, hoping that the bogeymen will somehow leave her alone.

Poor thing.

I thought we'd have the opportunity for one last dance.

The kind of dance where her feet would leave the ground, and the rope would tighten around her neck until the stars come out.

Well, no use lingering. The authorities will no doubt be combing the entire neighborhood, questioning anyone they encounter. Mind you, I never worry about such encounters. I've beaten a dozen lie detectors. But I'd rather not be stopped and questioned directly in front of the main suspect's apartment. Woe to those who crossed paths with Lee Harvey Oswald on that fateful November day!

I move east on Green, planning to clear the six blocks until I reach the Broad Street subway, which will take me north to the edge of the city. From there, I will disappear completely, like I always do.

But a few strides into my escape, a voice echoes off the brownstones.

"Hey! Jerkface!"

I'm elated. It's Patricia, ready to engage.

But where is she?

I spin around, trying to locate the sound of her voice. But she's not behind me on Green, nor is she in the street.

"Ha! I think I've finally figured out your weakness— you never look up!"

There she is. Up on the rooftops above Green Street. My trembling little shut-in patsy, pretending so hard that she's brave.

But she's failing miserably.

However, I now find myself at a disadvantage, because not only has she figured out the plot, but she's also seen my face. My true face.

And that is a loose end I cannot tolerate.

"Want to know something?" she continues.

"What's that?"

"You looked better in a dress."

My arm twitches instinctively, as if I still have my apparatus attached to my wrist. Wouldn't she be surprised to hear a whooshing sound and then look down to see the back end of an arrow protruding from her chest?

But of course the apparatus is now in the hands of the police. I have to rely on other weapons to take her down.

"What's the matter, tough guy? All out of arrows?"

I stare up at Patricia and merely smile, lulling her into a false sense of victory. Her strategy is easy enough to intuit. Just like in all of the bad TV cop shows, she thinks she can "keep me talking."

But she has no idea what is about to happen to her.

CHAPTER 38

HERE'S THE WEIRD thing about…well, me being so *weird* about venturing outside at night.

I realize now that all of my anxieties were focused on the front door of my apartment building. Over time, I'd convinced myself that I could never pass through it. Not even when the sun was tucked away on the other side of the planet, making it perfectly safe for me to step outside. The door was my prison warden. There was no way I could slip past.

But up here on the roof?

With an aerial view of my beloved Spring Garden?

Hell, this is the vantage point I'd grown to *love* over the past few months. The *Amelia* drones were simply my avatars; *I* was the one who was flying.

I climbed out here, once I realized my only choice was to escape via the roof, and suddenly, being out in the world didn't seem all that crazy.

As I climbed the stairs that would take me to the top

of the building, I came up with a plan that would give me a shot at proving my innocence.

All I needed was a way to lure the killer to a particular spot.

So, like I had with everything else in my life, I took the very little resources I had and I improvised. I moved along the tops of the neighboring roofs, mirroring the killer's progress down Green Street. Finally, I saw what I needed and decided to catch his attention.

After I called out to him, the killer spun around, like he had no idea where I was. Just like he failed to spot *Amelia* the first time. I get it now. He's so focused on things at the street level that he forgets to look up at the world above his head.

Then he finally spied me. I taunted him a little more, and he moved his arm out, like he wanted to shoot me with an arrow, just like he had shot my drone. Except, he's probably stashed his fancy little wrist crossbow in my apartment for the cops to find.

Oh, you should've seen the look on his bland little face when I goaded him for not having any arrows. He looked like he wanted to throttle me, stomp on my corpse, and then revive me just to throttle me all over again. But he made a good show of it, smiling like he didn't have a care in the world.

And then *BOOM*—he takes off like an Olympic sprinter at the crack of a pistol, headed straight for the building beneath me.

That's right, Archer. Come and get me.

The killer probably thinks he has me trapped. That

we're about to start this long cat-and-mouse chase across the rooftops of Spring Garden, as if it were something from the movie *Vertigo*. I'm leaping across chasms and scrambling over gables and I'll probably end up in some dark alley with my neck snapped.

Well, guess again, Archer.

I might be afraid of the world.

But I'm not afraid of heights.

CHAPTER 39

Target Diary—Day 13 (The Big Day, concluded)

THE MOMENT I step onto the roof is the moment I realize she's gone.

Vanished completely.

Did she jump?

I run to the edge of the building and skid to a halt, checking Green Street below for signs of her twisted, dying body. No such luck. Instead, I spy her using a metal drain pipe to climb down the front of this three-story brownstone. Hand over hand, feet pressed against the wall, guiding her way down.

This will not do.

There is no time to come back to the ground the way I came up onto the roof, so I follow her path over to the edge of the building. I use the drainpipe in the same way. The fittings are older than I thought, and they're caked in rust. This is not a path I'd ordinarily choose, but she's forced me into this position.

Patricia reaches the ground safely and sprints across

Green. I redouble my efforts to make it down to street level. I cannot allow her to escape.

There's one major difference between myself and Patricia, however: body weight.

And by the time I'm halfway down, the drainage pipe breaks loose from its moorings. I attempt to leap free, but I'm already falling by the time I'm twisting my body around, aiming for a relatively soft place to land.

My body slams awkwardly onto a small patch of front lawn, missing the spikes of a wrought-iron fence by a matter of inches. Lucky. But upon landing, the air is hammered from my lungs and my vision blurs. The wave of pain washes over me a microsecond later.

A quick and rudimentary self-exam reveals no broken bones, however. Which is good, because I'm going to need them intact when I choke the life out of this meddling woman.

I scan the block. My prey is jogging south on 19th Street in the direction of Logan Circle. Presumably toward those approaching sirens so she can give my full description to the police.

"They won't believe you!" I yell to her, limping slightly as I move down the street. "All the evidence points to you!"

Patricia looks back over her shoulder at me, sticks out her tongue, then faces forward and accelerates.

Did she honestly stick her tongue out?

I push aside the pain and break out into a full run. The city of Philadelphia fades away like the blurring roadside when you're moving eighty miles per hour down an interstate highway. Right now there are only two things in my world: predator and prey.

And the predator is gaining on its prey.

Without warning, she darts right onto Brandywine, which is a narrow and relatively secluded street, heading back in the direction of 20th Street. This is a poor choice on her part. She was doing better before when she was making her way down toward Logan Circle.

"There is no use running," I call out. "I run all night long. You wouldn't believe the stamina I've developed."

"Yeah, well, good for you," she says before quickly turning the corner.

The nerve of her.

I'm really going to enjoy ending her life.

CHAPTER 40

I'M RUNNING SO fast it's barely registered that I'm actually outside, in the fresh air, for the first time in three years.

So this is what freedom feels like.

Though I suppose it's easy to ignore your hypothetical fears when there's a professional assassin hot and heavy on your trail.

My heart is pounding and my temples are throbbing as I pump my arms and legs. I don't know how much longer I can keep this up. The sound of Archer's footfalls are like a boxer's gloves smacking a heavy bag, and I tense up every time I think they're getting closer. While I'm a fairly slender human being, I'm also woefully out of shape. It's kind of hard to do laps when your apartment is the size of a hotel room.

Fortunately, I don't need much in the way of stamina, because I don't have to run all that far.

When I reach the corner of 20th and Hamilton, I come to a full stop. Then I turn around to face my nemesis. Archer is so startled that he comes to an awkward, almost fumbling halt, pinwheeling his arms a bit. I'll admit it; it's nice to see this jerk out of control.

Still, he tries to recover his cool. "I'm surprised you gave up so soon. I thought there would be a little more fight left in you."

I shove my hands into my pockets and struggle to regain my breath.

"I know I can't beat you in a race."

"Very smart of you to realize that."

"But before you do *whatever* it is you're planning on doing to me," I tell him, "I just need to know one thing."

A bemused grin appears on his face. On most guys it would look charming. On this guy, it comes across as creepy.

"And what's that?"

"How you did it."

"Did what?"

"Take out a senator in broad daylight and then vanish into thin air."

He takes a moment to study me. I mean, *really* study me. As if my question boggled his mind. Finally, after a small eternity, he opens his mouth and speaks again. "You're serious," Archer says.

I bug my eyes out a little, as if to say, *Do you think I'm kidding around here?*

"If we had more time together," he says, "I'd be happy to walk you through the whole plan, step by step. I'm proud of my work. And I've done a lot of it in preparation for this mission. But the clock is ticking. Suffice to say that people always see what they want to see. They're not trained to observe the truly unexpected."

"Like the arrow that magically appeared out of your sleeve," I say.

Archer nods.

"But once the senator was hit, how were you not tackled by a dozen Secret Service guys?"

"Witnesses will swear they saw a woman take that shot. In the confusion, I simply ceased being that woman and transformed into just another panicked spectator. It's easier than you think. The basic principles have been around for centuries."

"Amazing."

Archer smiles. "I'm so glad you're impressed."

I laugh. "No, I'm not impressed by your nerdy Renaissance Faire assassination plan. Arrows? Seriously? No, I think it's amazing you just confessed."

Archer moves closer, attempting to box me in. There's an old storefront behind me. If I try to run in either direction, he'll definitely be able to catch me.

"It doesn't matter that I confessed to you," he says quietly. "You're the only one who heard, and in a few seconds, you will be dead."

"But that's the thing. I'm not the only one who heard."

CHAPTER 41

SAY HELLO, *AMELIA I*.

Yep, she's right above our heads, still caught in the ancient rusty sign on that rooftop where she crashed a while ago. With her little camera trained on this exact location. And she's captured *everything*.

While I was still on the rooftop a couple of minutes ago, I opened her app on my cell phone and saw that she had just enough power to pull this off. Then I texted the link to Officer Yates and told him to watch—This will explain everything.

And then, of course, I climbed down the front of a three-story brownstone and ran like hell, all with a trained killer nipping at my heels.

Oh, the look on Archer's face as he glances up and sees *Amelia I*, notices that there's a blinking green light near her camera, and instantly puts it all together.

What's that old saying? You can fool all of the people some of the time, and you can fool some people all of the time, but not all of the people all of the time?

Well, when a drone is watching you when you're trying to fool people, forget about it. You're screwed.

"What did you do?" Archer snarls. *"WHAT DID YOU DO?"*

I'm about to respond with a wisecrack, but I never get the chance. Because Archer immediately lunges for me.

CHAPTER 42

I'VE SUFFERED THROUGH multiple panic attacks this past week. Each time, I've likened the experience to "hands squeezing my throat" or some other metaphor for strangulation.

Well, let me tell you—a panic attack feels nothing like actually being strangled.

There are no "invisible hands." You feel every bony finger—especially the fat thumbs, crushing your windpipe like it's the cardboard tube inside a roll of paper towels.

Archer doesn't need arrows to kill. His hands are more than capable of pulling off this particular job.

The murder of a nosy shut-in.

Oh, I fight back, for what it's worth. I dig my nails down into his flesh, hoping to strike down into the bones of his hands. But the strength fades from my limbs before I can do anything resembling damage, and I'm sure Archer is so furious he doesn't feel a thing.

It really sucks that the last thing I'm ever going to see is Archer's red, trembling, angry face.

What happens when you die, you might ask? *Do you see stars or clouds? A long tunnel with a bright light at the end? Or simply black nothingness?*

In my case, it's none of the above. Instead, I see faces. Not the faces of long-deceased relatives come to take me home. Still, they are faces I recognize, even though I can't assign names to them.

Why do you all look so familiar? is my last thought before all of the lights turn out.

Later, I would understand why I knew those faces.

CHAPTER 43

THOSE FACES BELONGED to my neighbors in Spring Garden, the very same people I used to watch as they headed off to work in the morning, and then trudged home later that evening, tired or defeated. Some were the people who came home happy, looking forward to spending the night with someone they cared about. I saw them all through the eye of *Amelia* and experienced their lives vicariously.

Lawyer-types in their fine suits and even more expensive shoes who spent their days in air-conditioned conference rooms. Ordinary Philly dudes in jeans and button-down shirts trying to make it to 6 p.m. as fast as they possibly can...

I heard that about a dozen of them were running up to pull Archer off me. He wriggled like a maniac apparently, but there were just too many of them.

One neighbor, a nurse at Pennsylvania Hospital, worked on reviving me while the others subdued Archer, tackling him to the sidewalk.

You have to understand that in Philly, when we make reference to "subduing" someone, what we really mean is that we beat the holy crap out of them. Later, at the trial, Archer's face was still badly bruised and his jaw wired shut. The doctors said he'll never look the same.

Pity.

After all my neighbors saved me, Yates and Sears made it to the corner of 20th and Hamilton in time to slap the cuffs on Archer and read him his Miranda rights. They pretty much got instant credit for the whole thing.

Archer's real name, by the way, turned out to be...

You know what? I don't want to give that creepy guy any more notoriety than he already has. He can remain anonymous in my story.

Besides, to me he'll always be Mrs. Archer, the (supposedly) professional assassin in a dress who got his butt kicked by a shut-in.

CHAPTER 44

AFTER THE WHOLE story made the news, I became *sort-of* famous. You know what they call it now—"Internet famous." The kind of fame that lasts for a couple of minutes, tops, before the world is fascinated by, like, somebody in a Chewbacca mask telling knock-knock jokes or a dog who knows how to pump its paws to heavy metal.

Even Yates and Sears made it onto a few talk shows, even though they didn't do much aside from watch a link I'd texted them and show up to finish the job that my Spring Garden neighbors had started.

"We knew you weren't responsible for the senator," Yates later admitted to me.

"Yeah, we just thought you were nutty," Sears added.

Thanks, fellas.

But my brief hit of fame did bring a lot of my old friends out of the woodwork, and they all insisted on taking me out for a drink. Or five.

Which sounds great to me.

No, I'm not cured. My *solar urticaria* is still a consistent source of annoyance and a constant threat to my health. The only way I ever see my beloved city while the sun is shining down upon it is through the camera lens of a drone. And I use *Amelia I,* if you must know— the original.

Yates pulled the old girl down from that rusty old sign, knocked on my door shyly, and presented it to me as if it were a lost kitten. I felt like hugging the thing, but thought that might be a little weird.

As it turns out, I ended up giving Yates a hug instead. He's not so bad, once you get past the uniform and the beer belly. I invited him in for some instant coffee. Seemed to be the decent thing to do, even if he busted down my apartment door (and yeah, the landlord charged me for it).

"So what would you do if I were to ask you out?" Yates says to me one night, acting shy once again.

"I'd ask how you'd feel about a threesome."

"I'm sorry," he says, choking on his coffee, "w-what did you just say?"

"You heard me. Amelia's gotta chaperone. The thing is, I don't trust the police."

By now, I *have* made my peace with the outside world.

In fact, tonight I'm meeting a couple of my lovely Spring Garden neighbors at my new favorite joint, which happens to be BYOB. It's open only after sundown. There's an amazing view of nighttime Philadelphia, and yet it's never crowded. Best of all, it's a very short walk from my apartment.

Just four flights up.

THE CHARGES: EXPLOSIVE.
THE EVIDENCE: SHOCKING.
THE PEOPLE VS ALEX CROSS:
THE TRIAL OF THE CENTURY.

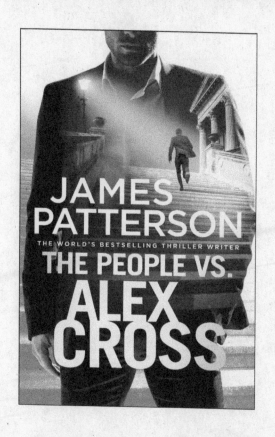

I LOOKED IN MY BEDROOM mirror and tried to tie the perfect necktie knot.

It was such a simple thing, a ritual I performed every day before work, and yet I couldn't get it right.

"Here, Alex, let me help," Bree said, sliding in beside me.

I let the tie hang and said, "Nerves."

"Understandable," Bree said, coming around in front of me and adjusting the lengths of the tie.

I have a good six inches on my wife, and I gazed down in wonder at how easily she tied the knot.

"Men can't do that," I said. "We have to stand behind a guy to do it."

"Just a difference in perspective," Bree said, snugging the knot up against my Adam's apple and tugging down the starched collar. She hesitated, then looked up at me with wide, fearful eyes and said, "You're ready now."

I felt queasy. "You think?"

"I believe in you," Bree said, getting up on her tiptoes and tilting her head back. "We all believe in you."

I kissed her then, and hugged her tight.

"Love you," I said.

"Forever and ever," Bree said.

When we separated, she had shiny eyes.

"Game face, now," I said, touching her chin. "Remember what Marley and Naomi told us."

She got out a Kleenex and dabbed at her tears while I put on my jacket.

"Better?" Bree asked.

"Perfect," I said, and opened our bedroom door.

The three other bedrooms off the second-floor landing were open and dark. We went downstairs. My family was gathered in the kitchen. Nana Mama, my ninety-something-year-old grandmother. Damon, my oldest child, down from Johns Hopkins. Jannie, my high-school junior and running star. And Ali, my precocious nine-year-old. They were all dressed as if for a funeral.

Ali saw me and broke into tears. He ran over and hugged my legs.

"Hey, hey," I said, stroking his head.

"It's not fair." Ali sobbed. "It's not true, what they're saying."

"Course it's not," Nana Mama said. "We've just got to ignore them. Sticks and stones."

"Words can hurt, Nana," Jannie said. "I know what he's feeling. You should see the stuff on social media."

"Ignore it," Bree said. "We're standing by your father. Family first."

She squeezed my hand.

"Let's do it, then," I said. "Heads high. Don't engage."

Nana Mama picked up her pocketbook, said, "I'd like to engage. I'd like to put a frying pan in my purse here and then clobber one of them with it."

Ali stopped sniffling and started to laugh. "Want me to get you one, Nana?"

"Next time. And I'd only use it if I was provoked."

"God help them if you are, Nana," Damon said, and we all laughed.

Feeling a little better, I checked my watch. Quarter to eight.

"Here we go," I said, and I went through the house to the front door.

I stopped there, listening to my family lining up behind me.

I took a deep breath, rolled my shoulders back like a Marine at attention, then twisted the knob, swung open the door, and stepped out onto my porch.

"It's him!" a woman cried.

Klieg lights blazed to life as a roar of shouts erupted from the small mob of media vultures and haters packing the sidewalk in front of our house on Fifth Street in Southeast Washington, DC.

There were fifteen, twenty of them, some carrying cameras and mikes, others carrying signs condemning me, all hurling questions or curses my way. It was such a madhouse I couldn't hear any of them clearly. Then one guy with a baritone voice bellowed loudly enough to be heard over the din:

"Are you guilty, Dr. Cross?" he shouted. "Did you shoot those people down in cold blood?"

A BLACK SUBURBAN WITH TINTED windows rolled up in front of my house.

"Stay close," I said, ignoring the shouted questions. I pointed to Damon. "Help Nana Mama, please."

My oldest came to my grandmother's side and we all moved as one tight unit down the stairs and onto the sidewalk.

A reporter shoved a microphone in my face, shouted, "Dr. Cross, how many times have you drawn your weapon in the course of duty?"

I had no idea, so I ignored him, but Nana Mama snapped, "How many times have you asked a stupid question in the pursuit of idiocy?"

After that, it took everything in me to tune it all out as we crossed the sidewalk to the Suburban. I saw the rest of my family inside the SUV, climbed up front, and shut the door.

Nana Mama let out a long breath.

"I hate them," Jannie said as we pulled away.

"It's like they're feeding on Dad," Ali said.

"Bloodsuckers," the driver said.

All too soon we arrived in front of the District of Columbia Courthouse at 500 Indiana Avenue. The building is a two-wing, smooth limestone structure with a steel-and-glass atrium over the lobby and a large plaza flanked by raised gardens out front. There'd been twenty vultures at my house, but there were sixty jackals there for my rendezvous with cold justice.

Anita Marley, my attorney, was also there, waiting at the curb.

Tall and athletically built, with auburn hair, freckled skin, and sharp emerald eyes, Marley had once played volleyball for and studied acting at the University of Texas; she later graduated near the top of her law-school class at Rice. She was classy, brassy, and hilarious, as well as certifiably badass in the courtroom, which was why we'd hired her.

Marley opened my door.

"I do the talking from here on out, Alex," she said in a commanding drawl just as the roar of accusation and ridicule hit me, far worse than what I'd been subjected to at home.

I'd seen this kind of thing in the past, a big-time trial mob with local and national reporters preparing to feed raw meat to the twenty-four-hour cable-news monster. I'd just never been the raw meat before.

"Talk to us, Cross!" they shouted. "Are *you* the problem? Are *you* and your cowboy ways what the police have become in America? Above the law?"

I couldn't take it and responded, "No one is above the law."

"Don't say anything," Marley hissed, and she took me by the elbow and moved me across the plaza toward the front doors of the courthouse.

The swarm went with us, still buzzing, still stinging.

From the crowd beyond the reporters, a man shouted in a terrified voice, "Don't shoot me, Cross! Don't shoot!"

Others started to chant with him in that same tone. "Don't shoot me, Cross! Don't shoot!"

Despite my best efforts, I could not help turning my head to look at them. Some carried placards that featured a red *X* over my face with a caption below it, one reading END POLICE VIOLENCE and another GUILTY AS CHARGED!

In front of the bulletproof courthouse doors, Marley stopped to turn me toward the lights, microphones, and cameras. I threw my shoulders back and lifted my chin.

My attorney held up her hand and said in a loud, firm voice, "Dr. Cross is an innocent man and an innocent police officer. We are very happy that at long last he'll have the opportunity to clear his good name."

NYPD RED 5

James Patterson
& Marshall Karp

The one who knows the secrets is the one who holds the power.

The richest of New York's rich gather at The Pierre's Cotillion Room to raise money for those less fortunate. Detectives Zach Jordan and Kylie MacDonald of the elite NYPD Red task force are providing security.

The night is shattered as a fatal blast rocks the room, stirring up horrifying memories of 9/11. Is the explosion an act of terrorism – or a homicide?

A big-name female filmmaker is the next to die, in a desolate corner of New York City. As the attacks keep escalating, Zach and Kylie realise the perpetrators may be among the A-list New Yorkers NYPD Red was formed to protect.

arrow books

Also by James Patterson

ALEX CROSS NOVELS

Along Came a Spider • Kiss the Girls • Jack and Jill •
Cat and Mouse • Pop Goes the Weasel • Roses are Red •
Violets are Blue • Four Blind Mice • The Big Bad Wolf •
London Bridges • Mary, Mary • Cross • Double Cross •
Cross Country • Alex Cross's Trial (*with Richard DiLallo*) •
I, Alex Cross • Cross Fire • Kill Alex Cross • Merry
Christmas, Alex Cross • Alex Cross, Run • Cross My
Heart • Hope to Die • Cross Justice • Cross the Line •
The People vs. Alex Cross

THE WOMEN'S MURDER CLUB SERIES

1st to Die • 2nd Chance (*with Andrew Gross*) • 3rd Degree
(*with Andrew Gross*) • 4th of July (*with Maxine Paetro*) •
The 5th Horseman (*with Maxine Paetro*) • The 6th Target
(*with Maxine Paetro*) • 7th Heaven (*with Maxine Paetro*) •
8th Confession (*with Maxine Paetro*) • 9th Judgement (*with
Maxine Paetro*) • 10th Anniversary (*with Maxine Paetro*) •
11th Hour (*with Maxine Paetro*) • 12th of Never (*with Maxine
Paetro*) • Unlucky 13 (*with Maxine Paetro*) • 14th Deadly Sin
(*with Maxine Paetro*) • 15th Affair (*with Maxine Paetro*) •
16th Seduction (*with Maxine Paetro*) • 17th Suspect
(*with Maxine Paetro*)

DETECTIVE MICHAEL BENNETT SERIES

Step on a Crack (*with Michael Ledwidge*) • Run for Your Life
(*with Michael Ledwidge*) • Worst Case (*with Michael Ledwidge*) •
Tick Tock (*with Michael Ledwidge*) • I, Michael Bennett
(*with Michael Ledwidge*) • Gone (*with Michael Ledwidge*) •
Burn (*with Michael Ledwidge*) • Alert (*with Michael Ledwidge*) •
Bullseye (*with Michael Ledwidge*) • Haunted (*with James O. Born*)

PRIVATE NOVELS

Private (*with Maxine Paetro*) • Private London (*with Mark Pearson*) • Private Games (*with Mark Sullivan*) • Private: No. 1 Suspect (*with Maxine Paetro*) • Private Berlin (*with Mark Sullivan*) • Private Down Under (*with Michael White*) • Private L.A. (*with Mark Sullivan*) • Private India (*with Ashwin Sanghi*) • Private Vegas (*with Maxine Paetro*) • Private Sydney (*with Kathryn Fox*) • Private Paris (*with Mark Sullivan*) • The Games (*with Mark Sullivan*) • Private Delhi (*with Ashwin Sanghi*) • Private Princess (*with Rees Jones*)

NYPD RED SERIES

NYPD Red (*with Marshall Karp*) • NYPD Red 2 (*with Marshall Karp*) • NYPD Red 3 (*with Marshall Karp*) • NYPD Red 4 (*with Marshall Karp*) • NYPD Red 5 (*with Marshall Karp*)

DETECTIVE HARRIET BLUE SERIES

Never Never (*with Candice Fox*) • Fifty Fifty (*with Candice Fox*) • Liar Liar (*with Candice Fox*)

STAND-ALONE THRILLERS

The Thomas Berryman Number • Hide and Seek • Black Market • The Midnight Club • Sail (*with Howard Roughan*) • Swimsuit (*with Maxine Paetro*) • Don't Blink (*with Howard Roughan*) • Postcard Killers (*with Liza Marklund*) • Toys (*with Neil McMahon*) • Now You See Her (*with Michael Ledwidge*) • Kill Me If You Can (*with Marshall Karp*) • Guilty Wives (*with David Ellis*) • Zoo (*with Michael Ledwidge*) • Second Honeymoon (*with Howard Roughan*) • Mistress (*with David Ellis*) • Invisible (*with David Ellis*) • Truth or Die (*with Howard Roughan*) • Murder House (*with David Ellis*) • Woman of God (*with Maxine Paetro*) • Humans, Bow Down (*with Emily Raymond*) • The Black Book (*with David Ellis*) • Murder Games (*with Howard Roughan*) • The Store (*with Richard DiLallo*) • Texas Ranger (*with Andrew Bourelle*) • The President is Missing (*with Bill Clinton*)

NON-FICTION

Torn Apart (*with Hal and Cory Friedman*) • The Murder of King Tut (*with Martin Dugard*) • All-American Murder (*with Alex Abramovich and Mike Harvkey*)

MURDER IS FOREVER TRUE CRIME

Murder, Interrupted (*with Alex Abramovich and Christopher Charles*) • Home Sweet Murder (*with Andrew Bourelle and Scott Slaven*) • Murder Beyond the Grave (*with Andrew Bourelle and Christopher Charles*)

ROMANCE

Sundays at Tiffany's (*with Gabrielle Charbonnet*) • The Christmas Wedding (*with Richard DiLallo*) • First Love (*with Emily Raymond*) • Two from the Heart (*with Frank Costantini, Emily Raymond and Brian Sitts*)

OTHER TITLES

Miracle at Augusta (*with Peter de Jonge*) • Penguins of America (*with Jack Patterson*)

FAMILY OF PAGE-TURNERS

MIDDLE SCHOOL BOOKS

The Worst Years of My Life (*with Chris Tebbetts*) • Get Me Out of Here! (*with Chris Tebbetts*) • My Brother Is a Big, Fat Liar (*with Lisa Papademetriou*) • How I Survived Bullies, Broccoli, and Snake Hill (*with Chris Tebbetts*) • Ultimate Showdown (*with Julia Bergen*) • Save Rafe! (*with Chris Tebbetts*) • Just My Rotten Luck (*with Chris Tebbetts*) • Dog's Best Friend (*with Chris Tebbetts*) • Escape to Australia (*with Martin Chatterton*) • From Hero to Zero (*with Chris Tebbetts*)